The Devil's Protection

The Devil's Protection

SUSAN CLITHEROE

St. Martin's Press New York

Library of Congress Cataloging-in-Publication Data

Clitheroe, Susan.
    The devil's protection / by Susan Clitheroe.
        p.   cm.
    ISBN 0-312-13466-5
    I. Title.
PR6053.L52D48   1995
823'.914—dc20   95-35371
                                              CIP

First published in Great Britain by Robert Hale Limited

First U.S. Edition: December 1995

10 9 8 7 6 5 4 3 2 1

One

The parsonage gig proceeded at a sedate pace along the winding country lane which linked the little village of Tadworth with the neighbouring market town of Harbury deep in the Hampshire countryside. Miss Geneva Hartwell had long since resigned herself to their dawdling progress, used as she was to the idiosyncrasies of the elderly grey cob.

Indeed under normal circumstances it would have been no hardship for Miss Hartwell. She enjoyed her occasional visits to Harbury and was usually in no great hurry to return. The small town was a veritable metropolis when compared to the sleepy village of Tadworth. Geneva liked nothing more than to stroll along its bustling streets, taking in the sights, sounds and smells of market day. If most of her shopping was of the window variety then she was too inured to her state of genteel poverty, and too sensible to allow envy to spoil her pleasure.

On this occasion however, Geneva had belatedly recalled rumours of a prize fight in the vicinity. The invasion of the area by numerous sprigs of the nobility, all bent it seemed on cutting a lark and enjoying their sporting day out to the full, brought with it inevitable evils for an unescorted young lady. But Miss Hartwell was not easily daunted, and she determined to make her purchases as speedily as possible and return home before the visiting hordes took to the road once more. The former she managed to do largely undisturbed, saved as she was from more importune attentions by the indefinable air of good breeding which somehow transcended the meanness of her transport and the dowdiness of her attire. The blue gingham gown was of good quality, but was low waisted and plain, and the navy half boots and woollen cloak were serviceable rather than fashionable.

Regardless of these seeming drawbacks, many an appreciative glance was cast in her direction, for the modesty of her dress could not disguise the vibrancy of her beauty. A mass of dusky curls framed a heart-shaped face of elfin charm. Large, wide-set violet eyes looked out on the world with a blend of innocence and intelligence. She was small in stature, and so slender that she could have been taken for a child had it not been for the tell-tale swell of her bosom and the seductive curve of her hip.

Despite her undeniable charms, Geneva was unaccustomed to the blatant admiration her appearance was provoking. As the daughter of the parson, a much-respected and well-loved personage, she was accorded the respect due to her status by the local population. It was with some relief then that she made her final purchase and prepared to depart. In this object however she was foiled. Stepping out of the draper's into the bright afternoon sunshine, a parcel of new chintz for the refurbishment of the best parlour under her arm, Geneva was accosted by Mrs Thorneygate.

Mrs Thorneygate was a tall, angular woman who wore an expression of perpetual disapproval. This in general became more pronounced in the presence of Geneva Hartwell. Like many of the gentlewomen of the parish, Mrs Thorneygate was of the opinion that it was almost indecent of the parson's daughter to possess such flamboyant beauty; though none of these ladies could say quite how the girl was to be blamed for her striking looks. It was more than her beauty however that these dames resented. While their daughters simpered and blushed, Miss Geneva Hartwell met every situation with her head held high and with a disconcertingly direct gaze. In consequence she was labelled bold, and by the more spiteful, fast. Mrs Thorneygate came into the latter category and it was with some malicious satisfaction that she espied Miss Hartwell leaving the draper's without even a maid to bear her company. Her stiff bombazine skirts positively rustling with disapproval she lost no time in hastening to that young lady's side, a martial gleam in her eye which boded ill for her victim.

For all her father's gentle strictures on tolerance and patience, Geneva could not bring herself to like or respect this overbearing woman. Mrs Thorneygate never wasted an opportunity to chastise Geneva and she began today's homily in her customary fashion.

'My dear, I hope you will not take this amiss, though I am sure you could not, for you must know that as a dear friend of your father, I have nothing but your best interests at heart.'

At this juncture, Geneva had to resist the temptation to reply truthfully that yes, she did take it amiss, and that she knew no such thing since the only best interests Mrs Thorneygate ever considered were those of herself. However, as always, she bit her lip and nodded meekly, mindful of the tales the widow would delight in relaying to her father given the least excuse.

Like many ladies hovering on the fringes of society, Mrs Thorneygate adopted a rigid propriety not seen among the more elevated sections of the ton. The daughter of a minor baronet of little consequence and an ambitious mother, Honoria Thorneygate had constantly striven to improve her social standing. A girl of no great beauty and less expectations would not have been expected to have enjoyed success in catching a titled husband, and such was the case. After two unproductive seasons, mother and daughter alike were happy to cut their losses and accept an offer from Mr Reginald Thorneygate, the wealthy owner of a Lancashire cotton mill. Mr Thorneygate was some years Honoria's senior but he came from hardy stock and Honoria was forced to wait twenty years before he made her a widow. When he finally obliged her he wasted no time in consigning Reginald Thorneygate and his mill to oblivion and returning to Harbury, the town of her birth, the possessor of a tidy fortune. She quickly established herself by sheer force of personality as one of the leading figures of the provincial society, and if anyone remembered her marriage to a cit, they had the wisdom not to mention so in her hearing at least.

Geneva, with her youthful idealism and honesty, found it difficult to forgive Mrs Thorneygate's hypocrisy. In her opinion such disloyalty to a husband who had if nothing else provided her with the means of her present success showed the Widow Thorneygate in a very poor light. But knowing how it would upset the Reverend Hartwell if she was anything less than polite to the lady, Geneva resigned herself to her fate and allowed herself to be bustled into the Harbury Tea-Rooms which Mrs Thorneygate thought a more suitable venue for their 'little chat' than a public thoroughfare.

The Harbury Tea-Rooms were a source of great local pride. They were the innovation of a local tradesman, Mr Samuel Blunkett who, having taken his large family on holiday to Margate one summer, had observed the success of a similar idea. The Harbury Tea-Rooms were on a smaller scale but were nonetheless spacious and had a pleasing elegance that guaranteed their popularity with the ladies of the area, who found them an excellent place to seek refreshment and exchange gossip after a rigorous morning of shopping.

Over a dish of bohea and what Geneva privately termed the sacrificial cake, Mrs Thorneygate expounded on Geneva's faults which, if she were to be believed, were many and varied. Having questioned the wisdom of a young lady out walking unescorted, the doubtful propriety of appearing in public with one's head uncovered and the folly of driving alone in an open carriage, Mrs Thorneygate was about to embark on a lengthy monologue on the lack of a stable female influence in Miss Hartwell's life, when she was apparently struck dumb. The finely plucked eyebrows almost disappeared beneath the hairline of her improbable nut-brown curls, thin lips were folded in a grim line and the tip of her long narrow nose literally quivered with offended propriety. Curiosity overcoming good manners, Geneva swivelled in her chair to see who or what could possibly have rendered her companion speechless. Her eyes widened at the scene before her.

Three young bucks, all, judging by their erratic progress and the disarray of their clothing, a trifle up in the world, swaggered across the room. On the arm of one was a female, whose appearance could leave no one, not even a parson's daughter, in any doubt of her profession. Unable to help herself, Geneva stared in fascination. A diaphanous gown of brilliant green gauze clung to the lady's voluptuous figure, its transparency revealing the lack of any discernible undergarments, and its hemline affording an excellent view of not only ankles but a great deal of calf encased in lavishly clocked stockings. The waist was so high and the neckline so low as to make the bodice brief in the extreme and a pair of heavily rouged nipples were clearly visible.

Before Geneva had time to fully absorb the effect of the woman's heavy maquillage and the splendid array of feathers with which she had chosen to adorn her coiffeur, Mrs

Thorneygate had recovered her powers of speech, and in arctic tones adjured her to 'avert her eyes'. This she did reluctantly, and as she did so her gaze for some reason rested on a gentleman sitting alone at a table across the room. Unlike the rest of the occupants of the tea-rooms, he was not transfixed with either shock or amused appreciation by the colourful apparition of the Cyprian. Instead he was looking straight at Geneva. The directness of his gaze brought a blush to her cheeks, and she quickly looked away. She had no opportunity to steal another glance in his direction since Mrs Thorneygate was herding her from the tea-rooms with some speed.

Once free of that scene of vice, Mrs Thorneygate gave full vent to her indignation at the assault on Harbury's sanctum of respectability by what she described as 'Satan's own minions'. Geneva, who would normally have derived secret amusement from the widow's outrage, listened with only half an ear, her thoughts, against her own volition, straying to the lone gentleman. She had seen him for only a fraction of a second, and yet his image was engraved on her mind's eye in startling detail.

He was not handsome in the accepted sense, but there was something about those pale aristocratic features with their expression of faint disdain that was strangely compelling. And his eyes! They were so dark as to appear black against his white skin. His hair was as black and sleek as a raven's wing, swept back severely from his high brow. Geneva, whose experience of London fashions was limited in the main to the reminiscences of Mrs Thorneygate, mistakenly classed him as a dandy. Indeed compared to the gentlemen of the parish he was like some rare exotic bird amongst a flock of country sparrows. But though careful to the point of fastidiousness in his dress, he was no clothes horse. The claret riding coat fitted to perfection, and displayed his excellent physique to advantage, palest buff breeches and glossy Hessians encased a pair of calves that needed no recourse to buckram to improve their shape. The hand that toyed abstractedly with the tassels of an amber-topped cane, though beautifully manicured, had strength.

But it had been his unwavering gaze that had most disturbed, even piqued Geneva. It had been unfathomable; not the frank admiration of the visiting young bloods, nor the shy adulation of the local swains; quite the opposite in fact, almost contemptuous.

With an effort Geneva banished the stranger from her thoughts and brought her attention back to Mrs Thorneygate's denunciation of the declining moral standards of the younger generation. This was one of her favourite bugbears and Geneva knew that she could maintain a one-sided oration on this topic indefinitely. Taking the opportunity granted by the lady's necessity to draw breath, Geneva quickly excused herself on the grounds that her father would be concerned as to her whereabouts if she did not hasten home. Mrs Thorneygate was obliged to relinquish her, and with some relief Geneva mounted the gig and rousing the dozing cob set off along the road to Tadworth.

Her unfortunate encounter with Mrs Thorneygate had made her considerably later than she had intended, the last of the late afternoon sun was gilding the fields and hedgerows, the clear sky was tinged with coral and indigo, and the air was still and balmy. Geneva loved these tranquil late summer evenings but she knew that in a matter of minutes the sun would disappear below the horizon and night would begin to close in. This held no fear for her, for she knew that the cob would find his way home with or without light to guide him, what did concern her was the worry it would cause her father.

The Reverend Charles Hartwell was an elderly man and he had never possessed a strong constitution. For several years now his frailty had increased and he was now virtually bedridden. Geneva's mother had died giving birth to her second child when Geneva was just three years old. The baby had followed her to the grave barely a week later. Consequently father and daughter had grown very close. Mrs Thorneygate may mourn the loss of a mother figure in Geneva's life, but Geneva herself rarely felt that lack. The parson had brought up his daughter with the help of their housekeeper, Mrs Hollins. With his kindly, unworldly, scholarly influence, and her practical down-to-earth devotion, Geneva had not fared ill. But the clergyman's days were drawing to a close and though it hurt her deeply, Geneva knew she must face the fact that she would soon be an orphan.

Beyond that the future was hazy, her world consisted entirely of her father and his parishioners. When her father's illness had made it impossible for him to fulfil all his clerical duties, Geneva had taken much of it on to her own shoulders. While her contemporaries spent their days with dancing masters and music tutors, since the age of seventeen Geneva's main occupation had been visiting the sick and needy of the district and helping Mrs Hollins to nurse her ailing parent. This was the reason for what the Harbury ladies unkindly termed boldness. Geneva's enforced independence had lent her a maturity and confidence deemed by the censorious to be unbecoming in a young lady of just twenty summers. But Geneva would need all her resources when the inevitable happened and Charles Hartwell passed from this world, for she knew that her time at the parsonage would then be limited. The newly ordained young vicar in the next parish was the father of a large family, and it was generally accepted that he would step into Reverend Hartwell's shoes when the time came.

The vicar and his young wife had made it clear that Miss Hartwell would be under no pressure from them to quit her home, but Geneva was too realisitic to think that such an arrangement would work. She was too used to being her own mistress to be able to hand over the reins to someone else and stand meekly by. No, she had determined to leave the parsonage directly after her father's funeral. Geneva knew she had a home with Mrs Hollins as long as she needed it, but she did not expect this to be for long. She would seek a post as a governess; she knew herself to be better educated than many young ladies of her acquaintance and felt confident she could fill such a role. In very occasional moments of doubt she wondered if she could be happy in the position of servant, especially if her employer should happen to be in the mould of Mrs Thorneygate for example. But mostly optimism would prevail, and the possibility that any matron would have serious doubts about introducing someone as young and lovely as Miss Hartwell into her household never occurred to her.

But while Geneva rarely let thoughts of her future trouble her, she knew that it worried her father a great deal, and she would have been willing to do almost anything in her power to relieve him of that burden. A sensible marriage, she knew to be the practical solution, but for some reason she shrank from the idea of settling down to a life as the spouse of a country squire.

Geneva longed to see more of the world, to visit London, to wear the latest modes, attend balls and routs and ridottos, to dance, perhaps even flirt a little.

It was a natural desire for any young lady of lively and imaginative disposition and for all her good sense Geneva could never quite subdue her restless yearning for a life filled with romance and excitement. For some inexplicable reason her brief encounter with the fashionable stranger had stirred up these longings once more. If she were to have a season in London would he be there? Would he ask her to dance? She found this thought oddly disturbing and resolutely turned her mind to more mundane topics.

She had just mentally rearranged the furniture in the breakfast parlour, and was about to plan the following evening's menu when the sound of a fast approaching vehicle jolted her back to reality. From around the bend Geneva had just negotiated came a sporting curricle travelling at full tilt behind a team of mettlesome chestnuts. In vain did she try to turn the gig on to the grass verge. The cob had his own way of reacting to approaching danger, which was to stand stock still, and no amount of urging could make him budge. The driver of the curricle, cursing volubly, tried without success to avoid the obstacle in his path. The lane was too narrow and the hedgerows too dense to allow it. As he thundered by, the wheels of his vehicle clipped the side of the gig, which despite its sturdy construction was not designed to withstand such an encounter. With a protesting creak it tipped sideways unceremoniously depositing Miss Hartwell into a dry ditch.

She lay still for a few minutes, momentarily winded by her fall. In the darkness above her she could hear the scraping of hooves on the hard surface of the road and the frightened whinnies of the chestnuts, as the driver of the curricle fought to regain control of his team. This he seemed to accomplish fairly quickly, for soon the hooves were still, and the only sound to be heard was the occasional jangle of harness.

Geneva was just attempting to scramble to her feet when a figure loomed over her. Startled she looked up sharply; a mistake, since still disorientated by her tumble, and hampered by the heavy folds of her cloak, this sudden movement caused her to lose her balance and she found herself once more in the ditch. The indignity of her situation roused an irrational anger against the person who had witnessed it.

'Well, whoever you are, having put me here you might at least have the decency to help me out instead of gawping like an imbecile!' she snapped.

The figure replied, his well-bred accents proclaiming him to be a gentleman, 'I hesitate to correct a lady, but the position you find yourself in is entirely down to that useless creature you see fit to put in harness. You should be relieved to hear that my cattle received no hurt.'

If the words themselves added fuel to Geneva's rage, then the studied indifference with which they were uttered incensed her. 'Your cattle! You concern yourself with the fate of your horses when I could be lying here with a broken neck for all you know or care!'

'You are remarkably eloquent for someone who has sustained such a serious injury.'

Geneva's fiery temper was she knew one of her most lamentable faults, but by the same token, as quickly as it flared did it subside. Her ready humour had not deserted her despite her mishap, and it occurred to her that she must make a very ridiculous picture, sitting in a ditch arguing up at a man she could not even see. She abandoned her outraged stance.

'Very well sir, you have made your point. Now will you please assist me?' She could not resist adding with heavy sarcasm, 'That is if you are quite sure your vehicle has sustained no harm.'

The reply was instant, 'The merest scratch, pray do not concern yourself!' and before Geneva could think of a suitably cutting rejoinder, a pair of strong arms plucked her with apparent ease from where she sat and restored her to the grass verge. The rising moon was large and bright allowing Geneva a clear view of her rescuer. She gave a gasp of consternation. There could be no mistaking those mocking black eyes and those pale features rendered more so by the cold moonlight. It was the solitary gentleman from the tea-rooms.

In her surprise at seeing him again, especially when he had intruded on her thoughts so recently, Geneva did not at once perceive the improper nature of their position. Having lifted her bodily from the ditch, the gentleman had made no attempt to release her. When she eventually came to her senses it was to discover herself clasped firmly to the stranger's chest, his hands resting easily on her hips. Geneva felt a tide of colour wash over her and she wondered briefly at the unfamiliar sensations his closeness was precipitating.

With difficulty she looked up and met his inscrutable gaze, and addressed him in frigid tones. 'You may release me now sir, I am quite recovered!'

He continued to regard her, and she fancied there was a glint of humour in his eyes. 'I would do so, but I fear you might turn shrewish, in which case I would be forced to return you to your ditch.'

Geneva strove to maintain her dignity, but their continued intimacy was making her uncharacteristically flustered. 'That is most unhandsome of you, sir. I think I am entitled to feel some anger at the treatment I have been dealt.'

The glint became more marked, and in the unreal light of the moon, his expression seemed to Geneva almost wolf-like. 'But have I not rescued you? Your gratitude is underwhelming. It seems I am forced to take my own reward.'

His grasp on her tightened, and some instinct warned Geneva of his intentions. The hawklike features loomed closer and Geneva thought desperately of some means of avoiding the inevitable. Struggle would be futile and undignified, and a quick glance at the groom soothing the fretful chestnuts was enough to convince her that she could expect no help from that quarter. The servant had tactfully turned his back on the proceedings, and obviously knew better than to interfere with his master's activities.

Geneva shut her eyes tightly and held herself tense in his embrace, hoping that her obvious unwillingness would minimize her ordeal. For what seemed an age nothing happened; she could feel his warm breath on her hair but he made no attempt to kiss her. Puzzled she opened her eyes and looked up at him. There was such a look of blazing anger on his face that she instinctively fought to escape his grasp. He released her so abruptly that she stumbled and nearly fell.

'Your beast seems to have elected to make his own way home. If you will direct me I will take you to your destination.'

Geneva hesitated, the cob had indeed made good his escape, the traces of the gig having broken in the collision. She doubted the wisdom of accepting the gentleman's offer, yet she had no wish to travel the remaining five miles on foot.

Correctly guessing her qualms, the man sneered unpleasantly. 'Your virtue is in no danger from me. Rustic maids hold
no appeal for me.'

Stung by his derision, Geneva recovered some of her spirit.
'Nor arrogant rakes for me, sir!' she retorted, and with her head
held high she marched to the curricle and waited for him to
hand her up. This he did, and within moments they were on
their way.

The first mile passed in silence, Geneva sat bolt upright, her
eyes firmly fixed straight ahead and her hands clasped tightly
in her lap, determined not to betray her anxiety at the reckless
speed at which they hurtled along the winding road. It was the
gentleman who spoke first.

'Do you intend to tell me where you wish to go? My talents
are varied, but psychic ability does not rank among them.'

'Nor do modesty or good manners, apparently. The village of
Tadworth if you please; it is but four miles further on so you
need only endure my rustic presence for a few minutes longer.'

He eyed her thoughtfully for a moment or two and then asked
bluntly, 'Who are you? From your speech you are no farmer's
wench.'

His high-handed manner irritated her beyond belief, but she
had no wish to be dumped by the roadside, which she did not
doubt his ability to do if she were to become 'shrewish'. 'I am
Miss Geneva Hartwell, daughter of the Reverend Charles
Hartwell, the Parson of Tadworth.'

The gentleman seemed to derive some secret amusement
from this. He tipped his curly brimmed beaver in mock salute.
'A title to be proud of indeed! And I am Lord Augustin Vance,
fourth Earl of Brewood, libertine, gambler, and ... er – arrogant
rake!'

Geneva's eyes widened at this information, and the earl
noted her reaction with ironic amusement. 'I see my fame has
proceeded me as usual, Miss Hartwell. Your restraint amazes
me. Most young ladies of virtue would have cast themselves
from my carriage rather than travel in my corrupt presence.'

'Perhaps I should, I am sure Mrs Thorneygate would say so,
but having already found myself in a ditch once today, I have
no desire to repeat the experience.' She answered matter-of-
factly but looked at her companion with renewed interest, after
all it was not every day that one met a local legend.

Geneva had indeed heard of Lord Augustin Vance; anyone living within a twenty-mile radius of Harbury could not have failed to hear of the notorious earl. His family seat Brewood Court was situated just beyond Tadworth, and though the present encumbent had not spent more than a sennight at the country mansion since he inherited the title fifteen years previously, his nefarious activities had been the area's chief source of gossip for the past ten years.

'I must say you are not at all what I expected.'

The earl's amusement was genuine this time, his gaze free from mockery. 'And what did you expect, Miss Hartwell?'

She considered him speculatively. 'Well I imagined you to be a great deal older, and to look, oh I don't know! More depraved.'

This made him laugh aloud. 'I shall take that as a compliment of sorts! Was it Mrs Thorneygate who described me thus? And who is Mrs Thorneygate?'

'Mrs Thorneygate is the wealthy widow of a man of business. Well he was actually a mill owner, but she does not care to be reminded of this, which I think is excessively silly. But no, to answer your first question, Mrs Thorneygate's description was far more colourful. If she were to be believed you are to be recognized by your forked tail and cloven feet! I believe you come into the category of one of "Satan's own minions".'

Geneva laughed up at him, her blue eyes sparkling mischievously, indignation and fear forgotten. 'But indeed, you saw Mrs Thorneygate! She was with me in the tea-rooms!'

Lord Vance's expression changed imperceptibly, but it seemed to Geneva that a barrier had been put between them. He turned away from her, ostensibly to concentrate on the road ahead, and answered in the bored, aloof accents with which he had originally addressed her.

'Ah yes, a very vulgar-looking female if I remember.'

Geneva felt crushed, she recognized a snub but was at a loss to know what she had done to deserve it. Since the earl made no effort to continue the conversation, and Geneva had too much pride to lay herself open to a further rebuke, the remainder of the journey was undertaken in silence. Only when the welcoming lights of the parsonage came into view did Geneva say in a colourless voice, 'You may set me down here, sir.'

Lord Vance brought his team to a halt, and assisted his passenger to the ground. 'Goodbye, Miss Hartwell, I doubt if we shall meet again.'

Geneva was not to be beaten for coldness. She dropped a small curtsy, and addressing his left shoulder said, 'Goodbye, my Lord, thank you for your assistance.' With that she turned and ran into the house without looking back. Had she done so she would have seen the earl watching her progress with that same inscrutabe gaze with which he had observed her in the tea-rooms.

Two

Out of habit Geneva entered the house through the back door which led directly into the parsonage kitchen. Her mind still buzzing with the day's events, she had done no more than register the fact that candlelight was streaming through the mullioned windows of the dining-room and front parlour. This was an uncommon occurrence and in normal circumstances it would have immediately captured her attention. The parsonage, though not a large house, had more rooms than the clergyman and his daughter had need of. The Reverend Hartwell's modest stipend required that they practise a degree of economy, and since in latter years the reverend's illness had meant they entertained infrequently, the two rooms at the front of the house were rarely in use. The reverend took most of his meals in his room, and if he did ever feel well enough to come down for dinner, he was happy to join Geneva and Mrs Hollins in the snug parlour at the rear of the house.

Only when Geneva had divested herself of her cloak and was warming her hands in front of the welcoming fire did she notice anything unusual. Normally at this time of the day Mrs Hollins could be found in the kitchen preparing one of the simple dinners that suited both the Hartwells' taste and purse. But today, though Mrs Hollins was not to be seen there were signs of her considerable industry everywhere. On the spit a plump goose was roasting and the broad oak table groaned under the weight of a raised game pie and a startling array of pastries, jellies and vegetable side dishes.

Geneva could not believe her eyes; the thought that Mrs Hollins had taken leave of her senses did momentarily cross her mind. At that point the housekeeper herself appeared, her plump figure clad in what Geneva knew to be her best dress, and though looking somewhat harassed, she seemed to be in full possession of her faculties. The sight of Geneva prompted a volley of reproaches and garbled explanations.

'Oh, Miss Geneva! Of all the days to go missing. I have been near out of my mind with worry. What with the young gentleman arriving, and your father insisting on entertaining him in the parlour. Then not five minutes since did that lazy animal not appear on its own, with no sign of yourself! I was just about to send Jed Blunkett out alooking, and what I was to tell your father I do not know!'

Geneva ushered the flustered woman into an armchair by the fire, saying soothingly as she did so, 'There, there, Holly! Not to worry, see here I am, and father need never be alarmed. I had a minor accident in the gig, but I am none the worse, and from what you say the cob has made his own way home. Jed may pull the gig from the ditch in the morning and that will be an end to it.'

Although she played down the incident to Mrs Hollins, something told Geneva that her meeting with the earl would not be so easily dismissed. She did not mention the cause of her accident nor the way she had travelled home. For some reason she felt a reluctance to share her experience with anyone until she had had time to resolve it satisfactorily in her own mind.

Mrs Hollin's agitation appeared to have subsided though she still fanned her round flushed face with her apron. Geneva gave the housekeeper a few moments to catch her breath, but then she could contain her curiosity no longer. She sank to the floor in front of Mrs Hollins and stilled the housekeeper's fluttering hands with her own.

'Now, Holly! Tell me what is to do! Has the Regent himself come to dine? For I can think of no other reason for all this.' She indicated the table's bounty.

'The Regent! Why for shame Miss Geneva, he may be our future king, but no Godfearing female would allow him near a gently bred young lady!'

Geneva stifled a giggle at this, for in her innocence she could not imagine what a young country girl could have to fear from a portly prince in his fifties. Mrs Hollins continued, 'Now the young gentleman is everything that is pleasing, such fine manners.'

Geneva thought that she would burst with the suspense. 'Oh,

Holly, do not tease me so, who is this paragon? And more to the point what is his business here?'

Mrs Hollins relented. 'Well Miss Geneva it would seem he is by way of being some sort of cousin of yours, though perhaps stepcousin would be a better description. As to his business, well how would I be knowing that? The reverend just gets it into his head that we are to dine in style tonight, though how I am not to blush with shame to be serving only three courses and him no doubt used to four or five.' This had the effect of recalling her to her domestic duties, and Mrs Hollins once more bustled about the kitchen. Geneva knew she would receive no more information from that quarter.

Resolving to satisfy her curiosity directly, Geneva made to go to the parlour, but in this she was foiled by Mrs Hollins, who knew better (she hoped) than to let Miss Geneva meet a young gentleman of fashion in muddy gingham and with her hair anyhow. So Geneva allowed herself to be bundled up the narrow stairs to her bedchamber.

'Now then Miss Geneva, you take of those dirty clothes and rest while Lucy fills your bath,' instructed the housekeeper. 'Dinner will not be ready for an hour yet, so you have plenty of time to make yourself presentable.'

With that Geneva was left alone to muse upon the possible identity of their guest. Geneva had never heard mention of a cousin or even stepcousin, but this did not entirely surprise her. She knew absolutely nothing about her mother's family, beyond the fact that they all lived in the wilds of Southern Ireland. At the age of seventeen, Geneva's mother had been sent to England to stay with her wealthy godmother in the hope that she would contract a suitable alliance amongst the English nobility. But although her beauty and sweetness had attracted a number of very eligible suitors, she had shown a strength which belied her gentle disposition and, in the face of family opposition, had married her young curate. Nothing had ever been said in Geneva's presence, but she had gained the impression that her mother had never quite been forgiven for this, certainly there had never been any contact between the two families since Mrs Hartwell's death. It seemed unlikely that after so many years of silence that a maternal relative would appear.

On the other hand, the Reverend Charles had lost contact

many years ago with the only surviving member of his immediate family, his elder brother. All Geneva knew of her Uncle James was that he had journeyed to India as a young man, intent on making his fortune. Charles and James had never been close, their personalities were too opposed. James was ambitious with a knack for business, and he was impatient of his brother's unworldly attitude and contemptuous of his scholarly interests. When James left for India, and Charles married and pursued his vocation, it was inevitable that they should drift apart. Could the young gentleman in the parlour below be a stepson of James Hartwell?

If it had not been for the intriguing presence of their unknown guest, Geneva would have relished the opportunity to soak in a steaming hot bath. Her tumble from the gig was beginning to take its toll, and the warm rose-scented water provided blessed relief for her aching muscles. But as it was, she bathed quickly and was soon dressed and seated at her dressing-table, frowning at her reflection and attempting to bring some order to her recalcitrant curls. She had little cause to frown, the dark ringlets framed her face delightfully, and the hot bath had brought a becoming glow to her faultness complexion. She had selected the only evening gown she possessed with any pretensions to fashion, but in truth, the simple white muslin with its broad sash of powder-blue ribbon was the perfect foil for her fresh beauty. Her toilette completed in a fraction of the time deemed necessary by a lady of fashion, Geneva descended the stairs to the parlour.

She paused on the threshold and noted with relief that the candlelight was kinder to the faded red damask draperies than the bright sunlight which had prompted her purchase of new chintz. Indeed the room was warm and welcoming, tasteful if old-fashioned in its decor. Time and loving care had lent the mahogany furniture a rich glow, pine logs burned merrily on the fire filling the air with the fragrant scent of the forest.

The Reverend Hartwell and his guest were seated either side of the fire, but both rose to greet Geneva, their guest with alacrity, the reverend with some difficulty, which caused his daughter to hasten to his side in concern.

'Father you should not be exerting yourself so!' Geneva scolded him gently as he lowered himself back into his armchair. He patted her hand reassuringly, but his skin had a greyish tinge and fatigue showed clearly on his lined face.

'Now, now child, you are forgetting your manners. Make your curtsy to our guest. Sir, allow me to introduce my daughter, Miss Geneva Hartwell. Geneva, my dear, this is Mr Leonard Boeman, my brother James's stepson.'

Geneva greeted Mr Boeman coolly, silent reproof in her expressive eyes for the man who had so wearied her father. Mr Boeman read her thoughts accurately and instantly sought to make amends. He took the hand extended to him in both his own and smiled warmly down at her. 'Miss Hartwell, I see I am in your black books already. Believe me when I say I would not have taken up so much of your father's time had I not known that the news I bring him was of the upmost importance to you both.'

Geneva was not so easily won over, but this speech, expressed with such apparent sincerity mollified her slightly and she looked upon their guest more kindly. Certainly, in his appearance there was nothing to offend. He was a well-made young man of above average height, though not, said a small treacherous voice inside Geneva, as tall as my Lord Vance. This thought was instantly quashed. In fact there was little similarity between the two men. Mr Boeman's looks were conventional rather than rakish in their attractiveness. His hair was golden blond and thick, and if Geneva had been acquainted with the Brutus cut she would have recognized a fine example of the style. He was dressed very correctly in the modest attire of the country gentleman. Buff breeches and a rust riding coat, with a white cravat arranged neatly but unostentatiously.

Everything about him indicated a pleasing diffidence, and yet Geneva had to resist the urge to snatch her hand from his. For a moment there was something about the way his pale-blue eyes rested on her which was anything but diffident, in fact she would have described it as almost predatory. But in an instant it was gone, and Geneva could not be sure that she had not imagined it. It coloured her response to his friendly overtures however, and she remained cool.

'You intrigue me sir, but my immediate concern, as I am sure you will appreciate, is for my father.'

Mr Boeman was either too pleasant or too acute to allow this mild snub to overset him, 'Your concern does you credit Miss

Hartwell, and indeed, as you may judge from my attire, my intention was not to intrude upon you for any longer than was necessary to pay my respects and impart my news. But your father and Mrs Hollins were insistent, and I would not offend that admirable lady for the world! Her hospitality had already overwhelmed me.'

Geneva knew that their visitor's geniality showed her in a poor light, but for some reason she felt disinclined to make amends. She was saved the necessity of replying by the intervention of her father.

'Indeed my boy, you are very welcome; however I fear my delight at meeting you has led me to overestimate my own strength. You will forgive an old man I hope, for deserting his guest? But please, stay and dine with my daughter, and let her hear your news from your own lips. Mrs Hollins will act as chaperone so there need be no fear of impropriety.'

No, thought Geneva, not even Mrs Thorneygate could object to such an arrangement, and yet the thought of entertaining Mr Boeman alone made her feel uneasy. Strange that she should accept the assistance of a renowned rake on the open road, and yet could feel reluctance at dining under her own roof with a young male relation.

But Geneva's antipathy for their guest was not as strong as the curiosity he aroused. This she could not contain, and as soon as the reverend had been helped to his room and they were comfortably ensconced in the cosy dining-room, Geneva broached the question she had been longing to ask from the start.

'You spoke of some important news, Mr Boeman. It must be very important indeed to bring you so many miles.'

Mr Boeman flashed her an understanding smile and said warmly, 'I see good breeding forbids you to ask outright what you must be longing to know. Never fear I will satisfy your curisity on one condition. Will you not call me Leonard? We are after all related.'

Geneva blushed and transferred her gaze to her plate. His words though innocuous seemed to imply something less innocent, as did the way his pale eyes rested on her.

'The relationship is very remote if it exists at all,' she prevaricated.

Mr Boeman was not so easily discouraged, and he replied

smoothly, 'But that, I hope, will not be a barrier to our friendship ... Geneva.'

No man had ever used her given name except her father, and Geneva did not like the sound of it on Mr Boeman's lips. But she had never been missish, and she was loath to make an issue of such a seemingly trivial point. Deciding to make light of it she said brightly, 'You leave me no choice then, *Leonard*, for I must admit your visit does intrigue me.'

Mr Boeman seemed satisfied by this, and he began by questioning Geneva's own knowledge of her Uncle James. When she confirmed his belief that she had never met with her father's brother, he said gravely, 'Then I hope that the sad news of his death will not pain you greatly beyond your proper grief at the loss of a relative.'

This was said with such a solemn look and such a heartfelt sigh, that Geneva immediately inferred that for Leonard Boeman, his stepfather's death had been a great personal tragedy. At once her kind heart was touched, and she was quick to offer her sympathy and condolences, saying earnestly, 'You are right in what you say, of course, and it would be a hypocrisy of the sort I cannot abide, to pretend otherwise. But believe me when I say I feel most sincerely for you and your mother at the loss of one who must have been beloved.'

Mr Boeman appeared touched by her sincerity and was moved to declare with unwonted passion that his eyes had not deceived him, and that the beauty of her appearance extended to her mind. Geneva was dismayed by his fulsome compliments, and could not help feeling they were inappropriate under the present circumstances. Her companion sensed her withdrawal and begged forgiveness. 'I am afraid I have let the strength of my emotions overcome my manners, but—' He seemed to check himself. 'I will not embarrass you further. I will continue my tale.' He then proceeded to tell her of the series of events which had brought him to Tadworth, and despite her instinctive dislike of him, Geneva was soon enthralled by the story he told.

Mr James Hartwell had indeed journeyed to India, and there his ambition and business acumen had assured his success. Ten years of hard work and a series of wise investments, while not justifying the description of Nabob, had left him in command of a sizeable fortune, one which allowed him to return to the land of his birth and live the life of a gentleman of leisure. This he duly did, acquiring the country seat of a nobleman whose own speculations had been less profitable than Mr Hartwell's. Another ten years passed seeing James Hartwell firmly established among the gentry of the small Bedfordshire town, first in wealth, and only second in rank to the local squire.

A vigorous man with a fondness for sport, he had enjoyed his bachelor lifestyle, and he seldom felt the want of female companionship. However, as he approached his forty-fifth year he began to see the benefits of a wife and family to comfort him in his latter years. Happily, this coincided with the arrival in the neighborhood of Mrs Boeman. The widow of a city banker, Mrs Lucasta Boeman had been forced by her straitened circumstances to leave her London residence and live quietly in the country with her young son on their reduced income. The reason for their penury Mr Boeman did not directly specify, but Geneva was given to believe that the late Mr Boeman had been grossly deceived by a business partner, thus preventing him from leaving his family well provided for.

The circumstances by which Mr James Hartwell, distinguished gentleman of the town, and Mrs Boeman, an impoverished widow twenty years his junior, had become acquainted, were again unclear. The result was in any case an early alliance, and from that day to the day of Mr Hartwell's demise, if Mr Boeman were to be believed, the three of them had lived in a state of enviable harmony.

At this point in his history, Mr Boeman paused to compliment Mrs Hollins once more upon her culinary expertise. This allowed Geneva to ask the question which had perplexed her from the outset, and which Mr Boeman's disclosures had not yet answered.

'You will forgive my impatient curiosity I hope, but while it is very good of you to have travelled such a distance to inform us of my uncle's death, surely you need not have put yourself to such trouble? My father, I am sure, would have expected no more than a letter.'

'You are right of course, and if that had been the only news I had to impart then it is doubtful whether I would have made the journey. But I have other news of such direct importance to yourself, that when I was informed of it by my stepfather's solicitor, it seemed my duty to relay it to you, in person. And having met you Miss Hartwell ... Geneva, I can say that I would have readily travelled twice the distance for the pleasure of making your acquaintance.'

Geneva acknowledged this gallantry with a slight smile, but secretly wished he could cease these absurd attempts at flattery and come swiftly to the point. He did not disappoint her.

'The truth is Miss Hartwell, while my stepfather was very content with his lot, when illness struck him he was plagued by a feeling of guilt. He felt he should have contacted his brother and perhaps shared his own good fortune with him and his family. Towards the end, this thought possessed his mind to the near exclusion of all others, and if his health had permitted it, I am certain he would have made this journey himself. That was not possible, but he determined nonetheless to put right the wrong he felt he had committed. With this in mind he named you, his niece, as a beneficiary in his will.'

Mr Boeman paused to see the effect of this revelation. Indeed Geneva was very much taken aback and expressed her surprise. 'I can with all honesty say that neither my father nor myself expected to be remembered in such a way. It was very thoughtful of my uncle!'

Mr Boeman gave a sharp laugh, but continued in the blandest of tones, 'You are expecting a trifling sum, no doubt. But my stepfather's thoughtfulness has made you a very rich young lady. My mother retains the house and receives a modest allowance, of the remainder you are the sole beneficiary. I would be astonished if the principal is less than forty thousand and you may expect a yearly income of some five or six thousand on your coming of age.'

If Mr Boeman had hoped to shock her, then he was not disappointed. His words rendered her speechless for a full minute, then she shook her head slightly in a gesture of disbelief. 'Surely there has been some mistake! I cannot believe that my uncle's intentions have been properly understood!'

'There is no mistake, Miss Hartwell. Believe me, Mr Hartwell was very clear in his instructions, there can be no doubt.'

Geneva could not reply. A thousand thoughts ran through her head; she knew this news would mean a great change but it would take time for her to fully comprehend its implications. Mr Boeman addressed her again. 'It is to be expected that such news cannot be absorbed at once. I can see you would wish to be alone with your thoughts. I shall leave you.'

This recollected Geneva to her responsibilities as hostess, and she rose quickly. 'Forgive me Mr Boeman! I will leave you to your port. Perhaps when you join me in the parlour I may have gathered my scattered wits!'

Mr Boeman had risen with her and he politely declined her offer of port. 'No, Miss Hartwell, I have trespassed long enough on your kindness. Besides it is getting late and I must ride to Harbury. I have bespoken a room at The George.'

Geneva protested, but out of politeness rather than any real desire to detain her guest, and he was firm in his resolve to depart. He pressed her hand warmly as he made his farewells.

'It has been the greatest pleasure to have met you my dear Miss Hartwell. I hope one day I may be able to repay your hospitality and invite you to pay us a visit. My mother I know would be delighted to meet you.'

Geneva said everything that was proper, and it was a relief when Mr Boeman had finally ridden off into the darkness and she was alone with her thoughts. These were many and varied, and she longed to discuss the day's events with her father. Such discussions, she knew must wait for the morning. Until then she must be content with her own speculations. It was only when she had prepared herself for sleep and lay snug in the darkness of her bedchamber, that the realization finally sank in that she was no longer the poor daughter of a country parson, but a considerable heiress in her own right.

In a single moment all her expectations of what her future held had been turned upside down. Her first thought was of the relief this change in their circumstances would bring to her father. He no longer need worry about the security of his only child once he had gone. To Geneva this seemed the greatest benefit to be gained from her good fortune. Beyond that she found it hard to imagine. She had so long been resigned to a future of servitude that at first she found it impossible to comprehend a life of ease and leisure. Her imagination did not desert her for long however. The dream of a London season with all its attendant pleasures and extravagances could no longer be suppressed. And as she slipped into that pleasant state between wake and sleep, a tall figure bowed elegantly before her in a ballroom lit by a thousand candles, a look of

appreciation replacing habitual mockery in his dark eyes as he
requested the pleasure of the next dance.

Long after Geneva's innocent dreams had claimed her and the
parsonage lay in darkness, a dim light glowed in the study of
Brewood Court. The Earl of Brewood lounged in a handsome
winged armchair, his long legs stretched negligently before the
dying embers of the fire. A bottle of brandy considerably less
than half full stood within easy reach on a mahogany
occasional table. The earl drank deeply, then twisted the
slender stem of his glass meditatively between long white
fingers, gazing unseeingly into the golden depths of the dark
aromatic liquid. A log shifted in the grate throwing a shower of
sparks on to the thick Aubusson rug, and rousing the earl from
his musings. He stood up abruptly, shaking his head with a
slight impatient gesture as if to dislodge some nagging thought
or image. But it proved persistent.

Why wondered Lord Vance, after living his life as he pleased
without a moment's reflection, should a pair of wide violet eyes
make him question his own conduct? When he had thrust Miss
Geneva Hartwell from him, instead of doing what he had
wanted to do, which was to kiss her soundly, his anger had not
been directed at her but at himself. Her obvious fear combined
with a brave dignity had shamed him.

Since the day Augustin Vance had inherited his father's title
and wealth, no woman had shown herself so totally repelled by
his advances. Oh, the ones of supposed good breeding made a
show of outraged virtue, but they invariably showed their true
colours in some way; he would be allowed to come upon them
skirts raised as they tied their garter, an artless movement
would afford him an excellent view of an ample cleavage. Yes
they advertised their wares as surely as a street corner whore,
and their motives were the same, to sell themselves to the
highest bidder.

But there had been no coyness, no pretence in Miss
Hartwell's rejection. But then maybe she had more wit than her
sisters he argued to himself cynically. Besides had she not
given herself away by admitting she had seen him in those
ghastly tea-rooms? He had been momentarily diverted by her
beauty; it was unusual to find such a diamond of the first water
in such a provincial setting. But she had caught his eye, and

that was all the encouragement Miss needed. No doubt that vulgar companion of hers had been quick to point him out, and then the innocent parson's daughter had laid her trap. It would not be the first time an enterprising damsel had staged some little accident designed to throw her into the arms of the eligible Earl of Brewood. Yet if he truly believed her to be a scheming minx why did he feel almost guilty for snubbing the girl?

He downed the remains of his brandy and set down the empty glass sharply on the stone mantelpiece with an impatient exclamation. Drink had addled his wits; Lord Augustin Vance and a clergyman's daughter were worlds apart. He would never see her again and would have forgotten her existence within the week. He rang the bell and instructed the sleepy-eyed butler to have his carriage ordered for early the next morning. He had completed the tedious but necessary estate business that had brought him to his country seat; there was no need to spend another moment in this provincial backwater. He would return to London.

'You are forgetting the young gentleman who brought you the news of your inheritance. Mr Leonard Boeman.'

A sense of foreboding began to steal over Geneva. 'My father has named Mr Boeman as my guardian?' Some of the horror she felt at this idea must have shown in her face, for Mr Edlington set down his teacup and looked at her sharply.

'Yes indeed, Miss Hartwell. I see this news disconcerts you, but it is really quite an unexceptionable choice. Your father decided against telling you, knowing how it would upset you to think he had such a short time to live.'

'Yes, yes. I understand that.' In her agitation Geneva had started from her seat and now paced back and forth, twisting her hands together nervously. 'But Mr Boeman can hardly be classed as a relative. Surely someone better known to my father would have been more suitable?'

Mr Edlington was surprised and disappointed by Geneva Hartwell's irrational response, but he tried to reassure her. 'Your father seemed very favourably impressed by Mr Boeman; he described him in glowing terms. Besides as the stepson of your benefactor he must be the obvious choice.'

Geneva strove to collect herself. She was being ridiculous; she had taken an unfounded dislike of Leonard Boeman, and she had allowed it to prejudice her reaction. In any case her twenty-first birthday was less than six months away; this information would not change her plans. She resumed her seat and smiled apologetically at the solicitor. 'Forgive me, sir. I was unprepared for such news, but really it is of little consequence. I intend to move to Harbury and live with Mrs Hollins and her elderly aunt in the short term. When I have gained control of my fortune I will reassess my situation. Mr Boeman is only my guardian in name; I am sure neither he nor I will wish to interpret it in any other way.'

For the first time, Mr Edlington failed to meet Geneva's eye. He shifted uneasily in his seat and cleared his throat. 'As to that, Miss Hartwell, having taken the liberty of corresponding with Mr Boeman to apprise him of the circumstances, I can tell you that the gentleman takes his responsibilities as guardian very seriously.' The solicitor felt in his pocket and produced a single sealed sheet. 'Mr Boeman requested that I give this to you in person.'

Geneva's hands shook a little as she accepted the letter. Her sense of foreboding had returned. Standing to gain the light of the candle on the mantelpiece, she broke the seal and quickly perused the letter.

My Dear Geneva
Firstly may I offer my deepest sympathies at the loss of your father. Having myself recently lost one who stood in that capacity, I venture to suggest that I am familiar with the feelings you must now be experiencing. When Mr Edlington informed me of Reverend Hartwell's decision to name me as guardian to his daughter, I welcomed that responsibility gladly as a chance to further strengthen the family ties that bind us, albeit loosely.

My mother is of the same opinion as myself on this matter, and she seconds my earnest wish for you to make your home with us here at Clayton House. Indeed, I intend to wield all the force of my guardianship on this point! I have taken the liberty of arranging for you to be conveyed here on the twenty-seventh of the month, for I know how painful it must be for you to remain in a house of which you are no longer mistress. I have engaged a maid to bear you company and the worthy Mr Edlington will acquaint you with all the details. I can only add that my mother and I eagerly anticipate your arrival.
Your Affectionate Guardian
Leonard Boeman

If Mr Edlington's startling revelation had discomposed Geneva, then her guardian's letter left her bereft of speech. She was obliged to reread the missive several times before its implications sank in. '*Indeed, I intend to wield all the force of my guardianship on this point!*' – a seemingly jocular way of pressing the invitation. But the fact that her removal to Bedfordshire had already been put into motion could put Geneva in no doubt of the serious intentions behind Mr Boeman's humour. She appealed to Mr Edlington. 'But the twenty-seventh is the day after tomorrow! Besides, I have never considered making my home with my late uncle's family!'

'I know it is short notice, Miss Hartwell, but I was only informed of Mr Boeman's wishes this morning, hence my calling at this late hour. As to where you should live, I can well understand your desire to stay in a familiar locale and with Mrs Hollins, the woman who has looked after you and your father for all these years. But Miss Hartwell your circumstances have changed considerably.' He paused delicately and Geneva looked at him, unable to comprehend his meaning. 'To be frank with you, Miss Hartwell, for the orphaned and penniless daughter of respectable parents, your plans would have been ideal, but that is not the case. You are a wealthy young woman, and though naturally you will not have entertained the thought of marriage, it is highly desirable that after a suitable period of mourning you are in a position to meet eligible young men. Your widowed aunt is the ideal chaperone for such a purpose.'

Geneva could not resist an incredulous smile at his words. 'Mr Edlington, if that is all the reason you have to support the idea of my leaving my home and friends to live with an aunt with whom I am not even acquainted, then I must say that I consider it no reason at all! I have no thoughts of making an eligible match. If I marry it will be for love or not at all, and I would certainly not use my wealth to gain a noble husband.'

Mr Edlington returned her smile but somewhat gravely. 'Your sentiments, though naive, do you great credit Miss Hartwell. However it is not my place to advise you on such a subject. But it behoves me to tell you that as far as the law is concerned your own personal desires carry little weight. As your legal guardian, Mr Boeman has every right to demand your compliance. Now I am sure if he is the man your father believed him to be, he would not dream of forcing you into something you disliked, but my advice is to accept his invitation, for I can see no polite way of refusing his hospitality.'

Geneva inwardly rebelled at having her actions dictated by a man she scarcely knew, and one moreover for whom she felt an instinctive distrust. But she was sensible enough to recognize the wisdom of what Mr Edlington said. 'Very well. I will follow the course you suggest. But may I ask one small favour of you?'

Relieved that Miss Hartwell had accepted her situation, Mr Edlington did not hesitate to inform her that he would do anything within his power to help her. 'Then may I ask you to send details to me personally of any correspondence you may have with my guardian regarding my inheritance?' Mr Edlington was taken aback by this irregular request, but seeing no real objection, agreed to it, and after telling Geneva to expect the post chaise at eight on the morning of her journey, the lawyer took his leave.

With a feeling of bored resignation, the Earl of Brewood set down his coffee cup and broke the seal on the stiff bundle of papers his butler had kindly set with his morning paper on the breakfast-table. The earl was breakfasting alone, his sister and aunt, the only other members of his household, never rose much before noon during the season, and preferred to take their chocolate and rolls in the privacy of their boudoirs.

Six mornings out of seven Lord Vance enjoyed his breakfast and paper in peace, but once a week, as regular as clockwork, he would receive Mr Donaldson's report. The earl took little interest in the workings of his large country estate, preferring to spend the majority of his time in town. But he was not a neglectful landlord, and had put the running of Brewood Court in the hands of a very capable manager, and installed a secretary, Mr Donaldson, to undertake any necessary communications with the earl during his Lordship's prolonged absences.

Mr Donaldson was very meticulous in his duties, and consequently Lord Vance received a blow-by-blow account of every event that occurred within the boundaries of the estate and its environs. Normally there was little in this to interest the earl but as he quickly flicked through the closely written sheets his attention was caught by a familiar name.

News has reached us of the demise of our local parson, the Reverend Charles Hartwell. His death comes as no surprise since for several months he has been bedridden and nursed by his only daughter and their housekeeper, his wife having died many years ago. However he was very well regarded in the neighbourhood and a message of condolence from your Lordship I am sure would be a much appreciated gesture. The funeral is to be at Tadworth Church on the twenty-fifth.

Hartwell! The memory of a beautiful, spirited girl in an outmoded dress, her dusky curls in disorder, her violet-blue eyes sparkling with indignation came flooding back to the earl. Every detail of her appearance was as sharp and clear as if she were standing before him. Lord Vance had a sudden urge to pay his condolences in person to Miss Hartwell. He felt a concern for her wellbeing that was entirely foreign to his nature. The girl was orphaned and probably as good as penniless. The alternatives open to a gently bred female with no family or income were depressing in the extreme. An offer of help from the Earl of Brewood would arouse speculation and do the girl more harm than good, but he found himself reluctant to abandon the girl to her fate. The funeral was on the twenty-fifth. That was today! Still he could travel on the morrow and visit the parsonage the following day. Surely his worthy secretary with his usual discretion could find Miss Hartwell some suitable position without the earl's name even being mentioned.

Mr Donaldson would have been only too pleased to have performed such a service, and Lord Vance need only have put pen to paper and it would have been as good as settled. But Augustin Vance was feeling bored and restless, and he found the thought of engaging himself on a matter not entirely concerned with the pursuit of his own pleasure strangely appealing. That he should decide to visit his estates during the height of the season on anything but the most urgent of business would astound and delight the inmates of Brewood Court.

It was no secret among the servants that the earl had no particular fondness for the place. Indeed it was with a sense of relief that Lord Vance had quitted Brewood Court on the occasion of his chance encounter with Miss Geneva Hartwell, and he had not returned since. The childhood memories evoked by those vast gloomy salons with their dark drapes and heavy old-fashioned furniture were not pleasant and on his return to his elegant town house in the heart of fashionable London, the earl had tried to dispel those painful recollections in a bout of debauchery and pleasure-seeking that was startling even by his standards. But he was aware of a nagging feeling of discontent. This dissatisfaction reached its zenith when he was subjected to an hysterical tantrum by the dazzling barque of frailty currently enjoying his protection, the latest in a long line of ravishingly beautiful and extraordinarily rapacious females.

The result of this display of temper was not what the fair Brigida had counted on, provoking as it did boredom rather than penitence. She was rewarded for her pains not with the delightful barouche lined in sapphire-blue silk she so craved, but by receiving her congé, albeit with a handsome parting gift. For the earl this was a familiar occurrence and one which he had always accepted. But for some reason on this occasion he was left with a nasty taste in his mouth, and now three months later he still had no desire to replace the voluptuous blonde.

The Earl of Brewood, now in his thirty-second year, had finally come to the wry conclusion that the pursuits of his youth had palled. This thought was speedily followed by one even less welcome. Augustin Vance despite his rakehell reputation had a deeply instilled sense of family pride, and he was well aware that it was his duty to marry some unexceptionable female of impeccable lineage and unquestionable virtue and secure the succession with a parcel of brats in his image.

It could not be said that this prospect appealed; he had been acquainted with any number of ladies who fitted that description over the years, and he had never felt the slightest desire to marry any one of them. But the earl was not and never had been a romantic youth; had he ever been so inclined, his own parents' disastrous union would have nipped such finer feelings in the bud. It was nearly eighteen years since his mother had created the scandal of several seasons by fleeing her husband's tyranny in the company of a dubious Italian count, but for Augustin it was still an open wound. A wound that had been allowed to fester with the result that Lord Vance viewed ninety-nine percent of women with contempt and suspicion and regarded the institution of marriage with harsh cynicism.

And so, coldly and rationally, the Earl of Brewood had examined the season's array of eligible damsels and selected his future countess in much the same way as he would have chosen a new saddle horse from Tattersalls. The debutantes were dismissed out of hand; Lord Vance had no intention of pandering to the vanity of simpering chits. If they wished for odes to their sweet lips and declarations of undying passion then they must look elsewhere; he had no intention of feigning emotions he had never felt nor expected to feel. This narrowed the field considerably; young ladies in their second or third seasons were invariably antidotes or without the benefit of either station or fortune. For the wealthy earl fortune was irrelevant, breeding paramount and though beauty was not essential Lord Vance felt that a good figure was not too much to ask. That the chosen lady should refuse he dismissed without a thought. All this may lead one to suppose that Lord Vance was an insufferable coxcomb, and indeed had he thought his irresistibility as a marriage prospect rested on his own personal attributes rather than the attractions of his title and his fortune, then that would certainly have been the case.

The lady fixed upon, without any particular enthusiasm or through any partiality for her company, was Miss Camilla Fortesque. Miss Fortesque, while not precisely at her last prayers, was in the unenviable position of being in her third season without ever having received an offer. This was surprising since she was undeniably an attractive girl in a pale, untouchable way. In fact she had been much courted on her debut but for some unaccountable reason none of her suitors had come up to scratch. True she had no fortune to recommend her, but her lineage was faultless, the Fortesques having, as Lady Fortesque never missed an opportunity to mention, come over with the Conqueror. And here was the crux of the matter.

Once any young gentleman moved to court the fair Camilla had spent any length of time in the company of Lady Helen Fortesque and her hapless spouse he was struck with an uncanny premonition of what life as Miss Fortesque's husband would be like.

Needless to say the earl was not so easily daunted – he had no intention of being hag-ridden like George Fortesque. But despite a rather half-hearted courtship over a period of months, despite his decisive nature and his jaded view of matrimony, Augustin had never quite brought himself to the sticking point. Lord Vance found Miss Fortesque's company insipid in the extreme: she behaved with the utmost propriety at all times, she was never vulgar or forward and was pleased to agree with the Earl of Brewood's opinion on every matter, and the Earl of Brewood had never been so intolerably bored in all his thirty-two years!

Lord Vance planned his journey to Tadworth with something almost approaching enthusiasm, and when his valet respectfully reminded him of his engagement to dine with the Fortesques on the following evening, he threw himself into the expedition with uncharacteristic zeal!

Between the departure of her guest and the arrival of the chaise, Geneva had little chance to dwell on the upheaval of all her plans. Her personal belongings must be packed and arrangements made for the storage of what items of furniture had been the personal property of Reverend Hartwell. Sad farewells must be made to her friends, and especially to Mrs Hollins, who had been quite overcome when she had learned she was to lose Geneva's company.

It was only when the last of the luggage was strapped to the chaise that the enormity of what was happening finally hit Geneva and she clung tearfully to Mrs Hollins. She was leaving behind all that she held most dear, and she thought her heart must break as she took her seat opposite the sullen, silent maid. The postillions gave their impatient horses the office to start, and gradually the red-brick parsonage and the plump, comforting figure of Mrs Hollins disappeared from view. Geneva was not given to indulging in self-pity, but it was some time before she could think of anything beyond her own misery.

It was Geneva's natural curiosity that eventually roused her from her melancholy introspection. In all her twenty years she had never travelled beyond Harbury, and inevitably her lively interest was caught by the new sights that greeted her as they bowled along through the countryside. It was fine and crisp, the sun shone cold and bright in a pale-blue sky and, but for the remnants of frost lying on the hedgerows and fields, it could have been taken for a spring day, rather than a morning in late November.

Geneva's companion, whose name she had discovered was Mary, was singularly uncommunicative, and after receiving only monosyllabic replies to her attempts to initiate conversation, Geneva gave up and turned her attention to the passing landscape. With so many unfamiliar vistas to occupy her, the stage passed quickly, but the sight of the posting house was nevertheless welcome as Geneva had made an indifferent breakfast and her appetite had returned with her spirits.

Four

While the ostlers hurried forward to change the steaming horses, Geneva gladly stepped into the snug parlour of the inn. It took a second or two for her eyes to adjust to the dim light after the bright sunshine of the yard, but when they did she received a shock. Sitting before the fire enjoying a hearty breakfast was Lord Augustin Vance.

For a moment Geneva stood rooted to the spot, her one desire being to leave unobtrusively and avoid what for her would be an embarrassing encounter. The snub he had dealt her on their previous meeting still rankled and she had no desire to give this insufferably arrogant lord the opportunity to humiliate her for a second time. But before she could retreat Lord Vance looked up from his repast and all chance of escape was lost.

The earl was not in the best of tempers. He had set off from London the previous morning in his curricle and four with the intention of reaching Brewood Court not long after dusk. The capital behind him he was assailed with doubts about the wisdom of his impulsive move. Why was the Earl of Brewood making a hundred and fifty mile round trip to go to the aid of a chit whom he had met just once and who, if she was anything like the rest of her sex, would be certain to deliberately misinterpret his philanthropic gesture? When one of his leaders cast a shoe and slowed his progress to such a degree that he was forced to spend the night in an inferior hostelry, he was a fair way to abandoning the whole misjudged expedition and returning to London not quite in time to attend the Fortesque dinner.

When he looked up and saw Miss Hartwell staring at him in what could only be described as wide-eyed horror, he rapidly revised his plans. His memory had not misled him; Geneva Hartwell was quite the most tantalizingly attractive female Lord Augustin Vance had ever set eyes on in all his long and chequered career. That the feeling was not mutual was plainly written all over her enchanting little face. The Earl of Brewood, though he might scorn the ill-concealed delight his appearance generally provoked amongst marriageable females and their scheming mothers, could not but be piqued by her obvious antipathy for his company. He felt a strong desire to see those violet eyes alight not with repugnance but with passion.

Lord Vance had intended to be distant and gracious in his dealings with Miss Hartwell, as befitted a member of the nobility offering assistance to the penniless orphan of the local clergyman, but the feelings her appearance was precipitating were anything but distant; in fact he had an overwhelming desire to be very intimate with Miss Geneva Hartwell. And angry that the mere sight of this girl could so wrong foot him, the earl was anything but gracious. He rose to his feet with slow feline grace that managed to make the usually polite gesture seem like a deliberate insult.

'Miss Hartwell! What a fortunate coincidence. I was on my way to pay my condolences to you. I am happy to see you are not prostrate with grief, though I hardly expected to find you racketing around the country so soon after your bereavement.'

The news that Lord Vance had actually intended visiting the parsonage followed so swiftly by such unmerited aspersions left Geneva confused and then angry. In the most disinterested tone she could muster she replied, 'Really my Lord, I had no idea you were acquainted with my father. There was not the slightest need for you to put yourself to the trouble of calling. I am sure you can ill spare the time from your...' – she paused delicately – 'your more pleasurable pursuits in London to be making such a journey.'

This attempt at dealing a crushing snub might well have been wholly successful had Geneva's temper not got the better of her and forced her to add in less measured accents, 'And I am not racketing round the country, not that it would have anything to do with you even if I were!'

The earl greeted this with a shout of laughter and mock applause. 'Bravo! But having put me firmly in my place, you should have left the room at once, very much on your dignity, and left me writhing in mortification. It is always a mistake to allow your anger to show.'

Geneva found she could not suppress an answering smile, and was dismayed at how easily this intolerably rude man could disarm her. 'Well you were very insulting with no provocation, and if I had any degree of sensibility I would certainly run screaming from your presence, but as it is I am very hungry—'

'And you have no intention of letting such a graceless coxcomb deny you your breakfast,' supplied the earl.

'Well I would not have used such language, but I see you take my point.'

The earl laughed again and, signalling a serving girl, gestured to the seat opposite him. 'Enough! I have a congenital dislike of coming to cuffs before breakfast. Will you not join me, Miss Hartwell? Then if you feel the need you may abuse me at will.'

Geneva hesitated; she found there was nothing she would like more than to accept Lord Vance's invitation. He was like no man she had ever encountered. She knew she should be shocked by his behaviour, but if she were honest she found his outrageous conversation exhilarating. But Geneva also knew that any gently bred female finding herself in such a situation would certainly leave the inn immediately. She was about to regretfully refuse when the maid, Mary, intervened, saying in an agitated whisper that was audible to all, 'We should leave at once, miss. I don't know what Mr Boeman will say if he hears you have been fraternizing with a gentleman in a public tap room.'

Nothing was more likely to resolve Geneva than this. 'Really Mary, I am sure Mr Boeman is not so gothic in his ideas! There can be no impropriety while you are here. I am having breakfast, not fraternizing.' She directed a dazzling smile at the earl and took the offered seat.

'And who might Mr Boeman be to object to your bearing me company?' asked Lord Vance, when Geneva was settled with a mound of buttered eggs and a generous slice of ham before her.

Geneva knew she should firmly depress such impertinent questions but the news of Mr Boeman's guardianship still chafed her, and she found herself wanting to confide in the earl. She controlled the urge to confess all her misgivings, knowing that they were without firm foundation and would undoubtedly be received with open contempt, saying non-committally, 'Mary is over-anxious; Mr Boeman could have no objection.'

But Lord Vance was not to be put off. 'That, my girl, does not answer my question.'

Geneva did not know whether to be amused or shocked at this familiarity. 'Your persistence borders on insolence, my Lord!' But as he did not reply or even look up from the large rare steak he was making considerable inroads into, Geneva sighed resignedly and gave in to the inevitable. 'Mr Boeman is my guardian, and I am at present on my way to take up residence with him and his mother.'

'Your guardian. Well, he is certainly right to object to you fraternizing with a man of my reputation. You may be sure if I learned that my sister, who is also my ward, was fraternizing with such a hardened rake, I would take steps to stop it!'

'Oh I wish you would not use that word!'

'What? Fraternizing? But does it not aptly describe what we are now doing?'

'No it does not! We are having breakfast. Fraternizing suggests something altogether more—' Geneva blushed vividly and came to an embarrassed halt.

But the earl was ruthless. 'Altogether more what? Miss Hartwell you have a very colourful imagination. Your interpretation sounds much more agreeable than mine. Only tell me the details and I will do my best to oblige.'

Geneva cast him a fulminating glance, but though her heart was beating wildly beneath her demure high-necked gown, she was determined not to let Lord Vance see into what a flutter his provocative words had thrown her. 'You are trying to trap me into saying something very improper, but I will not take the bait, my Lord. The weather is very fine for so late in the year do you not agree?'

The earl eyed her with surprised admiration. Even the most seasoned lady of the ton would have been thrown into simpering disorder by such an outrageous speech. Yet this country miss sat there calmly sipping her coffee and making comments on the weather. 'Very fine,' he replied 'So you have acquired a guardian. How does that come about?'

Geneva suddenly saw a way of putting all her doubts to rest.

She would give Lord Vance an unbiased account of her newly inherited fortune and guardian, and she would judge from his reaction whether there was any foundation for her fears. That there was anything strange in her relying on the judgement of a man of whom she knew nothing but his wicked reputation did not occur to her. Just as she instinctively disliked and distrusted the charming Mr Boeman, so she instinctively trusted the scandalous earl.

'Mary, will you please go and ensure that the chaise is made ready to leave, I will join you in a moment.'

'But, miss!' protested the maid. 'Mr Boeman was very particular in his orders. He told me as how I was not to let you out of my sight, not even for a minute.'

'Do not be so ridiculous Mary. What possible harm can come to me in a public inn in full daylight!'

'But Mr Boeman said—'

'Enough!' interrupted the earl. 'You heard your mistress, now take yourself off.' With much muttering the maid shuffled out into the yard.

'Your efforts to contrive to be alone with me, quite unman me Miss Hartwell. Dare I hope you have … er – fraternization in mind?'

Geneva judged it better to ignore this taunt and concentrate on telling her story. This she found hard to do, since the earl had taken the opportuniry afforded by the maid's retreat to leave his seat and lead Geneva to the wooden settle before the fire. For some unaccountable reason, the closeness of his presence made it very difficult for her to frame a coherent sentence. But taking a deep breath and studiously avoiding his disturbingly intense gaze she launched into her tale.

Lord Vance listened to her in silence and when she had finished did not immediately say anything. Geneva looked up at him enquiringly, and found he was no longer looking at her but rather gazing into space with a preoccupied frown increasing his rather saturnine appearance.

Eventually he spoke. 'And so now the disinherited stepson is your guardian; how very convenient for him.'

This so exactly mirrored Geneva's own thoughts that unconsciously she put a hand on his arm and, looking up at him eagerly, exclaimed, 'So it strikes you that way also?'

The touch of her hand was too much for the earl's

self-control. Before he knew what he was about he had bent his head and kissed her slowly and gently on her slightly parted lips.

For what seemed like an endless moment, Geneva could only sit transfixed by the earl's smouldering gaze, completely at the mercy of the tumultuous sensations the touch of his lips on hers had sent coursing through her veins. With a smothered oath Lord Vance gathered her expertly into his arms. But in doing so he broke the spell, and with an inarticulate cry Geneva fought to repel him. The earl released her immediately, coming to his senses as quickly as the girl in his arms.

Geneva jumped to her feet, colour flooding her cheeks. 'I-I must go. The chaise will be waiting.'

'Wait!' The urgency of his command stopped Geneva in her tracks. Lord Vance strode to her side and grasped her arms roughly. 'I came here thinking you a penniless orphan, intending to offer you my protection. I find you have a fortune and a guardian, but my offer still stands. If you have any doubts about your guardian you have only to say—'

But Geneva did not allow him to continue, the conflicting emotions that beset her crystallizing into a sense of outrage at his scandalous proposition. 'Your protection! My Lord, I may only be a provincial miss in your eyes and I may have no noble relatives to protect me from such insults, but penniless orphan or heiress, nothing would induce me to accept such a degrading proposal!' And with the strength lent her by the violence of her feelings, Geneva wrenched herself free, ran out into the yard, and without waiting for assistance, clambered into the carriage.

By the time the earl had recovered from his surprise and followed her out of the tap room, the post chaise had already turned onto the road and was rapidly disappearing in a cloud of dust.

Geneva gazed blindly from the carriage window, the landscape rolling by unseen. It was some time before she was able to marshal her disordered thoughts. Geneva was too honest to deny the attraction she felt towards the rakish earl. But as her fast-beating heart gradually calmed, she was able to analyze her feelings more rationally. She remembered all the whispered innuendoes of the ladies of Harbury over their afternoon teas. Rumours of dashing matrons risking their reputations and marriages for Lord Augustin Vance. If they were to be believed, the slightest attention from the Earl of Brewood was enough to make young debutantes lose their hearts and their heads. Geneva was sensible enough not to believe absolutely the gossip that surrounded Lord Vance, but there could be no denying the fascination he exercised over the opposite sex. It was not to be expected that Geneva alone would be impervious to his charm.

This conclusion reached, Geneva felt no less wretched when she recalled Lord Vance's proposition. The anger she had felt had only partly been directed at him, because for one insane moment she had been close to casting all her principles to the wind and accepting his protection. Geneva resolutely refused to allow herself to dwell on the possible outcome of that decision. The earl was left behind; Clayton House and her guardian lay before her and it was on them that she should concentrate.

Geneva turned her attention to Mr Boeman's strict instructions to her companion, Mary. It seemed a trifle odd that he should be so insistent on Mary keeping her always within sight. Indeed Geneva was becoming increasingly irritated by Mary's behaviour. She seemed to have taken her master's words literally and Geneva was continually aware of her unwavering gaze. Really, Geneva thought, it is as if she thinks I am liable to vanish in a puff of smoke should she not watch me constantly. This led Geneva to think of her guardian's letter. He seemed very anxious that his ward should reach Clayton House without any delay. Then she remembered Lord Vance's response to her story. He did not strike her as a man given to flights of fancy, and he obviously regarded her guardian's actions with something approaching suspicion. But then, a cynical voice suggested, it was entirely in his interests that you should relinquish Mr Boeman's protection for his own. Geneva almost exclaimed aloud with impatience. Her thoughts were running in circles, and all were based on the wildest of suppositions. She would endeavour to enjoy the remainder of her journey travelling as she was in unaccustomed luxury. What awaited her at Clayton House would not change through her hypothesizing.

The journey was some sixty miles, but they made excellent time, and it was four o'clock in the afternoon when they stopped at the bustling Cross Keys Inn to change their cattle for the final time. Geneva made to step down but Mary's big square hand on her arm prevented this. Geneva glanced at the woman in surprise.

'Begging your pardon, miss, but Mr Boeman said as how you should stay in the carriage at this inn. He reckons that the Cross Keys is not the proper place for a young lady to be seen unescorted.'

Geneva, who had no great wish to leave the chaise acquiesced, but she could no longer suppress the idea that Mr Boeman had sent Mary to act as the gaoler. Looking out at the crowded yard Geneva could see nothing to justify her guardian's poor opinion. From the outside at least the Cross Keys seemed to be a tidy, well-run establishment, and its customers appeared to Geneva's eye to be eminently respectable people. Coupled with Mary's attempts to prevent her conversing with the earl, Geneva could not help thinking that her guardian seemed to have an unnatural desire to prevent her from speaking to anyone on her journey, particularly when they reached an inn close to Clayton House. What would the customers have to say to her that Mr Boeman did not want her to hear? If the chaise had not moved off at that moment Geneva would certainly have descended in the face of Mary's protests and made some enquiries.

The Cross Keys left behind, Geneva found her spirits sinking and her sense of disquiet increasing. What after all did she know of her new guardian? Her father had liked him, but then for all his excellent qualities the reverend had not been an astute judge of character. He had always been eager to see the best in people, and being without guile himself, he had never suspected it in others. A thought that had occasionally puzzled Geneva over the past few months came back to her, only this time it seemed to carry with it sinister implications. If Leonard Boeman had been like a true son to James Hartwell why had the man left his entire fortune to a niece he had never set eyes on?

At this moment the chaise turned into a wide, gravelled driveway, lined on either side with tall rhododendrons. They had arrived at Clayton House. The sun was low in the sky and between the dense shrubs it was gloomy and silent. It was perhaps fortunate that Miss Geneva Hartwell preferred the novels of Miss Austen to the fashionable gothic romances of Mrs Radcliffe, or her apprehension would doubtless have multiplied tenfold.

The drive was only half a mile in length, so it was no time before the chaise emerged once more into the pale light of dusk. A modest circular lawn with an impressive fountain at its centre lay between the end of the driveway and a plain oblong house built of dull grey stone. It was unprepossessing, neither welcoming nor forbidding. Geneva was aware of a sense of anticlimax.

The sound of the approaching carriage had obviously alerted the household to their arrival, because before the postillions had brought their horses to a halt the double doors were thrown open and two footmen hastened to assist Geneva to alight. They were followed at a more stately pace, as befitted his station, by the butler. This august personage bowed low before Geneva and with much pomp conveyed her into the house, up the wide palladian staircase and into the Rose Room, where, he informed her, Mrs Hartwell and Mr Boeman would join her presently.

Geneva looked about her in wide-eyed astonishment. The grey nondescript exterior had not prepared her for the magnificence of the interior. The Rose Room, as its name suggested, was decorated in a rich shade of pink. Pink satin and gilt chairs were scattered over pink carpet, pink flocked wallpaper covered the walls and elaborate pink drapes hung at the long narrow windows. Added to this superabundance of pink was a profusion of gilt, and the effect was so dazzling as to hurt the eye. Even to Geneva's inexperienced gaze it was obvious that everything was of the finest quality, and if its overblown opulence was not to her taste, she supposed that it must be the fashion amongst the wealthier classes.

Geneva was not given long to take in her surroundings, and she had just gingerly seated herself on the edge of one of the fragile looking chairs, when the door opened to admit Mr Boeman. He was followed by a large woman, impressively decked out in a wealth of black satin, lace and jet beads. Geneva guessed this was her uncle's widow. When he saw her, Mr Boeman strode across the room, his arms outstretched, a warm smile of welcome pinned to his lips. 'My dear Geneva! How delightful to see you again.' Before she could divine his intention, Geneva found herself swept into a tight embrace. When he released her she was considerably discomposed, and he was instantly penitent. 'Oh forgive me, Geneva, I have so looked forward to seeing you in my home that I am afraid my emotions got the better of me. Mother will tell you, I have not been able to settle to anything all day!'

Geneva could frame no response to such a welcome, finding it unnerving rather than gratifying. Mrs Hartwell's greeting was cool in comparison. Casting a mournful smile in Geneva's direction, she walked slowly across the room and arranged herself on a day bed close to the roaring fire. A maid followed behind carrying a tray loaded with a bewildering array of silver-stoppered crystal bottles, containing a variety of smelling salts and other remedies, which she deposited on a gilt occasional table at Mrs Hartwell's elbow. Mr Boeman took Geneva's hand and led her across to his mother, saying eagerly, 'Of course there is no need for formal introductions but we shall abide by the conventions. Mother, allow me to present Miss Geneva Hartwell, my ward. Geneva, my mother, Mrs Hartwell.'

'I am very pleased to meet you, Mrs Hartwell, and very grateful for your kind invitation.' Geneva dropped a small curtsy.

Mrs Hartwell gave another faded smile and limply extended one plump pink and white hand. 'You are very welcome Miss Hartwell.' This was said with a faint die-away air very much at odds with her robust healthy appearance.

'Now, now! What is this? Mrs Hartwell? Miss Hartwell? Are we not all of the same family? Geneva, my mother has looked forward to your arrival as eagerly as I, and it is her dearest wish that you should call her Aunt Lucasta, is that not so Mother?' Thus appealed to Mrs Hartwell agreed, but with such a languid lack of enthusiasm that Geneva found it very hard to believe she had ever voiced such a wish.

Mr Boeman again took the lead. 'I will ring for the housekeeper to show you your room, Geneva. I am afraid my mother's frail constitution precludes even the mildest exertion, but you will find an able substitute in Mrs Chambers.' Geneva murmured something appropriate and privately thought she had never seen anyone in such obvious rude health as Mrs Lucasta Hartwell.

The able substitute proved to be as dour and taciturn as Geneva's travelling companion. The bedchamber set aside for Geneva's use was as sumptuous as the Rose Room. It was decorated in shades of yellow ranging from pale primrose to saffron with a great deal too much bright green japanned furniture. The centrepiece was a magnificent four-poster bed in the style of a Chinese pagoda, each of the posts crowned with a fearsome looking gilt dragon. Not exactly conducive to a restful night's sleep thought Geneva ironically. Mrs Chambers broke her self-imposed silence to inform Geneva that dinner would be in an hour, and that Mary would act as lady's maid.

Geneva received the latter information with a sinking heart. A lady's maid was an unheard of luxury, but given a choice Geneva would have rather done without than renew her acquaintance with the surly Mary. But she had no choice, and so when the maid appeared with a freshly pressed evening gown Geneva made the best of it. Mary was as unforthcoming as ever, and though Geneva had nothing with which to compare her, she seemed remarkably ill-suited to her post. Her big coarse hands fumbled clumsily with the ties of Geneva's gown and Geneva wisely attended to her own coiffure, having no wish to have her hair torn out at the roots by the maid's rough ministrations. Mary was obviously under instruction not to answer any question that Geneva might put to her regarding her new home. Even the most innocuous of queries was met with, 'I couldn't rightly say, miss' in a dull monotone.

By the end of an hour, Geneva had come to the conclusion that Mary was either not quite right in the head, or her terms of employment were very peculiar indeed. It was a relief when a footman appeared to escort her to the dining-room to escape the maid's company, but as she had not met with anything as yet to allay her suspicions regarding her guardian, she could only look forward to the approaching meal with apprehension.

Five

Geneva followed the magnificently liveried and bewigged footman to the dining-room, ruefully comparing his velvet and braid finery with her own outmoded black silk. She would undoubtedly appear a complete dowd in Mrs Hartwell's fashionable establishment. Geneva was the last of the three to arrive. Mealtimes, as she would soon learn, were the only occasions on which one could rely on Mrs Hartwell's punctuality.

Mr Boeman, very formally attired in black evening wear, came forward to greet Geneva saying in a low ardent voice that only she could hear, 'My dear, you are lovelier every time I see you.'

Geneva blushed but refused to let his intimacy throw her, extricating her hand from his eager clasp and saying clearly, 'I wish you would not talk such nonsense, sir! You must have a very poor opinion of me if you think I crave constant flattery.'

Geneva thought she saw a flash of anger in those pale eyes, but the smile never left his lips, and he replied smoothly, 'I speak only the truth. But if it distresses you then I must strive to contain my feelings.'

Feeling it was best to ignore this hint at the depth of his regard for her, Geneva moved forward to greet her aunt. Mrs Hartwell was resplendent in grey taffeta and garnets, a magnificent turban crowned with a single tall black ostrich feather completing her toilette.

It was possible that Lucasta Hartwell might once have been a handsome woman, but years of indolence and fine living had ruined her figure and left her features slack and bloated. With the heavy maquillage she favoured and startling *décolletage* Geneva was instantly reminded of the Cyprian who had so shocked the clientele of the Harbury Tea-Rooms all those months ago. Inwardly chastising herself for such disrespectful comparisions, Geneva addressed her aunt, hoping her face did not betray her thoughts.

'Aunt Lucasta, I hope you have not gone to all this trouble on my account!' With a movement of her arm she indicated the long dining-table loaded with plate, and the sideboard covered with an astonishing array of dishes.

Mrs Hartwell sighed heavily. 'You are very kind to say so, my dear, but really I am ashamed to be putting such a pitiful spread before a guest. But my circumstances are not what they were, and I must manage as best I may.'

Geneva could find nothing to say to this and for once was glad of Mr Boeman's intervention. 'Now, Mother you must not embarrass Geneva so! After all I am sure she would wish to be treated as a member of the family rather than as a guest, is that not so?'

Geneva agreed eagerly, but Mrs Hartwell did not look convinced, saying doubtfully, 'Well if we are dining *en famille* I suppose it is passable.'

Mrs Hartwell's idea of dining *en famille* set the pattern for every evening meal during Geneva's time at Clayton House, and seemed to her to carry enough pomp and ceremony for a state banquet at Carlton House. The long dining-table could have seated a dozen comfortably, but although there was never more than the three of them, the extra leaves were not removed. Easy discourse was further handicapped by the presence of the butler and no less than six footmen; two behind each chair.

Mrs Hartwell concentrated all her attention on the satisfaction of her prodigious appetite. Her only contribution to the conversation was to occasionally exclaim that, really, there was nothing that could tempt her fastidious taste, before resignedly saying that she supposed she must try her best so as not to disappoint her chef. The footman would then obligingly heap her plate and in this way Mrs Hartwell contrived to maintain the fiction of her delicate constitution without in the least impairing the enjoyment of her food.

Mr Boeman on the other hand set out to be the perfect host, devoting his energies entirely to the entertainment of Geneva. This consisted of him directing a series of solicitous questions at Geneva regarding her health, spirits, her journey to Clayton House and the comfort of her bedchamber together with a myriad of other trivial enquiries. Geneva reassured him on all points and tried in vain to ignore the warmth in his tone and the glow of admiration in his gaze, which she could only find irritating.

It was a relief to Geneva when the interminable meal came to an end, and she and Mrs Hartwell very correctly withdrew and left Mr Boeman to his port. They returned to the Rose Room where Mrs Hartwell at once disposed herself on her favourite day bed and Geneva was established less comfortably on a highly ornate giltwood armchair, upholstered in the obligatory pink-figured silk. Since her hostess made no effort whatsoever, the burden of conversation fell entirely upon Geneva.

'You have a very elegant home, Aunt Lucasta,' ventured Geneva, thinking that this at least might be a topic which would please her companion.

But Mrs Hartwell answered in the despondent tones with which Geneva was becoming rapidly familiar. 'It is very well in its way, but it is nothing compared to our London residence.' Geneva was surprised, she had heard no mention of a second property and said as much. Mrs Hartwell gave a heavy sigh. 'Oh no, it is quite five years since I was last in town. My late husband's health demanded my presence here and so the town house was disposed of. I felt the loss most keenly but of course duty must prevail.'

'Mr Boeman led me to suppose you had all lived at Clayton House since your marriage to my uncle.' Geneva knew she was bordering on ill-mannered curiosity, but she was beginning to suspect that Mr Boeman had been somewhat economical with the truth in his heartwarming portrayal of the Hartwells' marriage. Lucasta Hartwell did not appear offended by her interest but on the contrary was content to reminisce about the gay life she had led in the capital. This consisted of series of dull anecdotes concerning Mrs Hartwell's encounters with the upper echelons of society, all of which were wasted on Geneva who was largely ignorant of the people and places referred to. Mr Boeman's name appeared frequently during this monologue but Mr Hartwell was mentioned not at all which prompted Geneva to ask whether her uncle had enjoyed town life.

'Mr Hartwell preferred his country pursuits I am afraid to

say, and I was never able to persuade him to leave this house in
all the years we were married. Even when I was forced to take
the waters in Bath for the sake of my health, he could not bear
to drag himself away. But my dear Leonard has been a blessed
support to me, always bearing me company.'

This hardly accorded with the idyllic picture of family life Mr
Boeman had painted. On the contrary, it appeared to Geneva
that while her uncle had continued to live his solitary bachelor
existence, James Hartwell's wife and stepson had jauntered
around the fashionable resorts at his expense. His death had
brought that to an abrupt end. Geneva had no idea what
allowance Mrs Hartwell had been provided with, but it seemed
unlikely that it would keep her and her son in the style to
which they had become accustomed. Her aunt's next words
confirmed this.

'Now I do not know how we will go on. You must not think I
will miss it all for a minute on my own account! It is my poor
dear Leonard of whom I think. It will be impossible for him to
move in the same circles now our income is so cruelly reduced.'

'But has Mr Boeman no occupation? No means of financing
himself?'

'You feel the same as Mr Hartwell I see. But rightly or
wrongly on this I have always stood firm. Mr Hartwell told me
time and again that Leonard should be sent away to school and
then induced to take up some profession, but he was my only
son and I could not bear to be parted from him. Leonard has
inherited my own weakly disposition, and I swear he could not
have survived the rigours of an education away from his
mother.' At this point she abandoned her languor for a moment
and leant towards Geneva, her round face eager and
questioning.

'But you have seen him! It is impossible to imagine such a
refined and accomplished man obliged to soil his hands with
trade! Leonard has been brought up as a man of wealth and
position, it is too cruel that he should now be expected to
change.'

Geneva privately thought that Mr Boeman would have done
better not to have relied so entirely on expectations, which as it
transpired, had no foundation in reality. That Mrs Hartwell's
aim was to make Geneva feel guilty at her own good fortune,
she did not doubt, and indeed it was impossible not to feel

some embarrassment. However much she might personally dislike Leonard Boeman and deplore his making no push to find employment, Geneva could not believe that she was any more entitled to her uncle's fortune than he was.

At this point they were interrupted by the entrance of the butler, who had lost some of his customary imperturbability. He approached his mistress and murmured something in her ear. Geneva could not hear what was said, but whatever it was it considerably disturbed Mrs Hartwell, who leapt to her feet with surprising agility for someone so large and inactive.

'My dear, pray will you excuse me? I fear Leonard is – is not quite well. I must go to him.'

Geneva instantly expressed her concern and offered to help in any way she might, at the same time wondering what mysterious ailment could have struck Mr Boeman down since they had left him less than an hour ago. Mrs Hartwell was resolute in her refusal to allow Geneva to help.

'It is just an affliction of the nerves, nothing very serious but it is best if I attend him. Perhaps you would take tea in your room, I am sure you must be fatigued after your journey.'

At that moment a footman had discreetly appeared, bearing a branch of candles to escort her, so Geneva felt she had little choice in the matter, though it was barely nine o'clock and she was not the least bit tired. But Mrs Hartwell had taken her assent for granted and had already bidden her a hasty goodnight and left the room.

Geneva followed the footman up the stairs, lingering as long as she dared at the top on the pretext of tying the ribbon of her shoe, and straining her ears to hear the muttered dialogue coming from behind the firmly closed door of the dining-room, but to no avail. Then just as she was reluctantly hastening after the disappearing footman, there came a sound of glass breaking and a voice raised in anger came from the direction of the dining-room.

'Damn it! I don't want this pap! Can a man not get a drink in his own home? That old miser may have tricked me out of his money, but I am still the master in this house, and when I call for brandy you'll bring it and be damned sharp about it if you know what's good for you!'

The murmuring voices became more agitated but by this time Geneva was out of earshot. But she had heard enough.

The measured mellow accents had been replaced by the bitter slurred tones of drunken anger, but there could be no mistaking Leonard Boeman. Geneva struggled to maintain an unruffled demeanour for the benefit of the footman and her maid. But when she was finally able to dismiss Mary she wasted no time in leaving her bed, creeping stealthily to the door of her bedroom and quietly turning the key in the lock. Geneva was not lacking in courage but the thought of sharing a roof with Leonard Bowman, his true character brought to the surface by the excesses of port he had so obviously imbibed, filled her with dread.

Satisfied that for the night at least she was safe from his nefarious plans, Geneva returned to her bed and tried to piece together the fragmented clues she had gathered during the course of the day. That Leonard Boeman and his mother should resent Geneva she found understandable. But why the show of affection? Even though Mr Boeman was her legal guardian he had no access to her fortune. Then Geneva thought of his open admiration for her, his absurd flattery and his scarcely veiled hints of his hopes for a closer relationship, and the truth struck her.

Where he had failed with his stepfather he hoped to succeed with Geneva. Mr Boeman intended to court her and through marriage acquire the fortune be believed to be his by right.

Whilst this realization disturbed Geneva, some of the apprehension she had felt left her. Armed with this knowledge she was surely safe, for there had never been any danger of her succumbing to his gallantry, and after all he could not force her into wedlock. Comforted by these sensible thoughts Geneva was able at last to slip into a relatively untroubled sleep, and when she was awoken by bright sunshine streaming through the tall narrow windows of her bedchamber all the fears of the previous evening melted like frost under its cheerful influence.

Feeling a little foolish she unlocked her door and without bothering to summon the maid, dressed quickly in a simple day dress of grey dimity, and made her way downstairs. The omnipresent butler conducted her to the breakfast parlour, informing her as he did so that the master and mistress rarely came down before 10.30.

Geneva was too thankful to be spared the oppressive

presence of her aunt and guardian to be daunted by his reproving tones. She resolved not to waste her precious time alone, and after partaking of a little tea and toast, collected her cloak and set out to explore the grounds of Clayton House. At the rear of the house a series of terraces led down to a formal Italian garden. Gravel paths divided geometric flower beds, which in summer were no doubt a riot of colour. But in this season there was little to delight the eye and Geneva quickly moved on. She was attracted by the sight of a folly on the far side of the small ornamental lake, and decided to make that her target.

Geneva walked at a brisk pace, for although the sun shone brightly in a cloudless sky, the air was sharp. She reached the folly and elected to sit for a moment in its dim interior before returning to the house. She gazed half seeing at the house in the distance, her thoughts turning naturally to her father. Geneva would have given all her fortune if she could have only had her beloved parent with her for another hour. How she missed his quiet wisdom!

But Geneva was given no time to be alone with her grief, for she caught sight of a figure striding across the gently undulating parkland in her direction. With a sinking heart Geneva recognized her guardian. Since she had no desire to grant him the opportunity of an intimate tête-à-tête in the secluded folly, she set off back towards the house at once, resigning herself to their inevitable meeting on the way. When they did meet it was obvious to Geneva that Mr Boeman had lost some of his usual sang-froid, and when he addressed her it was with barely concealed annoyance.

'Geneva, what can you be thinking of to be walking alone so far from the house?'

'But still within sight of it! I cannot imagine what harm could come to me here.'

'Your safety is not the issue. I merely wonder at the propriety of such an expedition. Surely you have not forgotten your mourning state?'

Geneva could not contain her irritation at his pomposity. 'Mr Boeman, you may be my guardian in law, but you are mistaken if you think you can dictate to me on matters where my own conscience should be sufficient rule. I would hardly call a stroll within the boundaries of your estate an expedition, and I see nothing to offend propriety. Why, you would incarcerate me in the house!'

In the face of such anger Mr Boeman obviously thought it expedient to appease her, but his own wrath was clearly visible. 'My dear, I have no wish to incarcerate you as you so violently put it, but I must tell you that my mother has very strict notions and it would certainly distress her if you were to openly flout her wishes. If you care to stroll outside, the terraces provide an unobjectionable setting.'

The first heat of her anger passed, Geneva's good sense came to the fore. It would do nothing but harm to antagonize her guardian while she was still within his power. So she accepted his criticism with deceptive meekness, and even managed to apologize for her thoughtless behaviour.

The day progressed with relentless tedium. To Geneva's relief Mr Boeman took himself off to some undisclosed destination and did not return until dinner. To someone whose days had always been full of industry, Mrs Hartwell's ideas of employment were vapid in the extreme. Geneva could only marvel at her apparent contentment to spend the entire day reclining on her day bed with only a fashionable periodical and the society columns of the daily newspaper to occupy her.

Day after day followed in this manner, and at times Geneva thought she would scream from frustration. In desperation she offered to read aloud, and this was deemed an excellent idea. All the books in the library of Clayton House were stigmatized by Mrs Hartwell as a dead bore, and so a footman was dispatched into Malpeth, the nearest town and some three miles distant, armed with a list of the various lurid publications that excited the widow's interest. In vain did Geneva offer to fulfil this errand herself. Mrs Hartwell would not hear of it, saying that Mr Boeman would consider it most irregular.

The only event to relieve the stultifying boredom of Geneva's first week at Clayton House was the arrival of a letter from one of Mrs Hartwell's London acquaintances. This excited Mrs Hartwell to such a degree that for an entire afternoon she was quite loquacious, wondering and exclaiming at all the gossip this lengthy missive contained.

Geneva listening to her, was quietly entertained, for while she was unacquainted with the people under discussion it was pleasant to hear news from the outside world. Her attention was suddenly and fully caught by the mention of a familiar name.

'Well I do declare! I am sure no one expected this! Only listen, Geneva.' Mrs Hartwell read out an extract of the letter with a great deal of dramatic emphasis. ' "An interesting rumour is at present circulating the fashionable salons regarding that confirmed bachelor, the Earl of Brewood. It is said that he has singled out a Miss Camilla Fortesque in a most marked way and it is thought that he will offer for her before the month is out! That she will accept is of course beyond doubt, for she is practically an ape-leader. All the debutantes and indeed most of the young married ladies are wild with envy for you must know he is a tremendous catch and has had countless girls thrown at his head these ten years and never shown the least interest. Whether it is a love match I cannot say but it is thought to be a very respectable alliance on both sides".' Mrs Hartwell dropped her lorgnette in her lap and exclaimed, 'Well what do you think of that?'

Fortunately for Geneva this was a rhetorical question and so she was spared the necessity of forming a reply. Why the news of the impending marriage of Lord Augustin Vance should so affect her, Geneva could not say, but there was no denying that it entirely destroyed her peace for the remainder of the day.

The memory of the earl's offered protection still pained her, and when she had chance to think about it she decided that what she was feeling was nothing more than wounded pride. Of course she had no desire to marry that insufferable man, but it irked her that while Miss Camilla Fortesque was worthy of an offer of marriage, the top-lofty earl considered Miss Geneva Hartwell to be only deserving of a much less respectable proposal.

But Geneva's lowness of spirits could not easily be shaken off. Somehow, despite his insulting behaviour, Lord Vance had remained in the recesses of Geneva's mind as a figure to whom she could turn for help if her situation ever became desperate. Now she felt terribly alone, not even Mrs Hollins had answered her letters.

It had gradually dawned on Geneva that she was effectively a prisoner at Clayton House. She was entirely dependent on her guardian, and even if she could escape his suffocating wardship, she had no means by which to return to Harbury.

Ironically, despite her vast fortune, Geneva had no money apart from the few shillings housekeeping money she had brought with her from the parsonage. It hardly seemed likely that Mr Boeman, if applied to, would provide the funds for her escape. For the first time in her life, Geneva's natural optimism deserted her. Foolishly she had allowed herself to think of Lord Vance as a distant ally. But the news of his forthcoming betrothal clearly proved that while he might still remain in her thoughts, the Earl of Brewood had all too quickly forgotten the existence of Miss Geneva Hartwell.

It was with a heavy heart than that she took up the copy of Lewis's *The Monk*, and began to read aloud to Mrs Hartwell on a dull wintry morning ten days after her arrival at Clayton House. Mr Boeman, as usual, had ridden off after breakfast and the house was silent but for her own melodious voice reading the melodramatic prose, and the ponderous tick of the ormolu bracket clock.

Suddenly the soporific mood was broken by the vigorous jangle of the doorbell. This was such a rare occurrence that Geneva laid down her book and even Mrs Hartwell stirred from her somnolent state. Geneva had commented earlier in the week on the lack of visitors, and had been given her own state of mourning as an excuse. Now she waited with eager expectation as the butler's deliberate tread was heard crossing the marble hallway. The door swung open and the loud commanding tones of a lady immediately filled the house.

'Now you may stop looking down your nose at me, man! I am well aware that Mrs and Miss Hartwell are not at home to callers, but as I do not intend to stay above five minutes you need not bother to refuse me! I will find your mistress in that confectionery box she calls the Rose Room I suppose, so you need not announce me either!'

The effect of these strongly spoken words on Lucasta Hartwell was electrifying. She abandoned her languorous pose and reached for her smelling salts. Geneva looked with interest towards the door. This was flung open with a vigour in keeping with their visitor's forceful nature, and a statuesque, handsome woman, probably in her early fifties, strode into the room. She was strikingly attired in a rather mannish green serge riding habit, a plain black beaver crowning her short-cropped, iron-grey hair.

Mrs Hartwell rose to her feet, shedding a variety of shawls and wraps as she did so. 'Lady Bartram. What a pleasant surprise, but really we are not receiving callers.' Lucasta Hartwell came to a faltering halt under the basilisk stare of their visitor.

Lady Bartram's only answer to this feeble protest was a brisk 'Nonsense Lucasta!' before she turned her attention to Geneva, who was eyeing the invader with startled amusement. 'Miss Hartwell I take it! Well my dear, welcome to the neighbourhood, though it cannot be much fun for you with only Lucasta and that here-and-thereian son of hers for company.'

Geneva was not obliged to reply to this slighting reference to her hosts since Lady Bartram continued without pause, 'Sorry to hear of your father's death, Miss Hartwell. A clergyman I understand. James Hartwell often spoke of him with affection, wished they'd been reunited, but I'll say no more on that point.' And indeed she had no opportunity to do so, for at that moment she was cut short by Mr Boeman, whose quiet entrance had gone unnoticed, and whose silky voice sent an involuntary shiver down Geneva's spine.

'Lady Bartram, it is very kind of you to welcome my ward, but I must second my mother: we are not receiving callers. Allow me to escort you to your vehicle.'

Hard, pale-blue eyes met grey in a silent battle of wills, and it seemed to Geneva that the atmosphere crackled with unspoken words. It was Lady Bartram who weakened first, abruptly taking her leave. Geneva thanked her for her kindness and wished she might hear more of this redoubtable lady's forthright opinions, but Mr Boeman was hovering with ill-concealed displeasure.

At the last moment Lady Bartram returned to Geneva's side exclaiming, 'Oh I nearly forgot my purpose in calling. Miss Hartwell, I fear that you will find little reading matter at Clayton House to provide you with solace, and I see I was right.' She motioned disparagingly at *The Monk* 'And so I brought you a little book of sermons whose wisdom was a great source of comfort to me when I lost my own parents.' With this she pressed the little hide-bound booklet into Geneva's hands with such a significant look that Geneva could not doubt there being some secret message in her gesture.

True to his word, Mr Boeman escorted their visitor off the

premises and in the meantime, Mrs Hartwell endeavoured to turn Geneva's mind from the distraction by imploring her to continue with her reading as, she declared, she was positively on the edge of her seat to discover the outcome of Ambrosio's diabolical plans.

Geneva obligingly did not question Mrs Hartwell about Lady Bartram and when Mr Boeman said at dinner, with a searching look, that he hoped she would not set any store by that lady's absurd prattlings, Geneva replied that she supposed the lady was a little eccentric and immediately turned the subject. This seem to relieve her guardian considerably and he was very jovial and attentive all evening so that it was later than she would have wished when Geneva gained the privacy of her bedchamber and could at last, with trembling fingers, open the little book of sermons.

Six

Just at Geneva had hoped, when she opened the slim volume, a much folded piece of paper fell from between the pages. When opened out, this proved to be a note addressed to Geneva in Lady Bartram's large untidy hand. Geneva read it avidly, and its contents caused her heart to beat faster in her breast for they confirmed all her darkest suspicions and more.

Dear Miss Hartwell
Forgive this cloak-and-dagger style of correspondence which is not at all my style, but if my suppositions are correct your guardian will not risk allowing you to be private with me.

I will be brief and to the point. Mr Boeman is a scoundrel and his mother is a harpy. Mr James Hartwell discovered this too late to prevent an unhappy marriage, but I hope you will not be tricked into making the same error. That marriage is what he intends I have no doubt, and I beg you, do not be fooled into thinking he has any affection for yourself, it is all reserved for the fortune he has counted on as his own. I hope his villainy stops short of coercion, but I beg leave to doubt it.

There is much more I wish to say on the subject so if you feel the need of a friend, I hope to see you in Malpeth Lending Library at ten on the morrow.
Sincerely
Ann Bartram

It was well into the night before Geneva fell into a fitful sleep. That she had found a friend was a relief and her mind buzzed with stratagems to evade the close scrutiny of the household and reach the intended rendezvous. In the end she resigned herself to the fact that it would be impossible to leave by one of the more conventional exits if she wished to avoid detection. This only left one rather unconventional option. Geneva's bedroom was at the back of the house and although it was situated on the second floor, there was by happy coincidence a large and sprawling oak tree directly beneath her window. Geneva's tree-climbing days were long behind her, but desperate straits called for desperate measures, and this was fixed on as her point of escape.

The next morning when the scullery maid appeared at her usual early hour to lay the fire, she was greeted by a low moan. She immediately sought out Mrs Chambers and, with a skill for the dramatic she never suspected she possessed, Geneva quickly convinced the dour housekeeper that she was suffering from a sick headache for which the only cure was laudanum and complete quiet.

Consequently when an hour later, her skirts tucked up high, Geneva descended the oak tree with more speed than grace, the entire household was under the impression that Miss Hartwell was resting on her bed in a darkened room, and was not to be disturbed until lunchtime.

Lady Bartram was already awaiting her arrival and she greeted Geneva with a vigorous handshake, saying that she had known at a glance that she did not lack for sense. They wasted no time on trivialities, Geneva first apprising Lady Bartram of the events leading up to her arrival at Clayton House in much the same manner as she had told the Earl of Brewood.

'Just as I thought!' was Lady Bartram's response. 'Leonard Boeman is a bad man, as anybody for miles around will tell you, which is no doubt why he has kept you a virtual prisoner. The rumours that surround him are not nice and I'll not distress you by repeating them. Suffice to say he is not a fit guardian or husband for any gently bred female.'

'But what can I do?' asked Geneva helplessly. 'I have no relatives to whom I can turn, and as my guardian he has absolute power over me until I am twenty-one.'

'That's the rub! I told my husband that we should not as Christians leave you at his mercy. But Sir John has the right of it when he says the law is on Boeman's side.'

The two ladies lapsed into brooding silence which was eventually broken by Geneva. 'If I could just find somewhere to hide from him for the next few months, then I would be free.'

Lady Bartram greeted this plan with approval. 'Dash it! That's the answer! If you were to go somewhere and take a false name, in all likelihood he would never find you, at least not until it was too late.'

'But where would I go? The only friends I have are in Harbury which is the first place my guardian would look.'

Lady Bartram considered this for a moment and then exclaimed, 'Jupiter! I think I have it! Sir John and I are going down to London to visit our daughter. She is recently married and is increasing. Her husband is a diplomat and is often abroad so she gets lonely, poor thing. She would love to have a girl her own age to bear her company. And in London, living quietly, you would attract no attention.'

Geneva was immediately enthusiastic, and having been earnestly assured by Lady Bartram that her Louisa would be delighted to have her, she gratefully and eagerly accepted. It was decided that Geneva should wait until Sir John and Lady Bartram had returned from their short visit before Geneva made her escape. It would not do for Mr Boeman to connect the two.

Hearing of Geneva's financial dependence Lady Bartram quickly pressed a ten pound bill into the embarrassed girl's hand, and was more than rewarded by the impulsive hug she received in return. Then mindful of her limited time, Geneva set off to make enquiries as to the times of the London stagecoach, guessing that it was unlikely that she would be able to escape Clayton House for a second time so easily. This done she hurried back to her gilded cage, her spirits greatly lifted by the positive action she had taken.

Geneva was within half a mile of Clayton House when she espied the distinctive blue and red uniform of the post boy. A sudden idea struck her and she hailed him. On learning that he was at that moment on his way to the house with mail, Geneva offered to relieve him of his burden. The boy, conscientious in his duties, was initially dubious, but a shilling pressed into his grubby palm and the promise that it would be their secret quickly dispelled any qualms. A quick glance at the small bundle revealed two letters for Geneva. The rounded precise hand of one was recognizable as Mrs Hollins's, the other in a more florid style was unfamiliar. Resisting the temptation to break the seals at once, Geneva concentrated instead on retracing her route into the house.

The ascent was more difficult than the descent, but in a few minutes, and with nothing more to show for her pains than a rent in her skirt and a few superficial scratches, she was once more in the safety of her room. Geneva wasted no time in opening her letters. The one from Mrs Hollins contained nothing of immediate interest, covering as it did only various items of local news. But the first sentence of the final paragraph caught her eye. '*I am disappointed you have not found the time to reply to my earlier letters....*' So she had guessed aright. Mr Boeman had been intercepting her post. It seemed that Lady Bartram was correct; her guardian had no intention of anything jeopardizing his plans to gain her fortune.

Geneva turned to her second letter. It proved to be from Mr Joseph Edlington, and as she read it her eyes widened in horror and disbelief.

My dear Miss Hartwell,

You cannot imagine my delight at receiving your guardian's letter informing me of your forthcoming marriage. True it is a little irregular so soon after your father's death, but Mr Boeman informs me that Reverend Hartwell appointed him as guardian in the hope of this happy outcome.

I have as requested sent the marriage settlements to Mr Boeman, and all that is needed is your signature. I write to you as requested, but for the first and last time, since your concerns and your guardian's will soon be inextricably linked forever.

I wish you every happiness in your future position as Mrs Leonard Boeman.

I remain, your servant,

Joseph Edlington

Geneva's first reaction on reading Mr Edlington's astonishing and revealing letter was to seek at once the offered protection of Lady Bartram. But common sense warned her that the short distance between Clayton House and Bartram Grange would not be enough to deter Leonard Boeman. The words spoken by Joseph Edlington on their meeting at Tadworth Parsonage came back to Geneva with unwelcome clarity, 'As far as the law is concerned your own personal desires carry very little weight. As your legal guardian, Mr Boeman has every right to demand your compliance.' Whether her guardian's authority extended to constraining her into marriage, Geneva did not know, but she had no intention of staying around to find out. But it would place Sir John and Lady Bartram in an invidious position if Geneva sought shelter not a mile from her guardian's home. No, she must bide her time.

The Bartrams were to leave for London in four days' time; she would follow them three days later. Hopefully the interval would prevent Mr Boeman from guessing her intentions. With any luck he would begin his search in Harbury. By the time he had exhausted that possibility Geneva would, with the Bartrams' help, have assumed a new identity. Surely she could evade Mr Boeman for the remaining five months of his guardianship?

Geneva's last week at Clayton House was the longest of her life. That all her worst misgivings of her guardian's character and motives had been confirmed, made it doubly difficult for her to treat him with even common civility. Yet it was imperative that his suspicions were not aroused; she was watched closely as it was, she had no wish to find herself further restrained. So, much as it went against the grain, Geneva bit back the cutting retorts that sprang to her lips at Mr Boeman's ever more persistent gallantries. Instead she accepted his flattery demurely, lowering her eyes coyly and hoping the warm colour suppressed indignation brought to her cheeks was mistaken for maidenly gratification. Geneva's duplicity paid dividends, Mr Boeman had a large streak of vanity which made him believe completely in the irresistibility of his own charms. Consequently as the week progressed he relaxed his vigil, confident that he had won over his recalcitrant ward.

Playing the devoted suitor was not at all in Mr Boeman's line, and he was beginning to feel the strain. He much preferred the bawdier entertainments offered by the Brown Cow, an insalubrious establishment which in the main boasted cut-purses and vagabonds for its clientele, served blue ruin in pint pots and provided half a dozen slatternly jades for its wealthier customers. Mr Boeman in his conceit, judging his matrimonial plans to be progressing smoothly, decided to reward himself by sampling the delights of the Brown Cow and to Geneva's great relief took himself off for the evening of her planned escape, informing his fond parent that he intended to dine with a friend in the next village and would probably spend the night there.

Geneva forced herself to wait until midnight before she slipped from her room as only then could she be sure that the servants would be asleep. Besides, any earlier and she would have to wait even longer for the arrival of the stagecoach. Since her arrival at Clayton House winter had closed in with vengeance and now snow already lay several inches deep on the ground. As she sank ankle deep into the soft white blanket, Geneva felt a momentary qualm – it was not a night for travelling. Fat flakes were falling in earnest from the overcast sky and showed no immediate sign of abating. But Geneva was a resilient country-bred girl and she strode out briskly, cheering herself with the thought that at least the fresh fall of snow would hide her tell-tale footprints. Within an hour she reached the desolate crossroads where she intended to pick up the London-bound stage. The blizzard had gained strength and a new worry assailed Geneva: supposing the vehicle were to sweep by without even noticing the lonely figure at the crossing? But the inclement weather had forced the coach to slacken its pace considerably, and in her dark cloak Geneva stood out against the pale uniform landscape. Thankfully she paid her fare and climbed aboard, too relieved at finally beginning to put some distance between herself and Clayton House to object to an outside seat.

The chaise and pair, once free of the London traffic, quickened its pace. The bay job horses, though not of prime stock, were fresh and willing, and soon the lights of the metropolis were left behind. The moon shone large and bright in a clear sky, coldly reflected by the thin crust of fresh snow which covered the landscape, providing ample light for travellers.

The young lady, who had sat tense and upright throughout their frustratingly slow exit from the capital, relaxed and sank back against the worn squabs of the carriage. She pulled back the faded velvet curtains which had so far served to shield the occupants from the curious. A shaft of silvery light penetrated the dim rather musty interior, showing the lady to be becomingly if inappropriately attired for a long journey, in an evening gown of rose-pink silk, trimmed lavishly with blond lace. The shade of the gown admirably complemented the lady's creamy complexion and profusion of guinea-gold curls. If a worried frown puckered her smooth brow, and limpid blue eyes held a trace of anxiety, then it did little to detract from the lady's undoubted beauty.

The reason for her anxiety became clear when she addressed her sole companion. 'Oh Julien, can you not hurry this wretched driver along? I feel sure Augustin will be hard on our heels!' For while Miss Geneva Hartwell was running away from the joys of matrimony with all the speed she could muster, Lady Isobel Vance was equally bent on defying her guardian by plunging headlong into wedded bliss.

By his demeanour her companion did not appear to share her concern that the Earl of Brewood was hot on their heels. But then it was the habit of Mr Julien Armistead to greet life's fortunes and misfortunes with the same lazy insolence. He was slouched in the corner of the carriage, his chin, already showing a faint shadow of stubble, sunk into his cravat, his dark-blue evening coat hanging open to reveal a waistcoat startlingly patterned with pink cabbage roses. He was handsome in the dark Byronic way guaranteed to find favour with young impressionable debutantes, deprived as they were of that particular young lord's brooding presence. But there was a softness about him that suggested in later years he would run to fat, and despite his youth, the consequences of prolonged debauchery were already etched on his features.

He reassured the lady, but in the bored tones of one who had done so countless times already. 'Your fears are unfounded, Isobel my dear. There is no earthly reason why your brother should even suspect that you have flown. As far as he and the rest of your family are concerned you have simply taken to your bed with a sick headache after leaving the Lavenhams' ball early. We are safe until morning, by which time we shall be well on our way to the border.'

'Oh you make it sound so simple, but you do not know Augustin as I do.' With this cryptic statement, Lady Isobel

Vance sank into a fretful silence. It was impossible to explain, but when Augustin looked at one with those piercing dark eyes, one raised eyebrow registering faint disbelief, one could almost believe he could read what was in your very soul. Standing before him stammering her excuse for leaving the ball, when for the past month she had talked of little else but what she would wear and whom she would dance with at this, the most prestigious occasion of the season, she had been forcibly reminded of the last time she had attempted to deceive her brother.

At the age of sixteen she had invented a visit to an elderly aunt, so that she might keep her assignation with her young and persuadable music teacher. Augustin had looked at her in that same way, and promptly offered to escort her on this worthy expedition. There followed a tedious afternoon of listening to the rambling and disjointed reminiscences of Great Aunt Clara, whilst the besotted music teacher cooled his heels in the excessively romantic, but excessively chilly ruins of an old abbey, their appointed rendezvous. Fortunately on this occasion the earl had put no impediment in her way, merely calling for the family carriage and instructing the retinue of coachman, footman and lady's maid to ensure his sister and her chaperone were returned home safely. But Lady Isobel was very much struck by the similarity of the two situations and although there had not been the slightest hitch in the proceedings, she was unable to rid herself of the fear that Augustin would suddenly appear like an avenging angel to foil their plans. Consequently, when she had shunned the ministrations of her maid Betty and Miss Amelia Vance, her chaperone, it was with her heart in her mouth that, wrapped in a drab cloak and carrying a single bandbox, she slipped from her room down the servants' staircase and out into the narrow alleyway behind the house in Berkeley Square, expecting to see that familiar figure around every corner.

Indeed she was very tempted to relate the Great Aunt Clara incident to Mr Armistead as proof of her brother's omniscience, but decided on reflection that it might not be quite the thing to recount tales of past indiscretions to the man with whom one was presently eloping. Besides which, a glance at her beloved confirmed, to her chagrin, that Mr Armistead was in fact sound asleep. This fact added to the sense of ill-usage which had mounted within Lady Isobel as their adventure had progressed.

A lady of considerable spirit but of little sense, nothing had been more likely to drive her into the arms of her lover than the probable refusal of her brother to entertain his suit. This had been what Julien Armistead had counted on when he had paid her court. The youngest of two brothers, both renowned for their dissolute ways and their partiality for young heiresses of good family, Mr Armistead was under no illusion as to what the response of the Earl of Brewood would be if he should aspire to the hand of his younger sister. He had wisely refrained from putting his fate to the touch, knowing that their elopement (for he had planned this from the start) would stand a greater chance of success if there were no suspicion of an attachment between them. With the willing conspiracy of Lady Isobel's maid, a girl as empty headed as her mistress, an illicit correspondence had ensued. Poetic nonsense and shy admiration had won over a romantically minded miss, and this had quickly led to more fervent declarations of love from both parties. Mr Armistead deftly dramatized their situation into one of star-crossed lovers, worthy of the more lurid publications of the Minerva Press. It was then but a small step to persuade Lady Isobel that the only course of action open to them was flight.

But whilst Mr Armistead was well pleased with the way matters were progressing, Lady Isobel was rapidly becoming disillusioned. Their clandestine courtship had appealed to her sense of adventure and romance, as did the idea of an elopement. She was swiftly coming to the conclusion however that the idea and the actuality were two vastly different things. Far from whisking her off in a luxurious coach drawn by four fiery charges, Julien had appeared in this decidedly shabby vehicle with only a pair in harness, and instead of the expected outriders and postillions in smart livery, there was an eldery coachman in a none too clean frock coat. She had rather imagined that Julien would take her in his arms and cover her face with impassioned kisses, instead he had unceremoniously bundled her into the smelly chaise, since which time she might well have not existed for all the attention he had paid her.

And now he was asleep. Slouched in the corner, his mouth slack and falling open, the smell of stale drink on his breath, he little resembled the dashing beau she had dreamt of and wept tears for. A niggling doubt which she had quashed throughout began to rise to the surface. Was she really ready to give up her family and friends, to be shunned by society, and live in near poverty with this man? It dawned on her that no, she was not. But she could see no way of going back; for even if they turned around now, they would not reach London before sunrise, by which time their intention would be known, and she would be ruined. This revelation had the effect of reducing her to tears.

While the awe with which his sister regarded Lord Vance's perspicacity was exaggerated, it was in some respects well founded, and it is doubtful whether he would have accepted Lady Isobel's excuses so unquestioningly had his attention not been engaged by more pressing personal matters. In fact his sister's departure had allowed him to escape the ballroom in favour of the small salon set aside for cards; something for which he was profoundly grateful. He elected to observe rather than play despite being invited by a circle of the most inveterate gamblers to join them in a round of deep basset. The earl made it a rule never to play unless he could give his undivided attention to the cards, and this maxim had served him well for in general he rose a winner at the end of the night. Tonight however he was satisfied to lean negligently against a pillar, ostensibly watching the play but in reality considering events of the past few months.

Lord Vance had come to regret the impulse that had led him on a needlesss errand of mercy to Tadworth and into a second encounter with the parson's daughter. For some reason it had left him less than certain as to how his life should progress, and this irritated him. The earl prided himself on his sound judgement and his ability to make rational decisions where others allowed emotions to overrule their common sense. He knew that marriage to Miss Camilla Fortesque was a logical move, but illogically he had a gut feeling that it would also be a terrible mistake.

He had tried and failed to banish the memory of those sweet lips. It was cruelly ironic that on the one occasion of his life that he had offered his protection to a female with only the most pure and selfless of intentions, his motives should be so utterly misread. Despite what the gossips may say of him, he was not in the habit of offering his *carte blanche* to virtuous young ladies, nor of seducing innocents. Geneva Hartwell's reaction had angered him, and he had resolved to forget all about the tiresome minx, but his conscience would not let him. There was definitely something shady about this Boeman character; he would have to look into that. But for now the most pressing of his problems was the Fortesques.

The worst of it was, that having finally realized that he could not go through with his marriage to Miss Camilla Fortesque, he began to fear that it was too late to retreat. Lady Fortesque was already regarding him with a proprietorial eye and had rearranged the dinner the earl had hoped to avoid entirely around his availability. That the other guests were all family members made him feel distinctly uneasy, and he had made his escape as soon as he could politely do so. That they were laying bets in the clubs as to which way he would jump, the earl was well aware. That the lady herself lived in daily expectation of a declaration he could not know, but a conversation with Miss Fortesque a few minutes previously had gone some way to enlightening him.

The earl's bleak musings on the possibly unavoidable nature of this union were interrupted by his friend, Mr Oliver Worthington. To outsiders there seemed no more unlikely alliance than the friendship between the rakish lord and Mr Worthington, a model of gentlemanly sobriety. But it was a friendship that stood the test of time. The earl knew that beneath Oliver's modest demeanour there lay a sharp wit and shrewd intelligence, and while Mr Worthington might deplore the excesses of his noble friend at the same time he had a fair understanding of what promoted them and so was sympathetic.

'I hear the Fortesques are to join the droves in Vienna for the peace celebrations,' he said mildly, shrewdly divining the reason behind the earl's discontent.

'Within the week Miss Fortesque informs me,' replied the earl with heavy sarcasm. 'She also contrived, with the greatest ingenuity and without a breath of impropriety, to imply that she and her parents would be very glad to receive me should I choose to pay them a call before they depart.'

'Ah,' was the only reply evinced by Mr Worthington, whose whole attention appeared to be centred on the delicate task of taking snuff from an exquisitely enamelled snuffbox.

'Is that all you can say Worthington?' The earl held his temper in check with visible difficulty. After a pause he addressed his friend once more. 'Tell me the truth, Oliver, if I don't follow this thing through, will I be hurting the girl?'

Mr Worthington seemed to consider this carefully; in the end his reply was inconclusive. 'She is certainly justified in expecting an offer.'

'Cut line! That is not what I asked, though I cannot say that before tonight she gave me any indication that she regarded my intentions as serious.'

Mr Worthington relented, and returning the snuffbox to the pocket of his elegant black evening coat, gave the earl the benefit of his opinion. 'Miss Fortesque is a gently bred female who would most certainly shy from displaying an unbecoming awareness of a gentleman's intentions. However, she, like the rest of the ton, knows that you have never before solicited the company of a marriageable lady, and like the rest of the ton, she has undoubtedly reached the inevitable conclusion. As to hurting her, I very much doubt whether it would be possible to hurt anything but Miss Fortesque's pride.'

The earl responded to this with a look of profound relief, saying in a more sanguine tone, 'And I always suspected you were of the opinion that I should waste no time in getting myself leg-shackled.'

'Well, I still believe that should you meet the right woman, marriage would be the making of you.'

'So young and yet so wise!' jeered the earl. 'I doubt that such a woman exists; besides I am generally held to be beyond redemption.'

Mr Worthington smiled but made no answer. He linked arms with his friend and drew him back towards the ballroom, saying as he did, 'Come! I am promised to your lovely sister for the boulanger, and I would be much obliged if you would play that part of stern guardian and disperse the crowd of young puppies we will no doubt find clustered around her!'

'Oh, Isobel pleaded a sick headache and went home,' replied Lord Vance carelessly.

'What?' For once the perpetual air of calm reserve deserted Mr Worthington. He stopped dead in his tracks, a look of disbelieving horror on his handsome face. 'And you mean to tell me you allowed her to go?'

It was the earl's turn to be amused. 'My dear Worthington, had I known you had such a burning desire to dance the boulanger with my sister, then I would assuredly have insisted on her remaining, headache or no.'

There was no answering glint of humour in his companion's eyes. 'You mean to say you were taken in by such nonsense? I had not thought you such a slowtop Brewood! You know better than I how Lady Isobel loves these occasions. I'll guarantee that if we look about we'll find that scoundrel Julien Armistead has mysteriously disappeared.'

The truth of Mr Worthington's words quickly dawned on Lord Vance, and he cursed his own lack of insight. While the two protagonists had been convinced of their own discretion, the studied indifference they adopted when in company together and the occasional furtive glances he had intercepted, had been enough to arouse suspicion in the mind of Lord Vance, who was well aware of his sister's weakness for a charming rogue. He had not interfered, confident of his ability to put a stop to the connection before things got out of hand. But while very astute, Lord Vance was not blessed with the jealous eye of Oliver Worthington when it came to the *affaires* of Lady Isobel.

A quick tour of the ballroom and its surrounding salons confirmed their misgivings; Mr Armistead was nowhere to be found. Taking their leave leisurely of their hostess so as to avoid any possible conjecture, the two men then swiftly made their way to Berkeley Square

'I will kill that villain if he has harmed her!' exclaimed Mr Worthington with unaccustomed violence. The earl looked at him with sympathetic pity. 'I am afraid you will have to allow my prior claim as her brother and guardian. But if you will accompany me and stand my second I will be indebted to you.'

This was agreed and since Lady Isobel had been so obliging as to leave a letter for her relatives apprising them of her intentions, it was a remarkably short time before the earl's curricle drawn by four splendid bays was heading for the North road, barely two hours behind the fleeing lovers.

Seven

Lady Isobel's bout of self-pity continued until she was a further ten miles from the safety and security of her home. Isobel felt she would do anything to see the haughty features of dearest Gus and hear the fluttering tones of darling Aunt Amelia. That she had previously stigmatized them as a despotic tyrant and a wet hen respectively was now forgotten. She stared accusingly at Julien Armistead's recumbent form. Neither heartrending sobs nor disconsolate sniffs had roused him from his slumber and, irrationally, Isobel saw this as a further sign of his lack of proper concern for her welfare. But in the end she dried her eyes, for as she knew, nothing is more ruinous to a fair complexion than tears.

Gradually as her composure returned, Isobel began to notice that their progress was no longer smooth, and their pace had slackened. Bright moonlight no longer illuminated the carriage. Wiping the misted window with her swansdown muff. Isobel peared into the darkness. The reason for their erratic motion was immediately apparent; as they had travelled further north, the weather had dramatically deteriorated. The sky was now heavy with thick grey cloud, and in the mounting wind large snowflakes swirled dizzily, filling the air and making visibility increasingly poor.

Isobel knew she should be alarmed by this development, but was only aware of a rising hope that somehow something would happen to solve her dreadful predicament. Then as if in answer to her unspoken prayer, disaster struck. For several miles the road had been gradually inclining, now as they rounded a tight bend, it suddenly dropped away steeply. Although their pace was not fast, their momentum combined with the slippery surface carried them down the slope and into a deep drift.

The startled shouts of the coachman and the frightened whinnies of the horses were enough to wake Julian Armistead from his stupor. Groggy from sleep though he was, a cursory glance out of the carriage window was enough to apprise him of the situation. Forgetting the image of suave gentleman of the ton which he had cultivated so carefully for Isobel's benefit, he swore loudly and comprehensively. Coachman, horses, carriage and the English weather were cursed equally, in fact everything bar his own folly in attempting such a journey in an inadequate vehicle in the midst of a bitter winter came under attack. Isobel clapped her hands over her ears with an exclamation of shock, her eyes opened still further to the true character of the man she had agreed to marry. The sound of the coachman still fighting to calm the terrified horses could be heard; until he had achieved this, the occupants of the carriage could not escape, for the snow came a little over half-way up the carriage doors making it impossible to prise them open. In his rage, Armistead attempted to kick one door open but only succeeding in splintering the rotten wood. This did nothing to improve his temper, and Isobel shrank into the corner staring in horror at this brutish stranger.

At length the horses grew calmer and the crunch of heavy footsteps through the thick snow was heard. The round, ruddy face of the driver appeared at the window. 'Don't you fret now,' he advised in coarse country accents, 'I'll have you out of there in a brace of shakes.' He was as good as his word, and within ten minutes he had cleared away enough snow to allow the door on one side of the carriage to open. Mr Armistead, who had been fretting and fuming at his confinement, immediately climbed from the vehicle and continued his verbal assaults of the coachman in person. Lady Isobel, realizing she could expect no assistance from her beau, clambered out into the open, a difficult operation hampered as she was by long skirts, which did little to improve her state of mind. She emerged to find that Mr Armistead and the coachman had reached deadlock. Mr Armistead ranted in vain; the coachman was steadfast in his refusal to travel any further that night. Isobel's temper deteriorated rapidly as she listened to their fruitless argument. Icy snow had quickly penetrated her thin satin dance slippers, and the threadbare cloak she had purloined from the servants' hall was inadequate protection from the bitter wind.

'Oh for goodness sake, Julien!' she cried in exasperation. 'Even if the dratted vehicle could be moved, I refuse to journey another inch in it. I am chilled to the bone, and if we do not make a move to find warmth and shelter, then your silly bickering will be irrelevant for I shall certainly be dead from pneumonia!'

Mr Armistead spun round, his face made ugly by anger. Isobel's look of startled fright brought him to his senses and he bit back his natural response, which was to tell the interfering bitch to mind her tongue. But he had not yet achieved his objective, and in the light of their present dilemma it would be unwise to frighten her into doing anything that might ruin his plans. He schooled his features into a expression of solicitous concern. 'My dearest, forgive me! My fear that our plans may be in jeopardy drove all other thoughts from my head.' He strode to her side and chafed her numbed fingers between his own. 'My poor darling, can you forgive me?'

But the sincerity of Julien's words and the warmth in his eyes no longer fooled Isobel. She had witnessed a side to Mr Julien Armistead's character which repelled her, and from being ready to risk social ruin to wed him she now felt she would be willing to face even greater censure by returning home unwed. This thought Isobel wisely kept to herself, for she instinctively knew her wishes would not weigh strongly with this man. She accepted his apologies in a stifled little voice and forced herself to smile up at him. But those wide blue eyes betrayed her fear, and Armistead cursed his temper. His finances were in desperate straits and he had no intention of relinquishing such a prize at this stage in the game, but he would have preferred a willing accomplice to the end.

After a brief discussion it was decided that Julien and Lady Isobel would take the sound horse and hope to find some inn or hedge tavern further along the road. The luckless coachman was obliged to follow on foot leading the remaining horse which was dead lame.

Geneva set the heels of her sturdy walking boots on the fender of the large stone fireplace, and thankfully felt warmth creeping slowly back into her frozen feet. It was not what she had planned, but then she had reckoned without the weather. She had a roof over her head and she had put ten miles between herself and the evil machinations of her guardian. Geneva could only hope and pray that it was enough.

Her relief at successfully catching the stage had been shortlived. The coach's progress became increasingly laboured and when they reached the end of the stage, a mere eight miles from the crossroads, the driver was adamant in his refusal to travel any further that night. His decision was on the whole approved by the passengers who, having entered the welcome warmth of the Red Lion, were reluctant to brave the cold once more.

Geneva's heart sank. Her disappearance would be discovered as soon as the maid came to lay the fire in her room. It would not take Mr Boeman long to track her down. The Red Lion was a busy inn and a popular stop for coaches travelling in any direction. Whether her destination had been London or Harbury the likelihood was that she would have paused there. Instead of joining the undignified scramble for the few remaining rooms, Geneva quietly enquired whether there were any other hostelries in the vicinity. A harassed serving wench told her rather impatiently that the Wily Fox was about two miles along the road. Geneva collected her meagre luggage and unobtrusively slipped out into the night. After trudging wearily for over an hour and wryly coming to the conclusion that her informant had a very peculiar notion of distance, Geneva had eventually arrived at the Wily Fox.

Now she sipped gratefully from the generous tankard of mulled wine provided by the landlord's kind-hearted spouse. Together with the warmth of the room it was taking effect on Geneva's exhausted body, but she resolutely fought sleep, knowing she must devise some plan of action. It was a difficult problem and one she was no nearer to solving when suddenly the door of the tap room was flung open and a young couple hurried in, accompanied by an icy blast of air and a few scurrying snowflakes.

Geneva started, an irrational fear that her guardian had run her to ground already gripping her. But the couple were strangers. The quality of their apparel proclaimed them as gentry and while Geneva did not think the man particularly attractive she thought his companion was the prettiest girl she had ever seen. Geneva could not help overhearing the conversation between the young man and the landlord. In loud querulous tones he demanded two bedrooms and a private parlour for himself and his wife. He put a peculiar emphasis on the word 'wife' and the girl started and seemed about to say something but a warning frown from the gentleman silenced her. The landlord begged his pardon but said that he had no private parlour and only one free room. The man appeared to be about to argue the point but then changed his mind, and with a strange laugh answered the landlord, 'One room will be adequate, won't it my dear?' The girl made no reply but paled visibly.

Geneva might be an innocent country girl but she immediately sensed something was amiss. The poor girl looked petrified and, forgetting her own problems, Geneva stepped out of the shadows to offer assistance 'The young lady is welcome to share my room if she so wishes.' The girl's patent relief at this suggestion was enough to confirm Geneva's initial impression that all was not well. But the gentleman was not so easily foiled.

'Thank you for your offer, but as I said, one room will be quite sufficient.' The look of muted appeal in the girl's anxious blue eyes made Geneva determined to get her alone.

'I see your wife has no luggage and those clothes must be soaked through. If she would but step up to my room I think I can find something warm and dry.' The gentleman was clearly displeased by her interference, he nodded his consent. Geneva led the young lady from the room. Had she not put a warning finger to her lips the girl would have unburdened herself immediately. But only when they had gained the safety of the simply furnished bedroom with the door locked against intruders, did Geneva allow her to speak.

The girl immediately burst into incoherent speech at the same time clutching Geneva's hands in gratitude. 'Oh, please you must help me, for I cannot imagine who else I am to turn to!'

Seeing the girl was close to hysteria, Geneva was prosaic in her response. 'Well I will do all I can you may be sure, but first if you are not to catch a nasty chill you must take off those damp clothes. We are much the same size though I fear I can offer you nothing of such quality.'

'Oh, as if I cared for that!' exclaimed the young lady, but nevertheless allowed Geneva to divest her of the rose-pink silk and replace it with a round gown of navy wool. The mundane task of changing her clothes seemed to calm her and with a little prompting Geneva managed to get a fair picture of events leading up to the couple's arrival at the Wily Fox. She learned that her companion's name was Isobel and the gentleman claiming to be her husband was no such thing but a heartless deceiver by the name of Julien Armistead, who had first insinuated himself in Isobel's affections and then cruelly duped her, and now intended to compromise her and force her into marriage so that he may acquire her fortune. Geneva, in the circumstances, had a great deal of sympathy for her plight. She was less sure of the role played by Isobel's brother. The lady herself seemed alternately to dread his arrival and view him as her only possibility of salvation.

Isobel having bared her soul now looked at Geneva in despair crying, 'Oh what are we to do?' Geneva had been wondering much the same thing. By remaining firmly locked in the room they might be able to keep Mr Armistead at bay for a while, but not indefinitely. And what if Mr Boeman should arrive? Isobel had evinced no interest in what had brought Geneva to such an out of the way place, and Geneva had decided on reflection not to enlighten her. She could not place any reliance on the girl's fortitude if faced with the prospect of a second blackguard bent on coercion.

'I think that our only hope is to await the arrival of your brother. You say you left a note? Then undoubtedly he will follow you. In the meantime it would be better if Mr Armistead were not to suspect your change of heart, nor that you have taken me into your confidence.'

This sensible suggestion was rudely interrupted by a thunderous knocking on the door. Isobel gave a terrified shriek and clutched desperately at Geneva's arm.

'Isobel! What are you about? Supper is served and I am devilish sharp set!' called Mr Armistead impatiently.

Isobel, incensed by such a display of insensitivity, her fear momentarily forgotten in her ire, leaped to her feet exclaiming indignantly, 'Oh! of all the callous monsters! You have torn me away from my family, ruined me and all you can think of is your appetite. I hate you Julien Armistead! I hate you and I will never marry you, never!'

Geneva groaned inwardly as she listened to the violent curses Isobel's hysterical outburst generated. A locked door, albeit of stout construction, would not stand for long betwen this man and his goal. Taking a deep breath and hoping she could speak calmly she hailed him through the door. 'Mr Armistead, I should warn you that Isobel has left a letter for her relatives which will have been discovered long since. Indeed her brother may arrive at any moment, so I would advise you to leave off your threats if you wish to avoid his wrath.'

If anything this enraged Mr Armistead further. 'Good God! Was there a female who did not leave a note? But that will not deter me. I know Vance's habits, he will not leave his club before dawn, and by that time both you Isobel, and your damned brother will be begging me to make an honest woman of you!'

'I doubt if it will come to that, Armistead.' It was softly spoken like a whisper of cold steel, and it had the effect of capturing the attention of those on either side of the locked door.

'Vance!' came Armistead's incredulous voice, and then more determinedly, 'You'll not stop me now, I have gone too far to be stopped now!' There came the sound of the two men struggling and then suddenly there was the loud report of a pistol shot, a brief agonizing silence and then the sickening thump of a body hitting the wooden floor.

Geneva and Isobel could only gaze at the closed door paralyzed and speechless with horror. When there came another urgent knock on the door they both jumped, and Isobel let out a terrified whimper and pressed her hands to her lips.

'Isobel, it is me! Open the door!'

With a cry of relief, Isobel ran to the door and turned the key. 'Oh Gus, Gus! I am sorry, please forgive me!' and she cast herself tearfully into the newcomer's arms. The gentleman, who put her aside none too gently, had a far from forgiving look on his face, and he was about to launch into a scathing denunciation of his sister's conduct when he caught sight of Geneva standing rooted to the spot.

Geneva felt her heart skip a beat as she stared in bemusement at those familiar harsh features. Involuntarily, one hand stole to her lips as she remembered the soft pressure of his kiss. When the villain Armistead had exclaimed the name Vance, it had struck a chord, but in the turmoil of events Geneva had been given no time to register its significance.

Geneva felt sure all her emotions must be apparent on her face, but Lord Vance's expression was unreadable. He walked towards her and addressed her very formally. 'Miss Hartwell, you seem to have rendered assistance to my foolish sister. I am very grateful.' His voice was cool without a trace of emotion, and Geneva wondered helplessly at how, in contrast, she was hard put to frame a coherent sentence. She was spared the necessity of doing so by the intervention of Lady Isobel.

'Why this is famous! Do you mean to tell me Gus, that you are already acquainted with Geneva?' Then, eyeing Geneva's flushed countenance, she clapped her hands in delight and exclaimed mischievously, 'Why I believe I have discovered a romance! Of course I should not be surprised for Augustin makes a habit of knowing all the prettiest girls. He is a terrible rake you know, and I expect he has already tried to make love to you!'

Geneva, burning with mortification, wished the ground might open and swallow her up. Fortunately the earl cut in before Lady Isobel's thoughtless words could cause her any more distress. 'Your want of conduct, Isobel, never ceases to astound me. Good God! You have your mother's looks, I suppose I should not be surprised to find you have inherited her morals as well!'

Lady Isobel clenched her fists and stamped her foot in rage. 'How dare you! If you were not such … such a bully, I would not have been driven to this. If father was such a tyrant then I do not wonder that our mother left him.'

This display of filial respect was cut short by the entrance of a second gentleman, a few inches shorter than the earl and of stockier build, he had a pleasant open countenance which was at present marred by a worried frown. 'Armistead is dead,' he announced curtly.

The earl swore softly under his breath. 'Young fool. I would not have killed him if we had met. I have no desire to stand trial for murder.'

Lady Isobel meantime was still seething at her brother's insults, and at this announcement, cast a hand to her brow in a dramatic gesture worthy of Mrs Siddons. 'Oh, I might have guessed you would take a pleasure in blighting my only chance of happiness. To strike down in cold blood the only man I have ever cared for. I hope you may hang!'

Geneva could only blink in astonishment at this complete volte-face regarding the ill-fated Mr Armistead. The earl was more articulate. 'Spare me these Cheltenham tragedies, Isobel. I fear I know you too well. Besides I believe as a member of the aristocracy I will be beheaded rather than hanged.'

Abandoning her tragic pose, Lady Isobel flung herself on to the bed in a storm of passionate weeping. The earl's companion hastened to her side and attempted to placate her in low soothing tones. The earl looked with disgust at this scene, and would no doubt have continued his scathing attack had Geneva not forestalled him.

'My Lord, forgive me but your sister has had a traumatic experience and your browbeating her is not helping matters.'

Lord Vance spun round, his face like thunder, but Geneva refused to shrink from him, meeting his furious gaze squarely and saying with a defiant lift of her chin, 'And you need not think to make me tremble with your black looks, my Lord.' For a moment she thought she had pushed him too far, but then suddenly his harsh features relaxed and he gave a sharp crack of laughter.

'I should have known from our earlier encounters that you are not easily cowed, Miss Hartwell. But, grateful as I am for your help in this imbroglio, I will brook no interference. This is none of your affair.'

Infuriated by this comtemptuous dismissal, Geneva was stung into an angry response. 'Since it is none of my affair, I would be grateful then if you would kindly leave my bed-chamber, and take with you any corpses you may have left littering the corridor outside my door!'

The earl gave a wolfish grin, and said with some amusement, 'I am glad to see you are not reduced to a fit of the vapours by the presence of our dead friend.'

'I am afraid I am atrociously lacking in sensibility. But surely the landlord will be a little put out? Mr Armistead had not even paid his shot. Or do you intend to inform him in your odious way that it is none of his affair either?'

Lord Vance found himself enjoying this bizarre conversation, and was tempted to sample more of this fiery beauty's wit. But Geneva's words brought his attention back to the matter at hand. He addressed his gentleman companion peremptorily, 'Worthington! Leave my sister to her tantrums, we have more important matters to attend to,' and without another word he turned on his heel and stalked out of the room.

Mr Worthington was initially reluctant to leave Lady Isobel, for though the first paroxysm was over, she was stll sobbing quietly. Geneva was quick to assure him that she would remain with the distraught girl. He thanked her warmly holding out his hand and saying in a low voice, 'Miss Hartwell, is it not? Oliver Worthington. I don't know how you came to be involved in this confounded mess, but I am deeply grateful for the support you have given Lady Isobel.' He hesitated, before continuing with a slight blush, 'She has been a little foolish, but then she is little more than a child, and Armistead is – was – a cunning rogue. And Lord Vance, I hope you will not judge him harshly. His manner may be a little rough, but he cares deeply for his sister's welfare.' Mr Worthington did not wait for a reply, but followed the earl from the room.

Geneva drew up a chair to the bedside, and while her lips moved automatically uttering comforting nothings to the weeping girl, her mind was a frenzy of activity.

When the earl stepped out into the hall it was to find two stalwart grooms, under the direction of the flusterd landlord, moving the body of Julien Armistead into what had been, until his untimely demise, his bedchamber.

'A word with you, my good man,' said Lord Vance shortly, before descending the narrow wooden staircase to the tap room. He was met there by the landlord's wife, arms akimbo and with a belligerent look in her eye.

'Well my Lord, this is a fine to do!'

The agitated landlord hastened to his wife's side, saying in an anxious half whisper, 'Hush, Sarah! Remember whom you are talking to.'

This reminder of Lord Vance's social station did nothing to cow the pugnacious landlady who greeted her spouse's rebuke with a contemptuous snort before turning her attention once more to the earl. 'You may be the King of England himself for all I care, but when you come into a decent house, among decent people, and bring violence and murder with you, then you must answer to Sarah Ramsden!'

Lord Vance, perceiving that this stout-hearted dame would not be daunted by one of the freezing aristocratic stares with which he usually subdued the lower orders, and liking her all the better for it, treated her instead to one of his rare sweet smiles, and said that naturally, she was deserving of an explanation.

Mr Worthington and the landlord watched with amusement and admiration respectively as Lord Vance quickly won over Mrs Ramsden to his side. Within ten minutes she was praising his actions and bustling off to the kitchen for, unless she was mistaken, there was some of that nice game pie left over from dinner, and no doubt the gentlemen would be glad of refreshment after their long drive.

When she had gone, the earl turned to Mr Worthington, saying with an ironic smile, 'I hope the magistrate may be so easily convinced of my innocence.'

Mr Worthington looked shocked at this, saying incredulously, 'Surely you do not intend to stand trial?'

'But what else should I do? Rest assured my head is not at risk!'

'Oh no! You will be cleared all right! And in the meantime imagine the scandal and the damage this night's work will do to Lady Isobel's reputation if it ever gets out, which it certainly will if you do not make yourself scarce!'

The earl sat in meditative silence for a moment, before saying resignedly, 'You are right as usual, my friend. What do you suggest? If I flee the country then tongues will wag just as surely.'

Mr Worthington acknowledged the truth of this, but then said slowly, as if the idea was forming as he spoke, 'No, you must not flee the country. But if you and Lady Isobel were to travel abroad, perhaps to spend the season in Paris? With Napoleon safe on Elba the ton are flocking across the Channel so it would occasion no comment. And you may rely on me to smooth over matters here.'

Lord Vance was much struck by the idea. 'Yes it could work. But not Paris. I place little reliance on Bonaparte remaining on Elba. My Aunt Yarwood has taken a place in Vienna for the Peace Congress, and she has been begging me to bring Isobel over for a visit.'

Mr Worthington nodded enthusiastically, but then an unpleasant thought occurred to him. 'Vienna! But that is where the Fortesques are wintering! Imagine what the tattlemongers will make of you following the divine Camilla half-way across Europe!'

But the earl did not seem perturbed by this, only saying, with a devilish grin that convinced his friend that he was planning something outrageous, that the presence of the Fortesques would not cost him a minute's sleep. With that he left Mr Worthington to his game pie and his uneasy thoughts and ran lightly back up the stairs to knock quietly on Geneva Hartwell's door.

Lady Isobel had finally cried herself to sleep when Geneva answered the door to Lord Vance. She greeted him warily and begged him to keep his voice low in consideration for the sleeping girl. Once they were seated on either side of the fire, the room lit only by its dying embers, the earl came straight to the point.

'I gather from your presence in this Godforsaken place, Miss Hartwell, that you have shunned your guardian's care.'

Geneva's eyes flew to his face in surprise. Since the news of his probable attachment to Miss Fortesque, Geneva had convinced herself that the Earl of Brewood had long ago dismissed from his mind the problems of a mere parson's daughter. Lord Vance acknowledged her startled glance with a crooked grin. The flickering red light from the hearth cast dramatic shadows across his saturnine features, and to Geneva he looked almost devilish lounging with insolent ease in the chair opposite her.

Geneva in contrast sat bolt upright, her hands clenched tightly in her lap, praying he could not hear the erratic thump of her heart. Out of his presence, Geneva resolved to be cool and distant in her dealings with this disturbing lord. But his very nearness seemed to destroy those resolutions, and when he suddenly smiled kindly and said in a soft caressing voice, 'Will you not tell me the whole?' Geneva found herself recounting all that had happened.

Comforted by his sympathetic silence during her account, Geneva was moved to hesitantly suggest, 'If you are returning to London on the morrow, perhaps you might convey me to the Bartrams?'

'I do not return to London,' was the uncompromising reply. Geneva felt she had been doused with cold water. She rose abruptly saying, 'Then there is no more to be said. I bid you good evening, my Lord.'

Lord Vance ignored this pointed dismissal, saying patiently, 'I did not say I would not help you, Miss Hartwell, merely that I was not returning to London.'

But Geneva had been snubbed before, and she was not about to risk further humiliation. 'You are under no obligation to help me, Lord Vance. I wish you would forget all I have told you.'

'What I have to suggest will be to our mutual benefit, there is no question of obligation. I am going to Vienna and I want you to come with me.'

Geneva turned on him, wrath blazing in her magnificent violet eyes. How dared he! For the second time she had been foolish enough to confide in him, and for the second time he had abused her trust. 'To our mutual benefit! I have told you before, my Lord, that nothing would induce me to accept your – your protection. You are no better than my guardian, seeking to take advantage of my vulnerable position!'

Lord Vance remained entirely unmoved through this tirade. 'You know, it may be a cliché, but you really are very beautiful when you are in a rage. Did you know that your eyes turn almost purple when you are angry?' He paused, but Geneva remained unsoftened by his words, so he continued, 'Really, Miss Hartwell, you make a point of choosing to misunderstand me. Yes I am offering you my protection, but not in the sense you so obviously mean. I do not choose innocents or green girls for my mistresses. I am asking you to accompany me to Vienna in the guise of my betrothed.'

sturbing you, but Mr Boeman, my guardian, has this moment
rived, and…' she faltered awkwardly. How could she possibly
plain that her instinctive reaction had been to turn to the earl
 help?

Lord Vance continued smoothly, 'And naturally you came to
u fiancé for assistance. Give me a moment to make myself
sentable and I will deal with him.'

Oh, but I have not said—' exclaimed Geneva distractedly,
ly to be unceremoniously interrupted by the earl.

Time enough later! Now I believe it is customary in these
airs to ask the guardian's permission for the hand of his ward,
 I think we may in the circumstances dispense with the
aventions. I am sure Mr Boeman can be convinced of the
dom of putting no obstacle in my way.'

his last was said with such grim intent that a new fear
ailed Geneva. She caught his arm saying urgently, 'Oh pray!
u will not kill him?'

he earl smiled down at her reassuringly, 'Despite the
lence to the contrary, Miss Hartwell, I am not in the habit of
ing any man who dares to defy my will. Besides, from what
 have told me, Mr Boeman is nothing more than a worthless
y who will shrink from putting his own miserable life at risk.
v go back to your room and stay there until I come for you.'

eneva could find fault aplenty with this plan, but she was
nning to realize that opposing the earl was like trying to
 back the tide. So she returned to her room without demur
once there made haste to dress and pin up her hair into some
 of order, for she had no intention of sitting meekly upstairs
e down below the earl confronted her guardian.

eneva reached the concealing shadows at the foot of the
s in time to hear Lord Vance asking the landlord in bored
rcilious tones, what in heaven's name could have occurred
casion such a commotion.

e landlord greeted Lord Vance's arrival on the scene with
led relief and agitation. 'Well, my Lord, I am sorry if you
 been disturbed. This gentleman,' – at which point he
red the dishevelled Mr Boeman with a disparaging look
h suggested he took leave to doubt his claims to that title –
ted on seeing the young lady who arrived here late last
. Says he is her guardian, but he doesn't look at all the sort
ardian for a respectable lady.'

Eight

For one dazed moment Geneva thought the earl was actually
proposing to her, and she could only stare at him in stunned
incomprehension, her anger forgotten. When she eventually
found her voice, it was to say faintly, 'Your betrothed? But why
on earth…?'

'Why indeed!' cut in the earl brusquely. 'Well, if you will sit
down and cease gawping at me, I will tell you.'

This unloverlike speech had the effect of bringing Geneva
speedily to her senses, and she retorted tartly, 'I am not
gawping! But when you make such a ridiculous suggestion for
all the world as if you were asking me to do something totally
unexceptional, like – like take a walk in the park, you leave me
speechless!'

'Since we are stranded in the midst of a blizzard and it is
close on four in the morning, I would hardly call a walk in the
park the suggestion of a sensible man.'

Geneva not help giving an involuntary chuckle at this
prosaic humour, and Lord Vance smiled encouragingly. 'That's
a good girl. Now you have gathered your wits do please sit
down and I will explain all.'

Geneva considered taking exception to this familiar mode of
address, but in the end she felt unequal to the task and simply
sat down meekly as she was bid. The rigours of the evening
were beginning to tell. Events had taken on a dreamlike
quality, and as she sat in the dark bedroom of the inn, listening
to the Earl of Brewood explaining why she should fly with him
to Vienna and pretend to be his future bride, something in the
back of her mind told her that any minute now she would wake
up in her own bed back at the parsonage.

'Miss Hartwell!'

Geneva jumped guiltily. To her consternation she realized that she had not heard one word the earl had said to her. The comfort of the shabby armchair and the warmth of the room had lulled her to sleep. Hastily she resumed her upright posture, fixed her tired aching eyes on the earl's haughty face and said with assmued brightness, 'You were saying, my Lord?'

Lord Vance's features relaxed into a sympathetic smile. 'No, Miss Hartwell. Our discussion may wait until the morrow. I would advise you to get some sleep, if you agree to my proposal you will have a long and tiring journey ahead of you.'

Geneva nodded thankfully, rose and accompanied him to the door. 'Very well, but I should warn you, Lord Vance, that I cannot like the idea of practising such a deceit. I feel sure no good could come of it.'

Lord Vance shook his head slightly and put a slender white finger to her lips. Geneva looked up into his dark inscrutable eyes, her own wide and troubled. He felt an overpowering urge to kiss away the strain and worry from her face, but he controlled it. With infinite gentleness he brushed a tendril of hair from her brow before bending his head and pressing his lips to her forehead. Then he was gone, leaving Geneva puzzled but oddly reassured.

She thought she would never understand this provoking man or be able to analyse her own feelings regarding him. At one moment he would ride roughshod over her feelings, his eyes hard and mocking, his aristocratic features set in harsh lines, and she was sure that she hated him and everything he stood for. But then occasionally, as had just happened, he would smile down at her so unexpectedly that it was like a blinding ray of sunshine bursting from between lowering clouds on a stormy day, and suddenly her feelings were no longer clear cut. But she was too exhausted to contemplate his strange behaviour and even stranger proposition for long. Within minutes of sinking into the welcome downy softness of the bed, she fell into deep and dreamless sleep.

Lord Vance returned to the tap room, an ironic half smile on his lips. He was used to having damsels hanging on his every word. It was refreshing, though not very flattering to one's ego, to have a young lady fall asleep on him, especially when he had made her an offer most girls would have given their eye-teeth for.

But then that was why he had, and could o[...] the outrageous suggestion to Miss Geneva Har[...] female of his acquaintance would have lea[...] secretly confident that by fair means or foul t[...] the sham betrothal into an all too real marri[...] Miss Hartwell had received it with horror, [...] ridiculous, and it would no doubt take all of t[...] of persuasion to convince her of the sense behi[...]

Geneva felt that her head had barely tou[...] when she was awakened by the sound of a l[...] the yard beneath her window. Sliding cautiou[...] the covers so as not to disturb the sleeping La[...] pulled her cloak around her shoulders and [...] mullioned window. The snow had ceased to[...] was high in the sky, suggesting that the mo[...] fairly far advanced. But Geneva was in no mo[...] the weather or the time of day, for engage[...] dispute with the landlord was Leonard Boem[...]

Geneva automatically shrank from sight, a[...] feverishly pull on her slippers, she ran out in[...] the little narrow winding staircase to the a[...] hastily been prepared for Lord Vance and M[...]

Without pausing to consider the improp[...] gentleman's room dressed only in her nigh[...] with her luxuriant dark curls hanging dow[...] hammered urgently on the door. It w[...] Worthington, thankfully very properly, [...] attired in the previous night's evening d[...] noticed his startled look as he stepped a[...] enter.

Geneva came to an abrupt halt when cor[...] of the Earl of Brewood in his shirtsleeves, [...] lying carelessly open displaying the strong[...] Lord Vance paused in the act of tying his c[...] some amusement, his dark eyes glinting as[...]

Geneva felt colour flood into her cheek[...] cloak more closely around her in attemp[...] *déshabillé*, although in truth her nightgown[...] neck was far less revealing than the prev[...] wear. But this was no time to be missish a[...] ground saying in an urgent voice, 'I l[...]

Indeed, Mr Boeman was looking decidedly the worse for wear. He had enjoyed his evening's entertainment at the Brown Cow to the full, and when he had made his erratic way home as dawn was beginning to break over the snow-covered landscape, his only thoughts were of his bed. But instead of being allowed to slip unobtrusively up the back staircase and fall into a stupor, he had arrived at Clayton House to find the entire household in uproar. Mrs Hartwell, her refined manners forgotten, was cursing the stupidity of the servants, who were all adamant in vociferously denying their own culpability. Pausing only to add his own curses to those of his mother, Mr Boeman set off in pursuit of his ward, going over with relish in his mind the retribution he would serve her when he had compelled her to be his bride. He had tracked Geneva down to the Red Lion with little difficulty, as she had suspected he would, and then it was only a matter of time before he had learned of her presence at the Wily Fox, being that it was the only hostelry within walking distance of the Red Lion.

Now Geneva's eyes widened in disbelief as she took in Mr Boeman's sorry appearance, in such contrast was it to his habitual careful grooming. His cravat was crumpled and stained, stubble marred his chin and his top boots were scuffed and muddied. The genial mask he had always taken care to show to Geneva had been replaced by a decidedly ugly expression. This became more marked when the earl raised his quizzing glass deliberately to his eye and stared disdainfully down his aristocratic nose at him, a faint sneer on his lips.

'Indeed, I think you are right, Mr Ramsden. A very ramshackle fellow; I would not allow him indoors.'

Mr Boeman started towards Lord Vance angrily. 'I do not know who you may be, sir, but I don't care for your tone.'

'Really? I am afraid that is a matter of complete indifference to me. I do not care for your face, and would beg you to remove it from my sight.'

Mr Boeman clenched his fists but forced an unctuous smile. This man might dress like a London exquisite but there was a dangerous strength about him, and as the earl had suspected, Leonard Boeman was not a brave man. 'My Lord, I have no quarrel with you. I have merely come in search of my ward. A minor misunderstanding; you know how it is with young girls.'

Lord Vance's sneer became more pronounced. 'I am afraid I

don't know, but that is irrelevant. I should tell you Mr Boeman, that Miss Hartwell has not the slightest intention of returning to your care. You may offer me your felicitations, Mr Boeman. I have made Miss Hartwell an offer, which she has done me the honour of accepting.'

Mr Boeman shook his head and laughed mirthlessly through gritted teeth. 'I am afraid I cannot give my consent to such a match, and you do need my consent.'

The earl smiled faintly. 'But I understand your guardianship will come to an end within six months, and naturally we do not intend to marry before a suitable period of mourning for the Reverend Hartwell has elapsed. But in the meantime, my relatives are naturally impatient to meet my prospective bride and so I am taking Miss Hartwell to visit them.'

Mr Boeman turned pale, his jaw working in anger. 'You are making a grave mistake, my Lord, and one you will live to regret. Miss Hartwell is very fickle in her affections; you see she is already betrothed to me. I wished to spare her embarrassment, but I must tell you that it was something of a lover's tiff which caused Miss Hartwell to fly in the heat of the moment. I suspect she only accepted your offer in a moment of pique, and you may be sure she is already regretting it. You see...' Mr Boeman paused delicately. 'the strength of our feelings had already led us to perhaps go a little further than is considered proper for an unmarried couple—'

He got no further. The earl moved with lightning speed, his fist connecting squarely with Boeman's jaw sending him sprawling to the ground. Mr Worthington had been standing to one side watching this drama unfold in total bemusement, but the name Boeman triggered a memory. Now he stepped towards his friend, and seeing the blazing anger in Lord Vance's eyes, laid a restraining hand on his arm and himself addressed the floored man.

'I suggest you leave while you still can, Boeman. Unless I am mistaken, I believe Lord Neele would be interested to hear of your whereabouts, though I doubt if his unfortunate daughter wishes ever to set eyes on you again.'

Mr Worthington's calmly spoken words had a staggering effect on the prone man. The colour drained from his cheeks and fear showed in his pale eyes. Mr Boeman quickly scrambled to his feet and pointed a shaking finger at the earl.

'You may be sure this marriage will not go ahead, if it is marriage you intend.' He laughed nastily. 'I don't doubt Miss Hartwell will be glad to accept an honourable proposal when you have tired of her.'

Seeing the earl move ominously towards him, Mr Boeman retreated hastily, and within a short space of time there came the sound of a horse galloping away at speed across the hard-packed snow.

'He will certainly come to grief if he continues at that pace on this treacherous ground,' remarked Mr Worthington mildly.

'I hope he may break his horrible neck!' exclaimed Geneva heatedly, emerging from the shadows, her colour considerably heightened by Mr Boeman's slanderous insinuations.

Lord Vance spun around to face her. 'I might have known you would not do as you were bid!' he said roughly. 'Well if you have heard anything which you did not like, then you have only yourself to blame.'

'Brewood really!' protested Mr Worthington and then to Geneva, 'Miss Hartwell, it is a great pity that you should have been subjected to such unpleasantness. I need hardly say that the scoundrel's venomous words would be believed by no one.'

Geneva thanked him but said, 'I am glad to have seen his villainy completely exposed. His words cannot hurt me as they hold no truth. Besides as I have already told Lord Vance, I do not possess an excess of sensibility.'

'Bravely said!' exclaimed the earl. 'Now, Oliver, you appear to have played the trump card! What do Lord Neele and his unfortunate daughter have to do with the charming Mr Boeman?'

Mr Worthington glanced doubtfully at Geneva and said repressively, 'It is not a pretty tale, Gus.'

'Come! You heard Miss Hartwell, she has no sensibility. You may speak freely. But first may I suggest that the estimable Mrs Ramsden is prevailed upon to serve us breakfast?'

The landlord, who had been standing watching the play of events in helpless wonder, at once made haste to the kitchen, where he gave his opinion that gentry or no, a queerer set of folk he had never had under his roof. Whereupon his spouse sharply adjured him to mind his tongue and fetch ale for the gentlemen.

An excellent repast was soon forthcoming, and as the earl politely ushered Geneva to her seat he murmured provocatively in her ear, 'We seem destined to breakfast together, Miss Hartwell.' Geneva vouchsafed no reply beyond a slight lift of her chin, but simply begged Mr Worthington to tell them what he knew of her wicked guardian.

It was not, as Mr Worthington had warned, a pretty tale. Some five years previously, Lord Neele's daughter, a girl of just seventeen years and fresh from the schoolroom, had been sent to spend time in Bath with her elderly grandmother prior to making her debut in London society. Mr Boeman also happened to be making a sojourn in the fashionable spa town at the same time, and had very quickly insinuated himself into the good graces of the grandmother, and the affections of the young girl.

It was perhaps unfortunate that no male relative was on hand to discourage the attentions of a gazetted fortune hunter of doubtful background, and one moreover who had been mistaken in his prey. For it seems that Mr Boeman attached rather too much importance to old Lady Neele's vague hints of the dowry she intended to bestow on her favourite grandchild in the event of her marriage. When, under Mr Boeman's subtle questioning, it was revealed that this gift would consist of nothing more than a few pounds and a cameo brooch of little more than sentimental value, Mr Boeman's departure from Bath was remarkable in its swiftness.

For Lord Neele's daughter, the incident was not so easily forgotten; she was carrying his child. She was fortunate in that her family did not disown her, but she was shunned by society and all hopes of a respectable marriage were lost.

Geneva listened to this sad but all too common tale with rising indignation, which she could no longer contain when Mr Worthington was finally silent. 'Of all the infamous things! I knew he was wicked but I never suspected—' Geneva could find no words to express her outrage. 'That poor girl, how I feel for her!'

'Unfortunately the world does not share your sympathy in such cases,' remarked the earl grimly before changing the subject. 'Now I think you will agree, Miss Hartwell, that the further away from Mr Boeman you are the better. I do not place much reliance on your ability to avoid him, and I doubt the Bartrams, for all their good intentions, would have the means to protect you from him. You had much better accept my proposition and come to Vienna.'

Geneva could not but agree with him. Mr Boeman was a desperate man and totally unscrupulous. If she remained in this country she did not doubt his ability to pursue her and gain his ends by force. But to go to Vienna on the pretext of being betrothed to the Earl of Brewood! Surely that would be nothing short of madness?

Geneva shook her head helplessly. 'I do not know what to do for the best. I feel you are right that I would not be safe in London, but the alternative you give me is so drastic! Could I not simply accompany you to Vienna? I am sure I would have no difficulty in finding some employment for a few months.'

Even Mr Worthington was moved to protest at this idea. 'My dear Miss Hartwell, we could not allow that! I do not say that I agree with Lord Vance's outlandish proposal, but it would certainly be preferable to you being forced to find work.'

'Oliver is right on that score. My dear girl, I know you consider me selfish and insensitive, but I am not so devoid of common decency as to abandon a gently bred female to her own fate in a foreign country. If you find my suggestion too repugnant then you will of course stay as a guest in my aunt's house.'

But Geneva found that having been offered an ideal solution her conscience would not allow her to take it. 'I could not possibly impose on your relations in such a way! I am already so very much in your debt.'

The earl stared at Geneva in exasperation. 'Was there ever a more contrary female? If you feel so beholden to me then why not oblige me by masquerading as my betrothed?'

Geneva felt as if she was being inextricably drawn into accepting this outrageous role, and yet still she did not know the reason behind it, and said as much to the earl. To which he replied in a voice laden with sarcasm, 'Well if you think you can remain awake for long enough then I will be glad to explain.'

Geneva bridled at this, but was too eager to hear Lord Vance's reasonings to call him to account for this unfair jibe. Satisfied that he had her full attention, the earl began, 'I take it that the unfortunate circumstances surrounding Mr Armistead's death will be seen as sufficient reason for my own impromptu trip to Vienna?' Geneva nodded. She may have spent her whole life in the country, but she was no stranger to gossip. She could well imagine the lurid stories that would surround Lady Isobel if her brother was charged with the murder of Julien Armistead.

The Earl continued, 'Unfortunately, there is in Vienna a young lady who, through my own ill-judged behaviour, believes I am on the point of offering her marriage. This is not my intention, but should I travel hotfoot to Vienna so closely in her wake, then the gossip it would engender would make things very difficult for the young lady involved. However if I were to arrive at my aunt's already betrothed, such unpleasantness would be nipped in the bud.'

Geneva remembered Mrs Hartwell's letter and could have no doubt to whom Lord Vance was referring. The news that he had no intention of marrying made her feel unaccountably light at heart. 'You are speaking of Miss Fortesque, I gather.'

Here she succeeded in surprising his lordship, who exclaimed, 'Good God, if speculation has already reached the provinces then I would say this deception is all the more necessary!'

Geneva sat for a moment deep in thought. It seemed that the earl's motives were on the whole good. Indeed she was surprised to find him so considerate of Miss Fortesque's feelings. Even so, such subterfuge went against everything her father had taught her, but there again, she argued to herself, he could never have imagined she would find herself in such strange circumstances. She turned to Mr Worthington saying, 'Sir, I would value your unbiased opinion. Would it be very unpleasant for Miss Fortesque if I were to refuse?'

Mr Worthington was prompt in his reply. 'Miss Hartwell, you should not let that weigh with you. Consider your own position! Brewood, I am astonished that you should put Miss Hartwell in such an awkward position!'

'You have not answered Miss Hartwell's question, Oliver.'

Mr Worthington sighed and said somewhat reluctantly, 'Very well. Yes I am afraid Miss Fortesque would become the object of the most malicious gossip.'

Geneva took a deep breath and then asked the question that troubled her the most. 'Forgive me, but Lord Vance, is there anything – what I mean to say is, has anything passed between you and Miss Fortesque that would lead her quite rightly to demand marriage?' There it was said, and she resolutely fixed her eyes on the table as she felt hot colour pour into her cheeks.

The earl laughed unpleasantly. 'I wish I might know from where you have got this unflattering picture of me. If you intend to put me in the same category as your guardian then there is clearly no more to be said.'

Geneva was immediately contrite, for all his faults she had never really considered that the earl would be guilty of anything dishonourable, but if she were to go down this path then it was essential that she knew in what she was involving herself. 'Please do not take offence, but it is after all an unusual request.'

The earl found he was not proof to those pleading violet-blue eyes. 'Very well. Now do you have any more probing questions or will you let me have an answer?'

'Only one, my Lord. If I were to agree, how would we bring this bogus engagement to an end?'

Naturally, Lord Vance had an answer ready for this. 'You will jilt me of course. I will endeavour to do something totally unforgivable, and the world will applaud your good sense!'

At which Geneva, who felt that the earl had had the upper hand for far too long in this conversation, could not resist retorting, 'Oh, my Lord, I am sure you need not make any special effort!'

The earl laughed aloud at this and holding out his hand said, 'Then it is a deal, Miss Hartwell?'

Geneva hesitated before putting her hand in his. 'It is a deal, Lord Vance.'

Nine

The earl in typical fashion, having reached a decision wasted no time in putting his plans into action. It was not to be expected that the violent death of Julien Armistead could be concealed indefinitely, and when the landlord had come to clear away their breakfast dishes, he had very apologetically broached that delicate subject. His conscience could not allow him to do other than apprise Major Rawlinson, the magistrate whose manor lay a few miles north of the Wily Fox, of the unfortunate incident. He was told to rest easy on that score, since the earl and Mr Worthington fully intended to inform that venerable gentleman themselves.

Mr Ramsden could do nothing but accept this scheme, albeit with some reservations. He was an honest citizen, and something told him that it behoved him to keep the perpetrators of this crime within his sight while a more disinterested messenger was sent to the manor. But unlike his spouse, Mr Ramsden had a deeply ingrained awe of the nobility, and this prevented him from voicing his doubts.

Minutes later Lord Vance and Mr Worthington set off in the earl's curricle at a sensible trot. Their journey to Rawlinson Manor involved a slight detour to the Red Lion where Lord Vance was set down before Mr Worthington proceeded on his way at what could only be described as a meandering pace.

Lord Vance strolled into the tap room of the Red Lion and bespoke a post-chaise, informing the flustered landlord with his usual disregard for the problems such a request might create, that he would expect the vehicle to be ready to leave by the time he had refreshed himself with a tankard of the landlord's excellent ale. Consequently Geneva and Lady Isobel were comfortably installed along with the earl in the best chaise the Red Lion could provide, long before Mr Worthington was even in sight of Rawlinson Manor.

Even Mr Ramsden felt it was his duty to protest at this turn of events, but surprisingly it was Mrs Ramsden who came to the earl's defence, saying, 'Really, Mr Ramsden, what can you be thinking of? Naturally his Lordship is wishful of removing the young ladies before there is any more unpleasantness.' With that Mr Ramsden was pleased to be satisfied, and before long the earl and his party had left the Wily Fox behind, and were making good progress through the rapidly thawing snow.

The news that they were to travel to Vienna considerably improved Lady Isobel's spirits, and her unfortunate liaison with Mr Armistead was all but forgotten long before they reached London. It was close on midnight when the chaise finally drew up outside the house in Berkeley Square, and even Lady Isobel's excited speculations on the pleasures that awaited them on the Continent had petered out.

The earl allowed them only a few minutes to freshen up before he cut short the tearful reunion of Lady Isobel and her Aunt Amelia and their journey to the coast continued in the luxury of the Earl's travelling chaise, the Earl's groom and valet, and Lady Isobel's repentant maid in a second carriage. A second groom on horseback was despatched ahead to carry news of their arrival and the earl's sudden betrothal to their future hosts. Weary and resigned, Geneva simply made herself comfortable against the crimson squabs, pulled the fur-lined carriage rug around her, and with her feet resting on a hot brick went immediately to sleep.

Lady Isobel accepted their prolonged discomfort less philosophically, complaining pettily against her brother's cruelty. She was reminded in no uncertain terms that it was her lamentable behaviour which had brought them to this pass, and had the grace to relapse into silence, punctuated by the occasional muted grumble.

Once the Channel was behind them, the earl maintained a relentless pace across Eurupe. While Geneva could see the sense in this, she resented Lord Vance's high-handed way and the fact that while for the majority of the journey he elected to ride beside the carriage, Geneva was left with the impossible task of keeping Lady Isobel entertained.

The earl's sister was an indifferent traveller, and when she was not suffering from a headache or nausea, she was invariably bored and seemed to expect Geneva to relieve her ennui. Geneva thought she might have been able to do that quite satisfactorily had it not been for one circumstance. In vain did she point out the beauties of the landscape or suggest simple games to while away the tedious hours. Lady Isobel returned again and again to the one subject Geneva felt unable to discuss; her supposed engagement to Lord Vance.

It had been deemed necessary for the artificial nature of their attachment to be hidden from all bar Mr Worthington. Geneva had protested, believing it would be impossible to deceive Lady Isobel, but the earl was not to be gainsaid. With a lack of brotherly affection but with a certain degree of truth, he gave his opinion that his bird-witted sister could not be trusted to keep her tongue between her teeth and that if she was included in the secret, the whole of Vienna would know within twenty-four hours that the betrothal of the Earl of Brewood and Miss Hartwell was a hoax.

Which is all very well and good, reflected Geneva bitterly, but it is not my lord who is forced to endure Lady Isobel's constant probing. When she said as much to him, Lord Vance merely said that he was sure a person of her ingenuity would be able to think of something.

Justly annoyed by this typical lack of sympathy, Geneva took him at his word, and fabricated a whirlwind courtship designed to satiate the keenest appetite for romance. Lady Isobel listened to this fantastic tale of stolen kisses, clandestine meetings and secret correspondence with frank incredulity, exclaiming, 'Well! I would never have thought it of Gus! He has always held that kind of thing in the greatest contempt.'

Geneva, who could well believe this, merely suggested coyly that Lord Vance was perhaps as susceptible as the next person to Cupid's dart. Lady Isobel, who thought this highly unlikely, agreed politely but then added, 'Yes, but for all that, neither of you seemed at all pleased to see one another in that dreadful inn.'

Geneva was amazed that Lady Isobel, in the midst of her own torrid affair, had noticed the supposed lovers' decidedly cool reunion, and was forced to improvise wildly. 'Oh, it was such a surprise to us both, but you may be sure that privately we were both ecstatic. After all we had not seen one another for such a long time.'

Lady Isobel considered this and said she supposed their enforced separation could explain her brother's recent black humour, but went on to say candidly that the fact they were reunited had done little to improve his temper.

The result of Geneva's invention was all that she had hoped. When they stopped for the night at an inn just short of the Austrian border, Lady Isobel enlivened dinner with a series of less than subtle teasing references to the earl's fictitious courtship of Geneva. The earl, not surprisingly, chose not to take up any of his sister's hints, turning them aside smoothly with a skill Geneva was forced to admire. Throughout their exchange, Geneva kept her head firmly bowed, not trusting herself to meet Lord Vance's quizzical gaze. But when Lady Isobel went so far as to ask outright whether it was true that he and Geneva had disguised themselves as simple peasants so they might attend a country fair together, she gave an involuntary choke and looked quickly across the room at Lord Vance, her eyes brimming with humour.

His own eyes glinted dangerously in return, but he simply said blandly, 'Are you all right, my dear? Perhaps you would care for a glass of water?' Geneva shook her head wordlessly, resolutely biting her bottom lip in a desperate attempt to contain her mirth.

The earl then turned to his sister. 'Miss Hartwell and I often had difficulty in finding moments for ourselves. In fact I think that after dinner we might take advantage of the mild weather and take a short stroll. What do you say, my dear?'

This was all said in the pleasantest of tones, but Geneva knew that Lord Vance had revenge in mind, so she said sweetly, 'I own that is a tempting prospect, but we could not leave Lady Isobel on her own.'

But Geneva's attempts to thwart Lord Vance were ruined by his sister, who said magnanimously that she would not for the world spoil their plans. She then whisked herself from the room, saying with a dreadful archness that did nothing for Geneva's equanimity, that she could see they were dying to be alone.

There was a short pause before the earl remarked laconically, 'I suppose you will say I have received my just deserts.'

Geneva could maintain her self-possession no longer, and a

gurgle of laughter escaped her. But she quickly schooled her lips into prim lines and said innocently, 'But I merely followed your advice, my Lord, and used my imagination.'

'And as I have already had cause to note, you have a very vivid imagination.' He added in a pained voice, 'But disguised as a peasant? I dread to think how you may have described me! Wearing a smock and with hay in my hair I don't doubt.'

The picture he conjured up was too much for Geneva and she gave a peel of infectious laughter. With her eyes sparkling with mischief in her glowing face, those full rosebud lips parted in a delightful curve to reveal her perfect pearly-white teeth, she was an enchanting sight, and even the jaded earl was not immune to such fresh beauty. Quite suddenly he found he was looking forward to his visit to Vienna instead of viewing it in terms of an enforced exile.

'Come, my dear, let us take our stroll in the moonlight. After all we must not waste these precious moments alone.' His voice was loaded with irony but there was a gleam in those dark eyes that made Geneva feel suddenly breathless, and when he took her arm his touch sent a frisson of pleasure through her. Geneva knew she should regard the prospect of being alone in the company of a notorius rake with abject horror, but was ashamed to find that on the contrary she felt a little thrill of anticipation. She swiftly quelled this reprehensible emotion and sternly adjured herself not to allow the earl to lead her into saying or doing anything improper, which, it seemed was the inevitable consequence of her spending any length of time in his company.

Lord Vance sensed her apprehension and took pity on her, saying in business-like tones when they had left the shelter of the inn, 'I am glad of this opportunity to be private with you, for there are a few matters I would like to settle before we reach Vienna. Firstly I think it would be wise not to include Lord and Lady Yarwood in our charade.'

Geneva was relieved that their conversation had returned to more general matters, but she could not agree to this. 'Oh but I could not possibly practise such a deception on your aunt when I am already obliged to her for taking me in at such short notice. Indeed I should not wonder at her being quite put out by us descending on her in this way.'

'You need have no worries on that score. Aunt Liz loves

entertaining. Lord Yarwood is employed at the Foreign Office, so she is constantly on the move and required to entertain on a grand scale with much less warning than we have given her. She will be delighted to see us. I know you must find it repugnant to lie to her but I do believe it is for the best. It will be difficult enough for you to act this role, and I think you will agree that other people knowing of it could only make it worse.'

Geneva had to agree that it would, but she still could not feel happy about it. The earl, satisfied that the matter was settled turned to his next point. 'I also believe that it would be better if you did not appear to be in mourning. It would only lead to unnecessary speculation at the suddenness of our betrothal. If you appear in colours and attend social events, no one will be the wiser for I presume you have no acquaintances in Vienna.'

'I hardly see society's ignorance of my bereavement as a reason to forgo my mourning! My mourning clothes are a sign of my love and respect for my father, not simply a social convention,' protested Geneva hotly.

'My sentiments exactly. But is an outward show of grief necessary for you to preserve his memory?'

'Of course not! But every feeling revolts at so quickly entering society.'

'Under normal circumstances, yes. But these are hardly normal circumstances. Reflect for a moment, think of Lucasta Hartwell. Were widow's weeds and a quiet existence a true reflection of her grief?'

Geneva had to admit that they were not. She thought too of Mrs Thorneygate who constantly bedecked herself in unrelieved black, but who had little wifely affection for her deceased husband. Coloured gowns would not make the memory of her dear father any the fainter, nor blunt the edge of her grief. 'Very well, my Lord,' she said resignedly. 'You seem to have won on all points.'

'I merely wish to make things easier for yourself, Miss Hartwell. Now, I will turn to the real reason behind our little stroll. You know I cannot let you escape retribution for those delightful stories you have woven around our supposed courtship. I shall hardly be able to show my face in Vienna. My reputation as a hardened rake will be completely undermined!'

The earl's voice was no longer matter of fact, it held an

intimate bantering note that set alarm bells ringing in Geneva's head. She strove to answer him coolly. 'But I stressed to Lady Isobel that I was only telling her under duress, and in the strictest confidence.'

'Then you obviously have more faith than I in my sister's ability to keep such a prime piece of gossip to herself,' Lord Vance replied dryly.

Geneva's dismayed expression showed that she recognized the truth of this. No more than the earl did she want the nauseous tales she had invented to circulate the ballrooms and salons of Vienna. 'But I only intended—' Geneva stopped short. She could hardly admit that the whole episode had been designed to punish the earl for his dictatorial ways.

'To teach me a lesson,' finished Lord Vance obligingly. 'And now, in return I shall teach you one. Really, your powers of invention are quite extraordinary, but if anyone should question you more closely on those stolen kisses we have exchanged, I should not like you to have to rely entirely on imagination.'

Before Geneva could divine the intention behind this speech, a strong arm had encircled her slim waist and she was pulled inexorably towards him. A crescent moon appeared from behind the scudding clouds and shone briefly down on the couple, lighting up the earl's pale features and inevitably reminding Geneva of her first brush with him on the Harbury to Tadworth road. This time, however, there would be no respite, and Geneva realized with shame that this time she had no desire to be released from Lord Vance's disturbing embrace.

Lord Vance gazed down at her heart-shaped face, filled with apprehensive expectancy, and then very slowly and very deliberately he kissed her. It had been intended as a teasing punishment, but when he felt her lips soft and yielding beneath his own, and her body warm and pliant in his arms, all thoughts of punishment were forgotten and the earl began to kiss her in earnest.

Geneva knew she should be resisting him; somewhere at the back of her mind a small voice screamed that this was madness. But it was drowned by the sensations the earl's embrace sent racing through her body, and inexplicably, instead of pushing him away one hand had crept, seemingly of its own accord, to rest lightly on his shoulder.

It would have been so easy to have continued her education, but it was Geneva's vulnerability that caused the earl to draw back. Lord Vance was shaken by the feelings this girl was arousing in him and he set her aside abruptly, his usual aplomb deserting him as he said, 'I was obviously mistaken, you are in no need of tuition.' Geneva flinched as if she had been struck, and Lord Vance immediately regretted his cruel words. But it was too late to retract them. Besides, he told himself, it would be foolish beyond permission to allow an intimacy to develop between them. Their 'betrothal' was a business arrangement, devised for their mutual benefit. It would be totally ridiculous if the earl, endeavouring to avoid matrimony with one young lady, should be lured into indiscretion by the sweet lips and wide pansy eyes of another.

Geneva immediately sensed that Lord Vance had withdrawn behind an impenetrable barrier. She was confused and angry, both by her own reaction to his touch, and by his sudden rejection of her. But Geneva had too much pride to allow him to see her pain. 'I think we should return to the inn; it is late and I am tired from travelling,' she said in the most dispassionate tones she could muster. They walked back along the moonlit path in tense silence, each prey to their own troubled thoughts.

To Geneva's relief, Lady Isobel had been unable to stave off sleep, and so she was not besieged by a string of enquiries on her return. Geneva tossed and turned for several hours; her body ached with fatigue, and her mind refused to rest. To her shame, she found herself reliving that kiss over and over, and each time Lord Vance's cruel rejection was more painful.

Geneva awoke the next morning unrefreshed but determined not to let the earl's treatment depress her. In the still small hours she had finally reached the conclusion that the Earl of Brewood, deprived of more alluring game, was amusing himself at her expense. After all what possible attraction could an unsophisticated clergyman's daughter hold for the worldly and arrogant earl who could have the pick of society's elegant beauties if he so desired? But then her natural pride reasserted itself. Miss Geneva Hartwell was not going to lose her head over a heartless libertine. If Lord Augustin Vance thought he could enslave her with his kisses and wound her with his rebuffs, then he would soon discover that he had mistaken his quarry!

The remainder of their journey passed without mishap, since

both Geneva and the earl were equal in their determination to avoid one another's company. Their destination drawing ever closer, Lady Isobel was too excited to notice the distinctly unloverlike behaviour of the engaged couple, and so Geneva was spared any awkward questions.

On the seventh morning of their journey they finally emerged from the woodland of the low hills to the west of Vienna and came into the city itself. Geneva was immediately entranced. They passed through the newer part of the city with its elegant spacious palaces set in glorious gardens, through the ancient walls partly destroyed by the Turks in a previous age, and into the heart of 'old' Vienna. Here the streets were narrow and bustled with colourful life and Geneva and Isobel gazed in delight at the cosmopolitan scene.

Everything about Vienna was flamboyant. The architecture in contrast to the restrained classical style that prevailed the Regent's England, was rich and lavish. Winged and gilded cherubs, satyrs and nymphs decorated the intricate baroque and rococo designs. The pastel shades favoured by the ladies of London society were replaced by more vivid colours, as if the wearers wished to compete with the brilliant uniforms of the various personal guards who accompanied the numerous visiting foreign dignitaries.

A regiment of Hungarian hussars marched by, resplendent in their red uniforms, their tigerskin mantles flung over one shoulder.

'Don't they look dashing, Geneva? And all so tall and handsome!' exclaimed Lady Isobel. Geneva agreed, thinking with some amusement that if the earl had wished to keep his flighty sister out of mischief, he had certainly picked the wrong city!

At last their carriage came to a halt outside one of the tall palaces in the Josefsplatz. These elegant buildings had been abandoned by minor princelings of the Austro-Hungarian Empire, whose contributions to the wars against Napoleon had ruined them. Now they housed a few lucky visitors, the remainder having to settle for much less commodious dwellings.

Only as she was assisted from the chaise by a splendidly liveried footman did Geneva begin to realize the enormity of the deception she was practising. In an out-of-the-way ramshackle inn it was one thing to agree to such a charade, but faced with this dazzling city and its fashionable occupants, Geneva doubted her ability to carry it off. She had no 'town bronze' to help her through the pitfalls of society, and as the future Countess of Brewood she would be under constant jealous scrutiny. The scandalmongers and gossips would watch her every move, and if she put a foot wrong!

Geneva's face must have betrayed some of her anxiety, for when the earl drew her forward to be introduced to their hosts he gave her hand an encouraging squeeze and smiled down at her reassuringly. This slight show of support was enough to give Geneva the courage she needed, and she was able to approach the Yarwoods with apparent composure.

Geneva was immediately struck by the resemblance of Lord Vance to his paternal aunt. Lady Elizabeth Yarwood was a tall, imposing woman, in her late fifties and of erect bearing. She had strong handsome features and straight black hair streaked with silver and swept into a smooth chignon at the nape of her neck. Her complexion was rather sallow but her eyes glittered like pieces of jet beneath finely plucked and arched brows.

Lady Elizabeth's sharp tongue and rapier wit were famous within the beau monde, and many younger members of the ton had a lively dread of being singled out for one of her scathing remarks. But she obviously held no terrors for her nephew, who bowed mockingly over her hand and exclaimed, 'Why, Aunt Liz, every time I see you you become more the *grande dame*. I can see why Sally Jersey described you as the most frightening woman in London. Does the whole of Vienna quake at your feet yet?'

A smile quivered on Lady Yarwood's thin lips, but she answered tartly, 'Sally Jersey is a chattering bagpipe with more hair than wit! I would have thought you had more sense than to listen to her nonsense. Now introduce me to this young lady. I hope she may know what she is letting herself in for, the Vances make notoriously poor husbands!'

'Oh, I think Miss Hartwell is under no illusions as to my character, Aunt,' said Lord Vance with an amused glance in Geneva's direction. Lady Yarwood shot a penetrating stare at her nephew but said nothing, merely welcoming Geneva without effusiveness but with sincerity, shaking her hand firmly and offering a thin cheek to be kissed. Geneva was straight away attracted by her frank manner.

'You are very welcome, Miss Hartwell. Geneva is it? A pretty and unusual name and a pleasant change from the usual Carolines and Janes. You have an uncommon beauty as well, myself I do not see the attraction of insipid blondes.'

Lady Isobel, taking this as a personal insult, flushed, but she had been on the receiving end of her aunt's sharp tongue too often to tempt fate. Geneva meanwhile thanked Lady Yarwood warmly for her hospitality and expressed the hope that she had not been too much inconvenienced by their arrival.

'Not at all! Henry and I will be glad to have some young company, and obviously when I heard that Augustin was to be married I was very interested to meet the girl who had succeeded in captivating him.'

Geneva blushed rosily and could find nothing to say. Fortunately this was taken as maidenly modesty, and Lady Yarwood had already transferred her attention to her niece.

'And you, young lady! Well I always said to Gus that you would be far better off with me than that goosecap Amelia. Thanks to your brother's quick thinking it may be possible to salvage your reputation, but let me tell you Miss, I will not stand for your flighty ways. If you wish to be allowed in polite company you will learn to comport yourself with propriety.'

Lady Isobel looked mutinous but did not dare contradict her aunt; she did not doubt Lady Yarwood's ability to return her to the schoolroom under the least provocation.

Lord Henry Yarwood had stayed in the background while his forceful wife had her say, but now he came forward to greet the young ladies. Smiling kindly at Geneva he wished her welcome and taking Isobel's hand he said in a teasing manner perfectly designed to bring her out of the sulks that there would not be a hussar with his heart left whole once she had graced the ballrooms of Vienna. Lady Isobel was at once all smiles. Geneva warmed to this kindly man and could see why his quiet good manners and unassuming ways would be considered a valuable asset to the diplomatic service.

Lady Elizabeth led the way into the house, saying as she did, 'I suppose you will wish to freshen up after your journey, so I will show you your rooms. There is a cold collation in the dining-room when you are ready.'

Geneva could not suppress a twinge of guilt when she saw the bedroom she had been assigned. It seemed that as the betrothed of Lady Yarwood's favourite nephew, she was to be treated as a guest of honour. But neither could she contain her delight at the pretty elegance of the room. The walls were ornamented with paper delicately hand painted with exotic birds of paradise, bamboo and almond blossom on a pale cream background. The lofty ceiling was covered in fine rococo plasterwork, its swirls and scrolls picked out in gilt. Chintz floral drapes surrounded the bed and hung in lavish festoons from the window cornices.

What a contrast it was to the vulgar display of richness at Clayton House! Here the furniture was sparse, giving a pleasant uncluttered feel. Geneva noted with pleasure the pearwood dressing-table beneath the handsome gilt pier glass, and the satinwood escritoire set before one of the tall windows. 'Oh, it is perfect, Lady Elizabeth! What a truly enchanting room!'

Lady Elizabeth nodded, obviously pleased by Geneva's unfeigned delight. 'Yes I think it is my favourite room; it has an unpretentious charm. I think I have chosen well for you.'

Geneva did not reply but was secretly pleased to have gained the initial approval of the earl's aunt. Which is silly, she told herself sternly, for in a few months' time you will have no more to do with Lord Vance or his family.

Lady Yarwood left her to unpack, saying she would send her own maid, Conway, to help her. It did not take that superior person long to store away the meagre contents of Geneva's luggage, and it was plain that she considered it completely beneath her dignity to handle such unfashionable gowns as Miss Hartwell possessed. But when it came to dressing Geneva's hair, she revealed her true artistry. Her nimble fingers caught up the heavy tresses into a simple knot, allowing thick ringlets to fall from the crown of her head in artless disarray, revealing the swan-like grace of Geneva's slender neck.

Seeing the miracle the maid had wrought, Geneva turned to her, exclaiming impulsively, 'Oh thank you. How clever you are!' This caused Conway to unbend slightly and she even bestowed a wintry smile upon the girl.

The travellers refreshed, Lady Elizabeth said in her usual forthright fashion, 'Now, Isobel my dear I wish to go shopping with Geneva. I believe she packed in some haste and is in dire need of a new wardrobe, so I suggest you take the opportunity to rest. I know how travelling leaves you fagged to death.'

Isobel pouted and said she was well able to withstand an afternoon's shopping. The earl, correctly deducing that his aunt wished to spend some time getting to know Miss Hartwell, intervened, saying brutally, 'I am sure you are Isobel but you look quite hag-ridden and if I were you I would get some beauty sleep before you allow Vienna to see you.'

Isobel pulled her face and flounced to the door. 'Very well. But I must say,' she added indignantly, 'that I cannot imagine why so many ladies claim to find you charming, for I think you are positively rag-mannered!' And with that parting shot she left the room.

'Well you deserved that!' said Geneva laughingly before belatedly realizing that she was supposedly one of the nameless females who had succumbed to the earl's charms. Thankfully, Lady Yarwood was already busying herself with preparations for their shopping trip, and so the only thing to discomfort Geneva was the earl's provocative remark that he would obviously have to make a greater effort to please her.

Ten

Within minutes Geneva was once more driving through the bustling streets of Vienna, this time in Lady Yarwood's elegant barouche behind a pair of high-stepping greys. Geneva could not view the shopping expedition without reservation. Beside the niggling guilt at being tantamount to an impostor in the Yarwoods' residence was the embarrassment of her total lack of funds. It was unlikely that the contents of Geneva's purse would stretch to a length of ribbon to brighten up her grey dimity.

She was considering the best way of breaking this news to her companion, when Lady Elizabeth, with her usual bluntness, herself broached the subject. 'Gus has told me of the unpleasantness surrounding your guardian. He has instructed me to charge all expenses to him, so you may rest easy on that point.'

'Oh, but I could not possibly do that!' exclaimed Geneva before she had time to think how odd her objection might sound.

Lady Yarwood did look a little surprised but she sought to reassure Geneva. 'You are no doubt thinking it is a little irregular as you are not yet married, but really you should not let it worry you.'

Geneva would have liked to object further, but it would have been impossible to do so without sounding intolerably missish. She resolved nevertheless to have strong words with Lord Vance. How like him to arrange things without even bothering to apprise her! Geneva could not deny, however, that the prospect of abandoning herself to an orgy of spending in the scores of attractive shops that lined the streets and squares of Vienna would be a very pleasant experience. So, comforting herself with the thought that within a few months she would be in a position to repay the earl, she entered into the spirit of things with uninhibited pleasure. Their first port of call was a large fabric warehouse. Bale upon bale of fine material was examined, and it seemed to Geneva that they bought enough to keep her clothed for a lifetime, but from what Lady Yarwood said this was only the initial foray. Printed calicos and poplins for day dresses, ells of fine muslin, tarlatan, silks and satins for evening gowns, lengths of tiffany, georgette and gauze for over dresses and mantles, velvets and merinos for carriage dresses and pelisses. To Geneva the list of 'essentials' seemed endless. Finally when the barouche was loaded to the brim with bandboxes containing the precious fabrics, the busy thoroughfares were left behind and they turned on to the quiet side street where Lady Yarwood's very exclusive modiste could be found.

For the next hour Geneva was twisted and turned and measured and discussed as if she were little more than an inanimate doll. Madame Lysette was Hungarian by birth but like all the best modistes had trained in Paris and had adopted a French pseudonym to improve her fashionable appeal. Her appraisal of Geneva was succinct. 'Mademoiselle has a good figure, but she is too short.' Lady Yarwood nodded in agreement and the two ladies fell into a discussion as to how this defect might best be overcome. It was decided that simple lines were the answer, frills and flounces were to be avoided at all costs. Fortunately this agreed with Geneva's own taste, though she doubted whether her opinion was a factor of any account!

The various fabrics were displayed for Madame Lysette's benefit, and were greeted with approval. 'Ah yes! Strong colours for a vibrant beauty. With these materials everything I create will be the *dernier cri*. Mademoiselle Hartwell with the help of Madame Lysette will certainly become *un succès fou!*'

Geneva, who was beginning to flag, returned to the barouche with relief, inwardly chuckling at the memory of those fashionable French phrases pronounced with Madame Lysette's guttural accent. But as she sank into the soft leather squabs of the carriage, thinking longingly of the comfortable *chaise-longue* in her room, Lady Elizabeth was already planning the next stage of their expedition. The milliner must be visited and bonnets and evening caps ordered. Slippers, walking boots, shawls, reticules, gloves, mittens, parasols, handkerchiefs, in fact everything down to new lawn underthings and silk stockings must be chosen before they returned to the Josefsplatz.

The sun was already sinking behind the tall spire of St Stephen's Cathedral bathing the pale stone of Vienna's buildings in a golden glow, before they returned home. Geneva gladly acquiesced to the suggestion that she should rest before dinner, but once in the pleasing sanctuary of her room, Geneva found that sleep evaded her. So much had occurred in the last month! It was hard to believe that in that time she had been transformed from clergyman's daughter living quietly in the heart of the English countryside, to wealthy heiress, betrothed to one of the most eligible men in England and about to make her curtsey before the assembled Heads of State of Europe.

But of course, she hastily reminded herself, she was not really going to marry the earl. Indeed, she could not imagine anyone she would least like to wed, saving her wicked guardian that is. Lying on the chintz counterpane of her bed looking up into the canopy Geneva wondered what the future promised. She was forced to admit that she was attracted by the thought of the fashionable gaieties that were in store. After all the brilliance of a season in Vienna would she be glad to return to the bucolic existence of Tadworth? Or would provincial life seem sadly flat in comparison? Life would never be the same, of that Geneva was certain. The events of the last few weeks had opened her eyes to the ways of the world, her naïvety was lost. She could never recapture that serene trust in the goodness of all men that her father had been blessed with until the end of his days.

But neither had her experiences at the hands of Mr Boeman embittered her outlook, for she had met with such kindness as well. Mr Edlington, Lady Bartram and the Yarwoods, even the earl. For all his apparent selfishness it was rapidly becoming evident to Geneva that whatever he might say, the bargain they had struck was much more for her benefit that his. In return for the safe haven he had offered her, all she had to do was enjoy the luxuries and extravagances deemed appropriate for the fiancée of an earl.

That Lord Vance could have found a young lady more suited

to the role was soon obvious. Lady Yarwood was horrified to discover that not only had Geneva never attended a fashionable gathering, she had no knowledge of any of the dances currently performed in tonnish circles. The news of the Earl of Brewood's arrival and his betrothal had spread through the fashionable quarter of the city like wildfire; all of Vienna was eager to meet the young lady who had apparently succeeded where so many had failed in capturing the cold heart of Lord Augustin Vance. It was unthinkable therefore that Geneva should make her debut before she had some notion of how to go on in society.

A dancing master was sent for post haste, and hour upon hour of intensive instruction followed as Geneva was coached in the steps of the cotillion, the boulanger and of course the Vienna waltz. What with fittings at Madame Lysette's, sessions with the hairdresser and Lady Yarwood's tireless devotion to the task of educating her on matters of social etiquette, Geneva rarely had a moment to herself, and even more rarely did she the earl.

A slight indisposition caused by the long journey was the explanation given for Geneva's non-appearance in society. It would have been considered most improper for Lady Elizabeth to attend parties while her guest was, supposedly, confined to her bed, and so Lady Isobel was also obliged to remain at home. Lord Vance felt under no such obligation. Geneva had no wish to make a fool of herself by appearing in public before she was fully prepared, but she could not help resenting the fact that while she was forced to spend her evenings learning to play whist and silver-loo, and listening to Lady Isobel's constant complaints, the earl was apparently enjoying all the pleasures the city had to offer to the full. On the rare occasions that he did dine at the Josefsplatz, he inevitably left before tea was served to attend one function or another.

Geneva was dwelling on this point one afternoon in Lord Yarwood's library as she attempted to find a book to while away the hours until dinner. She had just curled up in a leather, winged armchair before the fire, having selected an anthology of Greek myths as the most tempting amongst the selection of rather dry political histories which Lord Henry favoured, when the library door opened and Lord Vance entered. He paused on the threshold, but then walked across to

Geneva who hastily untucked her feet from under her and assumed a more dignified pose.

'Do not let me disturb you, Miss Hartwell.' Lord Vance looked at the book's cover and quirked an eyebrow at her. 'I was not aware that you had a taste for the classics.'

Geneva smiled ruefully. 'I own I would prefer something a little lighter.'

'Poor Geneva, does your confinement irk very much?'

His voice had taken on that familiar caressing tone, but Geneva was determined not to let him unnerve her. 'I am looking forward to the day when I might go out and about, but in the meantime I have plenty to occupy me.' Adding with heavy irony, 'I am happy to see that my "indisposition" has not obliged you to forgo any entertainment.'

Lord Vance laughed and said teasingly, 'If I had known you missed my company I would have spent more evenings at home.'

Geneva was immediately defensive, this was the last thing she wanted him to think. 'That is not the reason at all! I simply think that considering we are supposed to be engaged, people would expect you to be more attentive to your poor housebound fiancée.'

'You are right of course. How selfish of me; how can I possibly redeem myself?'

'Now you are laughing at me!' said Geneva crossly. 'I wish you would forget I ever mentioned the matter.'

'No, how could I? Shall I stay in this evening and bathe your fevered brow with lavender water?'

'Now you are being ridiculous,' scolded Geneva, but her reproachful tone was belied by the irrepressible twinkle in her blue eyes.

The earl smiled. 'Yes I am. But seriously. The reason I have taken such pains to be seen abroad is to quash any rumours surrounding Julien Armistead's death. It would not do for me to appear to be in hiding.'

'Oh, how like you to have a ready answer!' exclaimed Geneva half laughingly.

'Does it seem that way? Well, I promise you that it is true. But you are right. If this betrothal is to pass without question then it would be as well for you to make a speedy recovery so that we may be seen together in company. Lady Yarwood is pleased with your progress and promises that you will not put me to the blush!'

Geneva did not dignify this unjust remark with a response, saying only, 'Well, it will be pleasant to venture beyond the bounds of the garden.'

'Then you shall!' said the earl with sudden enthusiasm. 'I have just acquired a pair of carriage horses and intend to put them through their paces. Can you be ready for ten or has life as a lady of leisure turned you into a lie-a-bed?'

There was never any danger of Geneva oversleeping, and at ten o'clock sharp she descended the wide staircase to find the earl awaiting her, very properly attired in top boots and breeches, a many caped coat accentuating his broad frame. The eagerness with which Geneva had looked forward to their outing she put down to it being her first opportunity to view the sights of Vienna. The unusual care with which she dressed could be explained by her desire not to appear to disadvantage among the fashionable throng. But neither could it be denied that Lord Vance's look of approval as he took in her appearance went some way to rewarding her efforts.

Indeed nothing could have been more complementary to Geneva's porcelain complexion and dusky curls than the cherry-red velvet three-quarter-length pelisse over a simple chemise gown of white muslin, the whole enchanting effect completed by a dashing deep poke bonnet of matching hue, its long cherry-red ribbons tied in a jaunty bow under her chin.

The earl bowed elegantly and took her gloved hand, saying simply in a voice devoid of its usual mocking undertones, 'You look bewitching, Miss Hartwell.'

Geneva accepted his compliment graciously; she was determined to be on her best behaviour. If the earl intended to taunt her into expressing herself with unbecoming warmth, then he would be sadly disappointed. Lord Vance would discover that Miss Hartwell's new modish appearance was more than skin deep. However it seemed that Geneva's resolve was not to be put to the test as the earl was also at his most urbane.

Much to Geneva's surprise Lord Vance proved to be a charming and entertaining guide. He tooled his high perch phaeton through the crowded streets with consummate ease, at the same time drawing Geneva's attention to the various points of interest and displaying an unexpected knowledge of the history and architecture of the city. She learned with interest that St Stephen's Cathedral's Gothic tower contained a bell weighing over twenty tons and cast from captured Turkish cannon, and shuddered with revulsion at the information that the Augustinian church contained the hearts of dead Habsburgs.

'I must say I had not expected you to be so well informed on such topics.' Geneva did not say 'you of all people' but the implication was clear.

The earl transferred his gaze from the splendour of the Hofburg's glittering turquoise dome to his companion's face, humour lurking in his dark eyes. 'But then you have always thought me a frippery fellow.'

The sophisticated damsel Geneva hoped to personify would have blushingly demurred and returned a light answer, but she was still her father's daughter and so she met his gaze squarely, her innate honesty forcing her to reply, 'No I do not, though no one could be blamed for thinking so when you take such pains to maintain your wicked reputation.'

She had succeeded in surprising him, but Lord Vance continued in his bantering tone, 'And you believe you have discovered hidden depths? I fear you are destined to disillusionment.'

But Geneva having voiced her opinion was tenacious. 'All I say is that while you like to give the impression of the heartless aristocrat, such a person would not have gone to such lengths to protect his sister's happiness.'

The earl gave a crack of derisory laughter. 'You may be sure that Isobel does not see it that way. She will tell you that my only concern is family honour.'

'Well I do not believe that, and neither would Lady Isobel if she considered it rationally,' argued Geneva staunchly. 'Besides, family honour was not at stake when you chose to defend me against my guardian. You were under no obligation to render me assistance.'

'You know as well as I that this hoax engagement is as much for my benefit as yours,' was the earl's reply. But this only served to provide Geneva with the winning thrust.

'And what is the purpose of this pantomime other than to protect Miss Fortesque from embarrassment? For if you intend to tell me that you care one jot for what people might say about you then I will not believe it!' rejoined Geneva triumphantly.

The earl shrugged his broad shoulders. 'Well if you are determined to view me in the light of an unsung hero, then who am I to argue? Were it not for the obvious difficulties presented by the construction of a high perch phaeton I would certainly take advantage of this rare moment and allow you to express your gratitude in a manner pleasing to us both.'

Geneva could have no doubt of their meaning, but although Lord Vance's words made her feel unaccountably breathless, she knew him too well to allow such an improper suggestion to discompose her. Instead she replied airily, 'Oh, I would not describe you thus, for you know there is a great deal of truth in what the gossips say; you are certainly a shameless flirt.'

The earl grinned appreciatively at this. The parson's daughter was rapidly learning town tricks; she would be no easy conquest. Lord Vance pulled himself up at this thought. He was in danger of allowing a pretty face and an artless manner to lure him into hazardous waters. Since that unfortunate moment during the course of their journey to Vienna when he had allowed passion to overrule common sense, the earl had strictly adhered to his intention of avoiding unnecessary intimacy with Miss Geneva Hartwell. But to his dismay, he found that his desire for her had increased rather than diminished.

Now he cursed his own stupidity. Geneva might describe it as an unselfish act, but Lord Vance knew in his heart of hearts that the overriding motive that had prompted him to embark on this ridiculous charade was far from altruistic. The Earl of Brewood had wanted Geneva Hartwell from the moment he had set eyes on her in those accursed tea-rooms, though what he had hoped to gain by involving her in this mad escapade he could not say.

Damned fool! Why had he not mounted her as his mistress in the first place? he thought savagely. His lust sated, his interest would have soon waned, and now he would not be constantly haunted by the memory of their all-too-brief embrace. Well he was suffering for his folly! He might be a rake but he was not such a loose screw as to seduce a gently bred female under his aunt's roof. Good God, he thought wrathfully, I wish I had never set eyes on the wench!

Lord Vance's anger at himself caused him to tighten his hands involuntarily on the reins. His horses, not used to such rough treatment threw their heads and pranced skittishly. Geneva glanced at him in surprise and was shocked to see the look of black rage on his face. Sensing her eyes upon him, the earl turned and smiled reassuringly. Confronted by that charming face with its wide questioning gaze, he found it impossible to regret his actions for long.

Geneva's drive with Lord Vance proved to be just the start of an eventful day. She returned to find Lady Isobel in high alt; Lady Yarwood had finally relented, Geneva and Isobel were to make their appearance in Viennese society. When Lady Elizabeth made up her mind to do something, she did not do it by half measures, and she had chosen Lady Eugenie Broome's ball for the debut of her protegées.

Lady Broome was renowned for her lavish entertainments, and as the wife of a prominent diplomat, the ball was guaranteed to attract the cream of the assembled foreign dignitaries. The ball was in just two days' time, and for that time Lady Isobel could talk of nothing else. Geneva's excitement was tempered by her nervousness at attending such an august gathering.

But when the evening of the ball arrived, and Conway had put the final touches to her toilette, it seemed to Geneva that it was not Miss Hartwell, parson's daughter, who would grace Lady Broome's ballroom, but a fashionable stranger.

Madame Lysette had been as good as her word and Geneva could hardly believe that such a stunning creation could really have been created for her. Shimmering folds of lavender-blue lustring hung in deceptively simple lines from a high-waisted, low-cut bodice. The only ornamentation was an intricate tracery of fine silver embroidery around the hem and on the bodice and tiny puffed sleeves. Sandals of Denmark satin, white kid gloves and a length of silver net draped *à la Ariane* over her elbows completed this elegant ensemble.

Geneva had been stubborn in her refusal to bow to the dictates of fashion and have her dark hair cropped short. Instead, the gleaming tresses were swept up and back from her face into a heavy knot, a profusion of glossy ringlets threaded with blue and silver ribbon framing her elfin features.

Satisfied that nothing more could be done to improve her charge, and privately thinking that this country-bred beauty would outshine all the supposed diamonds of the first water, Conway allowed Geneva to make her way down to the drawing-room.

Geneva paused at the head of the staircase and felt her heart skip a beat. Below her in the hallway stood the earl, a frown of concentration on his masculine face as he made infinitesimal adjustments to the astonishing intricacies of his cravat. Geneva set her foot on the first stair and as she did so Lord Vance, sensing her presence turned to greet her. The words died on his lips as he drank in the vision before him. With lithe grace she descended the staircase, the glossy silk of her gown softly caressing each perfect curve, its iridescent colour no more vivid than her sparkling eyes.

To Geneva, that descent seemed to last an eternity. Just as the earl's piercing eyes bored into her, so her gaze was irresistibly drawn to his tall, commanding figure. Never had she seen him look so striking. The superfine cloth of his corbeau coat was moulded to his athletic frame, cream kerseymere breeches clung like a second skin to his muscular thighs. A single fob hung from his waist, and his only jewellery was a heavy gold signet ring and a magnificent diamond pin nestling in the snowy folds of his cravat.

Geneva reached the foot of the stairs and stood before him, a faint blush mantling her cheeks, a shy smile trembling on her parted lips. Lord Vance forced himself to cover the ten yards between them at a leisurely pace, but when he reached her, all the contrived phrases and exquisite compliments that would normally trip off his tongue with practised ease seemed inadequate in the face of such breathtaking loveliness. All he could say was, 'God, but you are beautiful, Geneva!'

It was so rare for the earl to let his mask of cool dispassion slip that Geneva was quite unprepared for such intensity. She felt her colour heighten but her eyes did not waver. The sound of movement above stairs heralding the appearance of the remainder of the party brought them both back to reality. Lord Vance took Geneva's elbow and guided her into the drawing-room. Standing her before the enormous gilt mirror that hung above the broad fireplace, he drew a narrow velvet jeweller's case from his pocket.

'I have been very remiss. I should have given you a betrothal gift upon our arrival. I hope this will suffice until you may be measured for a ring.'

The sensitive skin of Geneva's throat tingled as the earl gently slipped the delicate filigree necklace around her slender neck, before resting his hands lightly on her bare shoulders. The necklace perfectly complemented her gown, a circlet of dainty silver flowers, each set with a brilliant sapphire.

'Oh, it is exquisite!' breathed Geneva, her eyes glowing with pleasure. 'Thank you! But I cannot possibly accept—'

'Hush!' interrupted Lord Vance, his lips brushing the nape of her neck so softly that she wondered if she had imagined his touch.

The door of the drawing-room was flung open and in danced Lady Isobel her face glowing with excitement. She performed a jaunty pirouette before the couple saying mischievously, 'Well, what do you think? Shall I break many hearts this evening?'

It seemed likely that she would. In contrast to the rich shade of Geneva's gown, Lady Isobel's was of palest pink muslin with an overdress of white spider gauze. With her blonde ringlets and fair skin the effect would have been almost ethereal had it not been for the vivacity of her disposition.

The earl looked at his sister with affectionate exasperation. 'You are a sad romp, Isobel. But I suppose it is useless to ask you to strive for a little dignity.'

This did nothing to depress Lady Isobel's high spirits, and she simply replied cheekily, 'Quite useless, Gus. Dignity has never been in my line as you well know!'

Geneva intervened at this point saying sincerely, 'Pay no attention to Lord Vance, Isobel! You look delightful.'

Lady Isobel accepted this tribute as her due, but said laughingly, 'How odd it is for you to be calling Gus Lord Vance in that proper way when you are engaged to be married.'

Geneva was completely at a loss, but the earl came smoothly to her rescue. 'Geneva only gives me my title when she is in disagreement with me. You may be sure that in private moments she does not stand on such ceremony.' With that he lifted her hand to his lips and quizzed her wickedly with his dark eyes.

Geneva could have cheerfully strangled him for this audacious remark, but she was obliged to acknowledge the truth of

Isobel's comment. It would be seen as very peculiar if the earl's future bride constantly addressed him by his formal title. Consequently when the earl handed her into the carriage a few minutes later, she was able to say with only the faintest trace of awkwardness, 'Thank you, Gus,' and was rewarded by an approving smile.

Eleven

Lady Broome's town house was situated in the Michaelerplatz, just a few hundred yards from the Yarwood residence, but naturally it was unthinkable that they should complete the short journey on foot. In a little over five minutes, Geneva found herself stepping out of the Yarwoods' town carriage into the damp December night before being swept along into the glittering world of the beau monde.

The next hour passed by in a whirl of introductions, and Geneva had to admit that without the earl's reassuring presence she would have found it a very taxing ordeal. But since Lord Vance punctuated his introductions with irreverent *sotto voce* remarks, Geneva was in more danger of succumbing to a fit of the giggles than being overcome by speechless awe.

It was hard to view the handsome boyish Czar Alexander with the respect due to his royal station when one knew that in a fit of pique he had challenged his rival in love, Prince Metternich, to a duel, and when that had been prevented, declined to speak to the Austrian First Minister for three months. Nor was it possible to be impressed by the insignificant figure of the Emperor Francis in his slightly grubby white uniform especially when one learned that his favourite hobby was making toffee.

But on the other hand it was impossible not to admire the stately presence of Lord Castlereagh or not to warm to his chattering wife in her home-made gowns. And Geneva could well understand what made the handsome Prince Metternich with his fascinating manners such a favourite with the ladies. Lord Vance rather improperly confirming her opinion that he was as much an intriguant in the boudoir as in the cabinet and was said to be a more successful liar than Napoleon!

The only introduction that caused Geneva any discomfort was the one to Miss Camilla Fortesque. Geneva had been inclined to feel sorry for this young lady as she found it increasingly hard to believe that she had been impervious to the earl's attentions. Her meeting with this proud beauty quickly set Geneva's mind at rest. She doubted if this cold, haughty lady with her white-blond hair and disdainful expression had a heart to break. In her pure white gown she looked as aloof and untouchable as an alabaster statue.

Flattering colour brought to her cheeks by the heat of a thousand candles, humour sparkling in her luminous eyes, Geneva attracted many an admiring glance, and when the dancing began she was soon besieged by potential partners. Initially a little nervous, Geneva soon found that if she paid less attention to the technicalities of the dance and allowed herself to be carried away by the rhythm of the music and the infectious gaiety of the occasion, she did not disgrace her partners.

Returning flushed and happy on the arm of a young Prussian nobleman from a set of particularly energetic country dances, she was surprised and delighted to see the familiar figure of Oliver Worthington standing beside the earl. She greeted him enthusiastically, taking his hand and saying, 'What a pleasure it is to see you again, Mr Worthington.' And then, remembering the unpleasant circumstances under which they had last met, said anxiously, 'I hope everything is well.'

Mr Worthington quickly reassured her and Geneva felt a tremendous relief. Here in Vienna, so far from England, it was easy to forget what had forced the earl to leave his country. But the earl had been cleared of any murderous intentions and these glad tidings were what had brought Mr Worthington to Vienna.

Not the only thing however, thought Geneva astutely as she watched how his eyes quickly sought out Lady Isobel. Feeling her sympathetic gaze on him he laughed ruefully and said, 'I am glad to see Lady Isobel has put the unfortunate episode behind her.'

Since Lady Isobel was at the heart of a very exuberant group of young people consisting mainly of officers of the Imperial Guard, it was fair to say that nothing could be further from her mind than thoughts of Julien Armistead.

'Isobel is still young,' replied Geneva. 'I doubt if she will give her heart to anyone for a few years yet. She is simply enjoying the novelty of being so admired.'

'So there may still be hope for a sober, middle-aged gentleman!' he exclaimed, only half jokingly.

Geneva smiled at him warmly. 'Indeed there is! For one soon tires of dashing military men and comes to appreciate more lasting virtues.'

'And in the meantime it would do my cause no harm to be seen dancing with the most beautiful ladies in the room?'

'Indeed not!'

'Then I shall take that as a yes!' And with that he led her on to the dance floor. Really, thought Geneva, if Isobel would only open her eyes, she would realize what a fortunate young lady she was to have captured the heart of this charming gentleman.

Lord Vance had led Geneva down for the first set but since then he had barely set eyes on her, she was in such high demand. But when the orchestra struck up the lilting chords of the waltz, he knew exactly where he could find her. He made his way through the small court surrounding her saying with lazy amusement, 'You must surrender to my greater claim, gentlemen.'

Not one of these dashing beaus had the slightest desire to incur the wrath of such a noted corinthian, and they melted quickly away leaving her to say with mock indignation, 'Well! I must say I think them very shabby fellows. What has happened to their protestations of undying devotion?'

The earl grinned wolfishly at her and whisked her with superb grace on to the dance floor. 'So you have been establishing your cicisbeos. I should, as a jealous fiancé put a stop to such shameless flirting.'

'Now you know I have no talent for flirting, my Lord.'

'My Lord? I thought we had progressed.'

'Very well, Gus,' said Geneva, blushing furiously and keeping her eyes firmly fixed on the top button of his white marcella waistcoat. She was finding that there was a world of difference between dancing with little Monsieur Geronde, the dancing master, and being swept along in the arms of the earl. With a few notable exceptions, Geneva had never been so close to him and she was finding it strangely disconcerting.

'The top of your head is very pretty, but I would prefer to

look at that enchanting face.' There was such unexpected tenderness in his voice that Geneva's eyes flew to the earl's face. The sudden movement unbalanced her and she stumbled. Lord Vance's arms tightened around her and suddenly Geneva was acutely aware of his physical proximity. His breath stirred her curls, the warmth of his hand penetrated the thin stuff of her gown, and as they circled the dance floor, she could feel his firm thigh lightly brushing against her body.

Geneva felt mesmerized. The brightly lit ballroom, the buzz and chatter of the hundreds of guests receded and faded leaving nothing but the sensation of the earl's arms around her. And then the truth hit her, almost blinding in its clarity: she was in love with Lord Augustin Vance, and she wanted nothing more than to spend the rest of her life enfolded in his strong embrace.

Mr Fabian Armistead propped his broad shoulders against a convenient pillar, his hooded gaze following the progress of the handsome couple as they circled the floor. Judging from the sardonic smile that played upon his sensuous lips, he derived some secret amusement from the sight. What exquisite irony! The proud Earl of Brewood had unwittingly supplied the means of his own downfall.

The news of his younger brother's death at the hands of Lord Vance had reached Fabian Armistead with astonishing speed. He had no great affection for his brother; he had deplored his boorish manners and considered his methods coarse, but he had a certain amount of family pride that would not allow him to see his brother's death go unavenged. Besides, there had never been any love lost between Augustin Vance and Fabian Armistead.

The earl, despite his abrasive manners and rakehell reputation, through his station and fortune, was still the darling of society. His appearance at a ball or soirée was considered to be quite a cachet for its hostess, and hopeful mamas viewed his arrival with scarcely concealed delight. The earl's sudden appearance in Vienna followed by the announcement of his engagement to an unknown beauty had provided Viennese society with a subject for endless speculation. Around the ballroom it was practically the only topic up for discussion.

Fabian Armistead resented Lord Vance's stature within the ton much more bitterly than he regretted Julien's death, and it was the former which fuelled his desire for revenge most strongly. Fabian Armistead was generally considered to be of good ton and was received everywhere. But his vanity demanded more. He had attained his acceptance through his undoubted good looks and his polished manner, but his lack of either title or wealth meant that he would never achieve a higher degree of note within the beau monde. That the earl, with his often open contempt for society's whims and artificialities, should be constantly fêted and toadied to, was a piece of injustice that Fabian Armistead found difficult to stomach.

But if the earl's chosen bride, instead of deeming it an honour and privilege to become his countess, should publicly jilt him in favour of one who had none of the earl's advantages, how he would fall in the eyes of the world. Lord Augustin Vance would become an object of ridicule and Fabian Armistead, the architect of his downfall, would jeer the loudest. Mr Armistead had devised this scheme long before he had set eyes on the engaged couple, but as he had watched Lord Vance's jealous vigilance of his betrothed, it seemed that his revenge would have an extra piquancy. For unless he was very much mistaken, the earl was head over heels in love with the chit, and when Fabian Armistead wooed his bride from under his very nose, he would be wounding much more than the earl's pride.

Mr Armistead shifted his position slightly and turned his gaze to the edge of the dance floor. Miss Camilla Fortesque, her back turned determinedly to the waltzing couple was engaged in desultory conversation with another young lady who also had the misfortune to be without a partner. The Fortesques' expectations regarding Lord Vance were not generally known in Vienna, but Mr Armistead made it his business to keep abreast of all the current *on dits*. He had lived by his wits for a great many years, and he knew that even the most innocuous piece of gossip might prove to be of worth at a later date. Now as the last strains of the waltz drifted through the perfumed air, Mr Armistead made his way unhurriedly to Miss Fortesque's side.

'Miss Fortesque, would you grant me the honour of the next dance?'

Miss Fortesque bowed her head and accepted graciously. The earl's rejection had not touched her heart but it had severely dented her pride, and she was woman enough to be gratified by the attentions of Fabian Armistead. He could not be considered as a marriage prospect but, besides being very handsome, he was an excellent dancer.

Mr Armistead took the blonde beauty's arm, and led her, not on to the dance floor, but to a small couch set in the relative privacy of a deep window embrasure. 'I hope you do not object Miss Fortesque, but the cotillion affords little opportunity for private conversation.' Miss Fortesque signalled her acquiescence but was intrigued. She was too pragmatic to suspect him of dalliance; her family was not wealthy and it was well known that the Armisteads hadn't a feather to fly with.

Mr Armistead talked mildly of general subjects for a few moments before saying carelessly, 'And so the Earl of Brewood is to marry little Miss Nobody. I think his choice must come as a surprise to all who know him. One always imagined his pride would only allow him to choose his countess from the ranks of the nobility.'

Mr Armistead felt the lady as his side stiffen but she answered him calmly enough. 'She seems an unexceptional girl, though I wonder if she knows what marriage holds in store. It must always be difficult for one not born into the aristocracy to assume the mantle of nobility.'

'You are so right, Miss Fortesque! Miss Hartwell is an undoubted beauty but she has not had the benefits of upbringing that, say, you have.'

Miss Fortesque looked at her companion sharply, her mind working overtime beneath her ice-cool façade. Surely Mr Armistead had not contrived this little tête-à-tête simply to ponder on the probable success or otherwise of the earl's marriage. Good breeding forbade her to question him outright, so she merely replied, 'One must suppose the earl is the best judge of what might suit him.'

This gave Mr Armistead the ideal opening. 'Yes indeed, if it were a judgement made rationally. It appears to me to have been something of a whirlwind romance; who is to say that either party might have a change of heart.'

Miss Fortesque had entertained the same idea but with little real hope. No gentleman could go back on a proposal of marriage, and Miss Fortesque, herself not blessed with a romantic disposition, could not envisage any young lady rejecting such an advantageous match. She continued to fan herself languidly. Mr Armistead had succeeded in capturing her interest but it would not do for him to suspect as much.

'I see no reason to suppose that the engagement will be broken.'

'Oh, none at all!' answered Mr Armistead, before adding in a voice steeped in meaning, 'If matters are allowed to run their natural course.'

This was a little too close to the bone for Miss Fortesque's liking, who shut her fan sharply and, giving a tinkle of false laughter, exclaimed, 'Really Mr Armistead, one would suppose you had a vested interest in preventing this marriage from taking place! Now if you will excuse me I am engaged to go down to supper with Count Marinsky.'

Mr Armistead was not fooled by her apparent disinterest. 'Perhaps I am taken with the *petite ingénue* myself. Whatever my motive, you would not be displeased if this engagement came to naught.'

Two spots of colour appeared in Miss Fortesque's pale cheeks, but she did not move. 'What is it, exactly, that you are suggesting?'

Fabian Armistead lifted his hands in a gesture of mock horror. 'Please do not suspect me of intrigue, Miss Fortesque. I merely suggest that perhaps if Miss Hartwell made the acquaintance of another gentleman who set out to charm her, and perhaps if she were to learn some of the less pleasant aspects of her fiancé's character, then perhaps she would not be so eager to take on the role of Countess of Brewood.'

Miss Fortesque looked at him calculatingly. It must of course be repugnant to her to collude with this man in a concerted attempt to break Lord Vance's engagement, but what he was suggesting was harmless enough. Miss Fortesque knew that the earl had represented probably her last chance to make a respectable alliance. If there was a possibility of resurrecting that opportunity would it not be sensible to pursue it? She did not believe for a moment that Mr Armistead had any interest in Miss Hartwell but neither did she have any inkling of his true motive. The details of Julien Armistead's death were not yet public knowledge, and as little as the earl did Fabian Armistead want his brother's chicanery exposed.

Miss Fortesque rose from the couch. 'This has been very

interesting, Mr Armistead. We shall have to see if your hypothetical scenario emerges.'

Mr Armistead bowed over her hand, 'It has been a pleasure, Miss Fortesque. Rarely have I encountered such excellent understanding.'

No more was said, but each was aware that a tacit agreement had been reached. The Earl of Brewood's path to the altar would not be without obstacles.

For Geneva that precious moment of discovery would remain engraved on her heart for ever. The moment when that delicate flower, which had grown secretly and unacknowledged within the darkest recesses of her soul, blossomed forth into brilliant and stunning realization, lighting every corner of her being with the golden glow of love.

Geneva wished she might preserve that instance for ever, but the dance must come to an end, and feet which had danced on air must return to the hard reality of the polished parquet dance floor. The shimmering rainbow background coalesced once more into the elite of European aristocracy, their voices and laughter merging in a multilingual cacophony that must intrude on the private world of Geneva and the earl. But while other gentlemen were escorting their partners from the floor, Lord Vance maintained his hold on Geneva and that scorching gaze never left her face.

Was it possible that the revelation that had struck her with such dazzling effect had been felt by the earl? Geneva felt the first tentative thrill of joy. Lord Vance's voice was low and urgent when he spoke. 'Come! I do not wish to relinquish you to the world just yet.' With that he led her through the crowds which lined the walls of the ballroom, deftly avoiding any acquaintance who might force them to halt and exchange greetings and break this spell that had woven its magic around them.

Geneva was powerless to resist. She too felt the indefinable force between them which must find expression away from the heat and clamour of the ballroom. At last the earl reached his goal, a small ante-room unlit except for a shaft of moonlight which stole in through the partially closed drapes. Lord Vance shut the door and the hubbub of the party was reduced to a distant murmur, all but drowned out it seemed to Geneva by the wild beating of her heart.

The earl gazed down at her, devouring her with those dark, hungry eyes, and then she was caught into his arms and his mouth descended on hers, hard and relentless. He was kissing her with a passion Geneva had never imagined could exist, but she did not shrink from its raw intensity, matching it, fire for fire, until they were both breathless and weak with desire. Geneva feeling her trembling limbs could not support her leaned against him and in a moment she was swept up in his arms and carried to a couch before the empty grate.

Lord Vance laid her down gently his eyes feasting on her luminous beauty which, even in the dimness of the room, glowed as if lit from within by the fire of her passion. Then his mouth claimed hers once more and this time there was such an aching sweetness in his kisses that Geneva could only cling to him her body arching against him of its own volition.

Sensing her response his hand moved over the bodice of her gown softly stroking the creamy swell above the low neckline before gently teasing aside the thin material to reveal the firm roundness of her breast. Only then did his lips leave hers, to trace a delicate trail of butterfly kisses down the smooth column of her throat. A low moan of pleasure escaped Geneva as his questing tongue found the rosy hardness of her exposed nipple, shooting quivers of ecstasy through the length of her body and intensifying the throbbing ache at the very core of her desire.

His hand, finding its way through the folds of her gown, travelled tantalizing over her stockings and beyond to caress the silken smoothness of her inner thigh.

'Oh, please, please,' cried out Geneva, knowing not what she pleaded for. But the earl knew, and the sound of her voice husky with longing brought him back from the cliff edge of his own overwhelming desire. The girl beneath him was no doxy to be taken at will, she was a gently bred lady of virtue, and he had been within ames-ace of forgetting that fact and bringing their passion to its natural ecstatic conclusion.

Breathing hard, the earl set Geneva tenderly aside. 'Good God, what am I doing?' he exclaimed half to himself. Then he looked down at the girl beneath him, her eyes dark and dilated with passion, her fair skin still flushed from his lovemaking, and he had to fight the urge to take her in his arms and continue where he had left off. But that would be madness, and so instead with gentle fingers he began to repair the ravages to her appearance, saying, 'We must return to the ballroom before our absence is noted. This is not the place; we shall speak on the morrow.'

For the last few moments Geneva had been lost to her senses, but the earl's words had their effect and she quickly struggled to her feet, smoothing her gown with shaking fingers. The enormity of what had passed between them began to dawn on her, and she burned with shame. Only Lord Vance's scruples had prevented the final consummation of their desire. But in her heart of hearts Geneva found she could not regret it; her passion had been an expression of her love, and surely that was also true of the earl? He had not said as much, but then he was right, this was not the place.

The remainder of the ball passed in a blur for Geneva. She danced and she chatted, but her heart and mind were on a different plane and if asked she would, much to her partners' chagrin, have been unable to say who she had danced with or what they had talked of. Only Lady Yarwood had noticed the couple's mysterious disappearance and read into Geneva's flushed countenance anything other than the natural result of the heat of the room and the exertion of dancing. She said nothing to the two protagonists, but remarked later when she and her husband were alone that the sooner those two were married the better!

Despite retiring at an hour much later than she was accustomed to, Geneva awoke early. Dawn had scarcely broken when, without bothering to summon a maid, she threw back the curtains and looked with pleasure across the city to where the wide meandering curve of the Danube burned red with the fiery reflection of the rising sun.

The events of the previous evening flooded back to her and for a few minutes Geneva sat, gazing unseeingly at the dark wooded hills beyond the walls of the city, hugging to herself the new-found knowledge of her love. Daylight had brought no change to her feelings, rather it had strengthened her certainty. Hers was not a fickle disposition, and where she loved she loved fiercely and forever. Geneva knew that whatever the outcome of their bizarre circumstances, in Lord

Augustin Vance she had found the only man who could ever claim her heart.

It was not in Geneva's nature to remain inactive for long, and this morning especially she was filled with a restless energy. She longed to see and speak to her love, but she would not while away the hours before they might meet with idle romantic speculation. It lacked just two days to Christmas Day, and this seemed to Geneva to be the ideal opportunity to put to good use the pin money Lord Vance had so kindly bestowed on her by going in search of gifts for her hosts.

Geneva's cotton nightgown was soon replaced by a very becoming sprigged muslin day dress, a broad primrose yellow sash around its high waist. A short fitted spencer of twilled sarsenet of the same delicate shade and trimmed with ruched white satin completed the outfit, and a charming chip straw bonnet lined with pleated silk and trimmed with yellow ribbon set off her dark curls to perfection.

Still a country girl at heart, Geneva was oblivious to the comments the appearance of such a beautiful and fashionably attired young lady with neither maid nor footman for company might give rise to. Fortunately she had chosen an unfashionably early hour to do her shopping and she encountered only tradespeople and servants about their daily business.

Within an hour Geneva's arms were full of gaily wrapped parcels, and she was beginning to regret that in her eagerness to be out and about she had not had the forethought to bring a footman to assist her. Besides a very elegant fringed shawl for Lady Elizabeth and a pair of Moroccan leather slippers for Lord Henry there was an exquisite bricassée fan for Lady Isobel, a collar of Mechlin lace for Lady Bartram and fine lawn handkerchiefs for Mrs Hollins and Conway.

The only person there remained to buy for was Lord Vance, and Geneva had to admit that it was the gift to which she gave most time and thought. She had remembered an idle conversation between the earl and Lord Yarwood during which the earl's collection of snuffboxes had been mentioned. But although she had visited half a dozen fashionable jewellers, as yet nothing had taken her eye.

Beginning to feel quite frustrated by her lack of success, Geneva left one such establishment, and as she did so collided with a gentleman walking in the opposite direction. Packages flew in all directions and with a cry of dismay Geneva bent to retrieve them. The gentleman was too quick for her. Apologizing profusely he quickly gathered them all up.

'There is no need to apologize, sir,' said Geneva smiling and holding out her arms to collect her shopping. 'I must confess I was wool gathering and not at all paying attention to where I was going.'

The gentleman smiled warmly in return but retained his hold on the bundle of gifts. 'It is very generous of you to say so, but the fault was mine. Not that I can regret my blunder since it has enabled me to meet such a charming young lady.'

This was said with just the right degree of flattering admiration, and while a more experienced lady might have quickly depressed the pretensions of a gentleman to whom she had not been formally introduced, Geneva was too kind-hearted to snub such an obviously well-intentioned man.

'Thank you, sir. But really I must go, so if you would just hand me my parcels....'

'Certainly!' replied the gentleman, 'if that is what you wish. But I cannot help but notice that you are unaccompanied. Can I not make amends by escorting you home? It seems to me that a young lady should not be obliged to carry such a bundle when there is a gentleman able and willing to do it for her!'

Geneva was not impervious to his debonair charm. Tall and well built, and undoubtedly handsome, he was dressed unostentatiously but was obviously a man of fashion. Nevertheless Geneva shook her head, saying laughingly, 'Really there is not the slightest need! I am not such a poor creature that I cannot manage a few light parcels. Besides my shopping is not complete.'

The gentleman seemed about to give in when a thought seemed to strike him. 'Then perhaps I may assist you in some other capacity? You are having difficulty in finding what you want? You see I know you must be a newcomer to Vienna, such beauty could not remain undiscovered for long.'

Geneva hesitated, she knew she should be firm in her refusal, but the question of the earl's gift was beginning to plague her. Surely there could be no impropriety in asking this gentleman's advice? 'Very well, sir. You have guessed aright. I am looking for a particular gift for my fiancé and I am afraid that my German is so lamentable that I have had little success.'

'Then I am at your command!' said the gentleman sketching a mock salute and nearly dropping the parcels once more.

Geneva laughed and held out her hand, 'Thank you again, sir. And since there is no one to introduce us, I must risk being thought very forward and tell you that I am Miss Geneva Hartwell.'

The gentleman bowed over her hand and looked a little rueful. 'Then your betrothed is Lord Augustin Vance. I fear I should not have been so persistent.' He paused and looked somewhat embarrassed. 'You see, I am Fabian Armistead.'

Twelve

The significance of this revelation was not lost on Geneva. From the moment she had met him she had felt there was something familiar about the stranger's features; now it became clear. His face was not marred by the same signs of dissolution, but other than that the similarity to Julien Armistead was strong.

Fabian Armistead sensed her instinctive withdrawal. So she was in Brewood's confidence. That would make his task more difficult, but if he adopted the right strategy who was to say that it would not work in his favour?

'I see my brother's reputation proceeds me. I blame myself for his downfall. I should have made a greater effort to curb his excesses, but alas I thought them only the wildness of youth. But I cannot ask you to sympathize or even understand. I will remove myself from your presence without further ado. Good day to you, Miss Hartwell.'

Impulsively Geneva laid a hand on his arm to detain him. True, the revelation that he was Julien Armistead's brother had immediately prejudiced her against him, but she knew that to be unfair. 'Mr Armistead, I am afraid I can have little sympathy for your brother, his actions were not those of an honourable man. However I see no reason why you should be blamed for his shortcomings. If you still wish it, I would be happy for you to escort me.'

Mr Armistead smiled gratefully and inwardly congratulated himself on the effectiveness of his tactics. 'It will be my pleasure, Miss Hartwell.'

Fabian Armistead proved to be a pleasant companion, and while he made his admiration for Geneva clear, he neither said nor did anything to embarrass her. When he heard of her quest for an unusual snuffbox, he said he knew just the place. His command of the German language was excellent, and the keeper of the tiny back-street jewellers, at his request, produced the very thing. It was an elegant oval box composed of intricately engraved gold and deep-blue enamel with a porcelain lid on which a scene had been painted in brilliant jewel colours. The design was by no means out of the common way, but it was the subject of the painting that attracted Geneva. It depicted one of the famous Lipizzaner stallions of the Spanish Riding School. These beautiful grey horses were trained and kept within the Hofburg and were renowned all over Europe for the grace and control of their dressage displays. Not only would the box make a charming addition to the earl's collection, it would also be a pretty souvenir of Vienna.

The purchase of the snuffbox made a severe dent in the remains of Geneva's money, but she could not regret it. Well pleased with both the success of her expedition and her companion, she returned to the Josefsplatz on Mr Armistead's arm, any fears that he might share his brother's low character completely dispelled.

Geneva was just thanking Mr Armistead for his assistance and laughingly retrieving her many parcels when the sound of hoofbeats approaching at a brisk trot caused her to look up. Geneva felt that familiar flutter of joyous expectancy as she recognized the tall figure of Lord Vance astride a raking bay hack. She lifted her head to smile up at him, her thoughts filled with memories of their last meeting, but the smile froze on her lips as she encountered his thunderous expression.

'Geneva, my aunt has been quite concerned as to your whereabouts.' The earl spoke abruptly and it was evident he was keeping his temper on a tight rein.

Geneva was immediately contrite. 'Oh, I am sorry if I have worried Lady Yarwood. But I rose early and decided to go shopping. Mr Armistead kindly escorted me home.'

The earl turned to Geneva's companion. 'I am obliged to you, sir. You may now leave Miss Hartwell safely in my care.'

Mr Armistead accepted his dismissal with good grace, bowing punctiliously over Geneva's hand and bidding her an elegant farewell. Turning his back on the couple he allowed himself a small smile of satisfaction. Yes, a good morning's work. He had not expected his ploy of stationing a servant to

spy on the Yarwood residence to have paid dividends so speedily. Now unless he was very much mistaken, Miss Geneva
Hartwell was a young lady of spirit who would not take kindly to
being read a lecture on propriety by the arrogant earl.

The earl was in a towering rage. His morning ablutions had
been disturbed by a mildly worried Lady Yarwood. The news
that Miss Hartwell had apparently left the house at an early
hour, unaccompanied and without a word to anyone, came as a
considerable shock to Lord Vance. Lady Yarwood, who had not
been inclined to refine too much on the circumstance, rapidly
revised her opinion when she saw what a sickening blow it had
dealt her nephew.

'I am sure we need not be overly concerned, Gus,' she said,
adding reassuringly, 'I see by your expression that you fear the
worst, but I am sure you are mistaken. Conway tells me that
none of Geneva's luggage is missing.'

This had failed to comfort the earl. It would be typical of
Geneva, harbouring some misplaced scruple, not to take with
her the wardrobe purchased with Lord Vance's money. Grim-
faced he had called for his horse, cursing his own stupidity. He
had allowed the strength of his passion for Geneva to overcome
his judgement. At the time he had believed her desire equalled
his own, but it was all too probable that he had frightened her. If
he could only find her and reassure her.

For the next two hours Lord Vance had visited every coaching
house in Vienna, and at each one he had drawn a blank. Finally
he had been forced to admit defeat. Weary and sick with despair
he had turned his horse homeward. The relief of seeing Geneva
safe and well on the doorstep of his aunt's house was swiftly
followed by overpowering anger. To return from scouring the
city to find that far from evincing any signs of maidenly qualms,
Geneva had obviously put all thoughts of the previous evening
behind her and was engaged in flirting with that scoundrel
Armistead, was too much for the earl's volatile temper.

Fabian Armistead summarily dismissed, Lord Vance threw
the reins of his horse to his groom and gripping Geneva's arm
painfully, propelled her into the house, with every intention of
delivering a thundering scold. But as Mr Armistead had
correctly surmised, Miss Geneva Hartwell had no intention of
succumbing meekly to such Turkish treatment. Rather than
engage in an unladylike struggle before the servants, Geneva

allowed herself to be marched into the drawing-room. But once the door was closed behind them, she wrenched her arm free and turned on the earl, her fine eyes sparkling with indignation.

'How dare you, sir! I admit it was thoughtless of me to worry Lady Yarwood, but that is no excuse for you to treat me thus, nor for you to be so abominably rude to Mr Armistead.'

This stretched Lord Vance's temper too far. 'You have the temerity to question my behaviour, when you are so lacking in decorum as to jaunter around town in the company of a man you have never met before in your life!'

'I was not jauntering around town, as you put it! Mr Armistead was kind enough to help me with my shopping, there was nothing in the least improper.'

'A service that would not have been necessary if you had thought to take a footman with you.' The earl curled his lip. 'Unless, of course, that was a deliberate oversight. Playing the damsel in distress is most certainly your favourite ploy, Miss Hartwell.'

Geneva was furious. The inference was clear: to think that he supposed her to be the kind of odious female who would stage such incidents in order to bring herself to the attention of eligible men.

'If by that you mean to suggest that my accident on the Harbury road was designed purely to put myself in your way my Lord, then your arrogance knows no bounds!'

'It is you who couple the two incidents together, not I,' replied the earl contemptuously.

'You are wrong, my Lord Vance. There can be no comparison. On this occasion my rescuer was truly the gentleman and demanded no reward for his deeds,' flashed Geneva with bitter sarcasm.

The earl sneered unpleasantly, 'That must have come as a bitter disappointment to you. And it is you who are wrong, Miss Hartwell. If you remember, I exacted no reward.'

Geneva was aware that somewhere inside her, the earl's cruel words were causing immeasurable pain. But at the moment, fury was uppermost and she sought to wound him as he wounded her.

'On that occasion no. But since that day you have hardly missed an opportunity to manhandle me.'

Lord Vance laughed harshly. 'It is a little late to be taking a stance of outraged virtue, wouldn't you agree? I would not describe your response to my advances last night as one of repugnance, in fact quite the opposite. I must congratulate you. I had thought myself wise to such trickery, but you came very close to achieving your objective.'

'My objective?' Geneva shook her head in bewilderment, she had no idea what he was suggesting.

'Must I spell it out? Had our delightful encounter continued unchecked then I would certainly have been obliged to stand by this sham betrothal. I wish you better luck with Mr Armistead, but I should warn you that he is a very poor catch. A girl of your talents could aim a lot higher.'

'This is infamous!' Geneva was almost speechless with rage. 'I compromise you? Let me tell you Lord Vance, I would rather die than marry you!'

'There is no need for you to go to such lengths, Miss Hartwell, let me assure you. But while society believes you to be my intended bride, you will oblige me by being a little more discreet in your attempts to catch a husband.'

Geneva could contain her anger no longer and she raised her hand sharply. She would remove that look of haughty disdain from his face. The earl was too quick for her; catching her slender wrist in an iron grasp, he jerked her towards him. Geneva struggled in vain, the earl's grip on her was relentless. With one hand he pinned her tightly clenched fists behind her back, with the other he forced up her chin. For a brief moment their blazing eyes met and then he was kissing her, savagely and mercilessly.

Geneva willed herself to remain rigid and unresponsive in his arms, but as his kisses deepened she felt awakening desire in her treacherous body. The earl's grip on her loosened as he felt her lips soften and part beneath his, and for a moment Geneva had not the will to resist him. But then her anger reasserted itself and wresting herself free from his embrace Geneva ran from the room, blinded by hot tears of rage and shame.

Reaching the sanctuary of her bedchamber, Geneva flung herself on to the bed, pummelling the pillows in impotent rage. How dare he! How dare he insult her so! But her anger was soon spent, and all that was left was a sense of bitter despair. All her burgeoning hopes and dreams had come crashing about her ears leaving only desolation. What a fool she had been to mistake the earl's lust for love. Well she was well served for her naïvety. Lord Vance had made it quite clear that he classed her as a scheming mercenary female, deserving only of his contempt.

This hurt and angered Geneva deeply. While she had learned to love and even in part to understand him, Lord Vance had obviously never thought her character worthy of consideration. She had been nothing but a convenient tool, rescuing him from an unwanted marriage and providing him with a brief amatory diversion. Well, no more. She would put an end to this farce of a betrothal and leave Vienna.

The prospect filled Geneva with bleak despair. For all her anger, she did not love the earl any less, and the thought of never seeing him again filled her with pain. Geneva's tearful musings were interrupted by a soft knock on the door, followed closely by the entrance of Lady Elizabeth.

Lady Elizabeth had encountered her nephew on his way out, and one look at his forbidding countenance was enough to inform her that all was not well. Geneva's ravaged face confirmed this. But Lady Elizabeth was not herself given to bouts of self-pity, and nor did she encourage them in others. Summoning a maid, she requested brandy, and forced the weeping girl to sip the fiery liquid.

Gradually Geneva's sobs lessened and only then did Lady Elizabeth speak. 'You and Gus have had a tiff I gather.'

Geneva could almost have laughed at this miracle of understatement. 'It is a little more serious than that, Lady Elizabeth. I intend to break the engagement.'

'Now, now,' said Lady Elizabeth in bracing tones, 'surely it is not as bad as all that? I've no doubt Gus has said a great many things he is now regretting. All the Vances have terrible tempers you know.'

If only she could tell her kind hostess that her optimism was misplaced since there had never been a betrothal in the first place. But Geneva's pride would not allow her to admit that she had been foolish enough to fall in love with the earl, when he had never pretended to feel anything in return.

Lady Elizabeth persisted. 'You know Geneva, it would be a terrible tragedy if this marriage was called off over a misunderstanding that could be resolved if you were not both so stubborn. I saw pride ruin my brother's marriage, and I would hate history to repeat itself.'

Geneva could not trust herself to respond to this and so seized the opportunity to turn the conversation into a different channel. 'What happened between Lord – I mean Gus's parents? I gather from something Isobel once said that her mother left the late earl.'

Lady Yarwood looked at Geneva in surprise. 'Do you mean to say that Gus has never told you?'

Geneva blushed. After all why would the earl feel the need to confide in her? 'Forgive me for asking. Perhaps Lord Vance would not wish me to know.'

'On reflection I can believe Gus might have found it difficult to talk about. You see it affected him very deeply at the time, and still does. As to my not telling you, I am sure you may hear it anytime you like from the gossipmongers. It must be preferable for you to hear it from a member of the family rather than through spiteful rumour and conjecture. Besides it might enable you to understand Gus's behaviour a little better.'

Lady Elizabeth poured them both a generous splash of brandy and settled herself more comfortably. 'It all really begins with my father, Gus and Isobel's grandfather. Lord what a high stickler he was! He brought up my brother Justin to be the same. In those days it was unheard of for the scion of a noble family to marry other than to oblige his parents. When Justin reached his majority, a bride was duly selected for him, a Miss Katherine Stapely.

'Kate was from an excellent family and brought a handsome dowry with her. She was a beauty too; Isobel is the image of her so you may judge for yourself. Beauty, breeding and fortune. Everything one could ask for in a future countess. But in every other respect Justin and Kate were totally ill-matched. Kate was an only child, and she had been cosseted and spoilt all her life. She had never had cause to consider anything but her own pleasure, and she saw no reason why that should change when she became Countess of Brewood.

'Justin, as you may imagine, had quite other ideas. Our father had reared him in the Gothic belief that a wife was little more than a chattel. But Kate was spirited and wild to a fault, and though Justin tried to tame her his tyranny only made her more wilful.

'The sad irony is that I am convinced that he loved her, and had he only set aside his foolish pride then maybe Kate would have grown to love him too.'

Lady Elizabeth lapsed into brooding silence, memories of past griefs filling her mind. Geneva waited patiently for her to resume. How well she could imagine Lord Justin Vance and his flighty young wife! She had only to think of Lady Isobel's rash elopement and the present earl's unbending reaction to it. While Isobel had clearly inherited her mother's thoughtless ways, Lord Vance had taken after his father. Geneva remembered Lord Vance's harsh words and autocratic treatment. Did they too mask a hidden love? But Lady Yarwood was continuing and Geneva forced herself to abandon such pointless speculation and attend to the narrative.

'The marriage was a disaster from the start. Kate duly produced the Brewood heir, and considered her duty done. She wanted to remove to London and cut a dash. Justin, with typical Vance male stubbornness, refused to let her. Oh the rows! And poor Gus ceaselessly pulled this way and that by them both. It is little wonder he rarely visits Brewood Court, for it must contain naught but bad memories.

'Well, battle raged almost unabated for fourteen years, and then Isobel was born. Finally, Kate got her way. She moved to town, leaving her family behind, and became one of the most noted hostesses of the day.

'Unfortunately she never had the wit to be circumspect about her little *affaires de coeur*, and inevitably news of her indiscretions filtered back to Brewood Court. Well you may imagine Justin's fury; Vance pride alone could not suffer such blatant infidelity. He demanded Kate's return, and when she refused, threatened to ride down to London himself and physically carry her back to Brewood.

'Never was there a more ill-judged start! Nothing was more certain to drive Kate into the arms of her latest lover. By the time Justin arrived at Berkeley Square his wife had absconded with an Italian count – though by all accounts it seems doubtful if he had any claims to a title, and it was said he made his fortune running gaming houses on the Continent. The scandal! It was talked of for years! Isobel was too young to be affected but for Gus things were very bad. He was at Eton when the scandal broke and I believe his peers made things very hard. Despite all her faults, Gus had always loved his mother.'

Geneva's heart immediately went out to that young boy, teetering on the edge of manhood and bearing all the emotional scars of an unhappy childhood. How well she could imagine him. His head held high, his dark eyes sparkling with that Vance pride, silently daring anyone to say to his face the muttered innuendoes and sniggering remarks that abounded when his back was turned. And beneath that show of pride, how his mother's desertion must have hurt. He had carried that hurt and resentment throughout his adult life, and inevitably it had coloured his view of the world and of women.

It was hardly surprising that he should have such a poor opinion of the opposite sex. An older and wiser man might have been able to understand Lady Kate's flight, but to an adolescent youth subject to the taunts of his schoolmates, it was an unforgivable betrayal.

Lady Elizabeth brought her tale to an end, 'After Kate had gone, Justin went to the devil. Three years later he broke his neck in a hunting accident; he was three parts drunk at the time. Of Kate there has been no sign. The occasional rumour surfaces, but nothing concrete. Gus has never shown any interest in tracing her whereabouts, and Isobel cannot remember her existence.'

Lady Yarwood drained her glass and turned to face Geneva. 'So you see, my dear, for all his apparent self-assurance in some respects Gus is still that young boy, scared that his love might be betrayed. Can you not forgive his cruel words and give him another chance?'

Geneva's generous spirit easily forgave the earl. Her anger towards him had melted into pity as Lady Yarwood's story had progressed. But Lady Yarwood's conclusions were based on the assumption that the betrothal was genuine, and moreover a love match. How tempting it was to let herself believe that Lord Vance's anger was indeed promoted by a jealous love. But no, that was a false hope, and one which would only lead to greater suffering. Lord Vance neither loved nor trusted her, and Geneva did not think she could bear to remain if her love was to be returned with only scorn and contempt.

'I do not know, Lady Elizabeth. I think you will find that Lord Vance is as keen as I to end our ... our attachment,' said Geneva hesitantly.

'Nonsense!' replied my Lord's aunt in rallying tones. 'You may be sure that Gus knew his own mind when he proposed this marriage. Heavens! It has taken him enough years to come to this point! He is not some fickle youth forever fancying himself in love.'

No, thought Geneva smiling wryly, Lord Vance knew exactly what he was doing when he suggested their 'betrothal', and love had never come into it.

Lady Elizabeth chose to take her silence as acquiescence, patting Geneva's hand reassuringly and saying, 'Good girl! I knew you would see sense.'

'Oh, but I have by no means decided—' protested Geneva only to be cut short by her companion.

'At least postpone your decision until after the Christmas festivities.'

Geneva relented. After all, where would she go? She was a brave girl, but the thought of being stranded in a foreign country, friendless and penniless was enough to daunt her. It would be painful to be constantly in the earl's company, but she hoped she had enough self-esteem remaining not to wear her heart on her sleeve.

In the event, Geneva was spared the discomfort of the earl's presence until the following day. Lord Vance, storming out of the house in a foul temper, had made his way purposefully to one of the many elegant and discreet gaming salons that had sprung up as if by magic since the arrival of the European dignitaries and their aristocratic entourages in Vienna.

There he intended, with the aid of liberal quantities of fine French brandy, to banish the infuriating Miss Hartwell from his mind. He failed miserably. Try as he might to concentrate on the game in hand, the vision of her lovely face constantly intruded. A few hours later and several hundred guineas the poorer he cut his losses and made his slightly erratic way home. The Earl of Brewood was feeling far from proud of himself. It had come to him part way through the evening, when his anger had finally abated, that he did not believe for a minute any of the appalling accusations he had made regarding Geneva's character and motives.

If the hour had not been so advanced he would certainly have sought her out and made the most abject of apologies, but unfortunately his excellent valet took a hand and steered him inexorably to his bed. The earl's last waking thought as he laid his befuddled head on the pillow was that on the morrow he would beg her forgiveness, on his knees if necessary.

Inevitably the morning brought with it sobriety and a return of the doubts and inhibitions that plagued Lord Vance. When Geneva answered the summons to attend his lordship in the drawing-room, it was to find the earl very much on his dignity. She entered the room quietly, her blue eyes warily regarding the earl's unreadable expression.

Lord Vance greeted her with stiff formality and tried to ignore the allure of her slight figure in the simple muslin day dress she wore. He addressed her in a voice entirely devoid of expression. 'Miss Hartwell, I must beg your pardon for my behaviour yesterday. My temper caused me to speak immoderately. I will understand perfectly if you feel unable to maintain our charade.'

Geneva resolutely swallowed the lump that had risen in her throat. This cold civility was more unbearable than any of his rages. For a brief foolish moment when she had heard Lord Vance wished to see her, Geneva had allowed herself to hope that he would beg her forgiveness and confess his love for her. His well-rehearsed, lukewarm apology betrayed no such strength of feeling. However, in the hours that had followed their last meeting, Geneva had regained some of her fighting spirit. She was determined that the earl should not suspect how deeply he had wounded her. Geneva shrugged her shoulders in a gesture of indifference.

'Your opinion of me is hardly flattering, Lord Vance, but I am not in a position to reject your protection. Lady Yarwood has persuaded me to remain until after Christmas. I will review the situation then.'

The earl was taken aback. He had expected tears and reproaches, indeed he deserved them, but not this cool detachment. He forced himself to match her pragmatism. 'Then you will continue to play the role of my future bride?'

'For the time being at least, since it serves both our purposes.'

There was nothing more to be said. The earl and Geneva parted, both equally disappointed at the outcome of their conversation.

Christmas Day for Geneva passed without any of the little domestic joys she had cherished in former years. The service at St Stephen's Cathedral was certainly magnificent, but to Geneva it seemed that the nobility who gathered there did so rather to see and be seen in all their finery, rather than through any particular devoutness. She thought wistfully of the Christmas Days of her childhood, when Reverend Hartwell had been well enough to lead the worship at Tadworth's humble church. Gentlemen and farm labourers had stood side by side and raised their voices to the glory of God in union. How different it had been from this artificial show of piety.

But there was nothing artificial about the good will and gaiety around the Yarwoods' dining-table that evening. They dined early for they were to attend a lavish ball and firework display being held at the Royal Palace, and the festive spirit seemed to infect them all. After dinner, presents were exchanged, with a great deal of exclamations and thanks. Geneva was pleased to see how well her modest gifts were received, but it was with a little awkwardness that she shyly handed the neatly wrapped snuff box to the earl. It was the first time they had come into direct contact all day.

Lord Vance accepted the parcel with a word of thanks and in turn proffered his own gift. Wishing her hands would not tremble so, and bowing her head to conceal her flushed cheeks, Geneva untied the elaborate bow and parted the thin sheets of tissue to reveal three handsomely bound volumes. Geneve could not contain an exclamation of delight when these proved to be the novels of Miss Austen, including *Mansfield Park*, her latest publication.

Forgetting their recent quarrel, Geneva lifted shining eyes to the earl's face. 'Oh, thank you! How could you have known? These are just what I would have wished for!'

Lord Vance, who had been admiring the exquisite snuffbox with much the same sentiments, smiled at her and said in a low voice, 'It seems that however much at odds we may be, we have come to know one another reasonably well.'

Geneva's heart leaped. Oh how she had missed that smile, the tender warmth in his voice when he spoke to her in that intimate way! Their attention was immediately claimed by the announcement that their carriage awaited them. But the brief moment did not go unnoticed by the eagle-eyed Lady Yarwood, who remarked with some satisfaction to her husband, that unless she was very much mistaken that marked a definite thaw in the relations between the Earl of Brewood and his bride-to-be.

Thirteen

Christmas behind them, Geneva found herself strangely reluctant to abandon her role as the earl's betrothed. She knew this to be a deplorable weakness but consoled herself with the thought that while prolonging the charade would do nothing for her emotional wellbeing, her physical wellbeing would certainly be under threat should she leave the protection of Lord Vance and his relatives.

But although Geneva might have succumbed so far to temptation, while she remained within Lord Vance's orbit she was determined to keep a firm hold on her heart's yearnings. The earl had made his opinion of her very clear, and despite the uneasy truce which now prevailed, Geneva was not about to let herself be lured into harbouring false hopes with regard to his feelings for her. If she could only avoid being alone in his company, Geneva found she was able to maintain her outward composure at least.

This posed few difficulties. Geneva had only to throw herself into all the gaieties Vienna had to offer. Routs, ridottos, Venetian breakfasts, musical soirées, concerts and balls. One followed another in a never-ending whirl of entertainment. Mornings were spent paying and receiving calls, afternoons shopping or riding in the Prater, and every evening there seemed to be three or four different invitations to choose from.

Lady Isobel was in her element, but for Geneva, despite her apparent enthusiasm, the heady excitement soon began to pall. The earl occasionally made up one of his aunt's party, and Geneva did not know whether to be glad or sorry when he did so. She would always find his presence disturbing, and yet without him any evening suddenly seemed unaccountably flat.

While Lady Isobel might delight in the extravagant

compliments and desperate flirtings of dashing young officers, Geneva considered them foolish, and the arrival of Fabian Armistead always provided a welcome diversion. Since their inauspicious shopping expedition, Geneva had seen a good deal of Mr Armistead, and she found herself enjoying his company more and more.

Mr Armistead was well pleased with the way his plans were progressing. While there was no sign of obvious hostility between the earl and Miss Hartwell, it had not escaped his notice that they were rarely seen in company together. He would have been less satisfied had he known the reason why Geneva enjoyed his company.

Fabian Armistead, while possessing considerably more finesse than his ill-fated brother, shared at least one weakness with him: vanity. It was inconceivable to him that any lady whom he set out in earnest to charm could remain indifferent.

Quite correctly he surmised that Miss Hartwell was not the kind of female to appreciate the absurd gallantries of his younger rivals. Instead of constantly worshipping at her feet, Fabian Armistead was decidedly more casual in his courtship. He was not to be found at every single event Geneva attended, and if he was present, there was no telling whether he might single her out or simply exchange a polite greeting before moving on. Mr Armistead's intention was to intrigue, and to add a little spice to their occasional conversations with just a hint of slightly mocking flirtation. This subtle manipulation might have found success with a lady whose heart was not already irrevocably given, but to Geneva, Fabian Armistead was nothing more than an amusing companion whose understated admiration and lack of any serious designs made him a pleasant change from her more ardent admirers.

But while Geneva might be convinced of the innocence of his intentions, it was not to be supposed the world at large would view it in such terms. The friendship between the Earl of Brewood's beautiful fiancée and the handsome and slightly dangerous Mr Armistead provided the *haut monde* with a delicious morsel of gossip.

Lady Yarwood frowned on the connection but was at a loss as to how to end it. To mention the matter to her nephew would be foolhardy in the extreme. Gus would in all probability lose his temper and forbid Geneva to even acknowledge

Fabian Armistead. Nothing would be more likely to break the uneasy peace that existed between the engaged couple. Lady Elizabeth tried to drop a hint in Geneva's ear herself, but met with little success. When she tactfully suggested that it would be perhaps advisable to spend a little less time in Mr Armistead's company, Geneva was inclined to view her request as nonsensical.

'But why?' was her laughing reply. 'I am sure I have not spent more than fifteen minutes at a time in his company, and you are quite out if you think he is attempting to fix an interest with me. He never pays me any lavish compliments or tries to flirt with me.'

Lady Isobel, who was present at the time, was unwise enough to voice her opinion. 'Really, Geneva, I am surprised that you should even be civil to that man when one considers his brother's infamous behaviour!'

This immediately brought Geneva to her friend's defence. 'I think it is very unkind of you to judge Mr Armistead by his brother's conduct.' Adding, as she thought of her own odious guardian and step-cousin, 'I am sure it would go very hard on us all if we were condemned by our relatives' actions.'

Lady Yarwood swiftly changed the subject. She was satisfied that up to now at least, Geneva was immune to Fabian Armistead's attractions. But it would not do for Geneva to set herself up as his champion, which she seemed very likely to do if anyone were to cast unfounded aspersions on his character.

But Lady Yarwood was well aware how quickly scurrilous rumour could rise from the most innocent of sources. Since Geneva had made her debut, Lord Vance had been absent from nine out of ten of the functions they attended, and the gossipmongers had been quick to seize upon this. Coupled with the obvious interest of Fabian Armistead the more malicious wits were beginning to speculate on the possible shakiness of the earl's betrothal.

Lady Yarwood had taken an immediate liking to Geneva Hartwell, whom she recognized had just the spirit and quickness of mind to meet Gus on equal terms. Lady Elizabeth was aware that her nephew had inherited a good deal of her brother Justin's pride and she had dreaded Gus choosing for his bride some milk and water miss with no opinion of her own, or even that cold-hearted Fortesque creature who thought of nothing but her own consequence, simply to secure the succession.

Lady Yarwood strongly suspected there was more behind Lord Vance's sudden betrothal to an unknown parson's daughter than he had led the world to believe, but even if the pair of them did not know it as yet, she was in no doubt that it was a love match. They were quite obviously made for one another, and the engagement would not founder through any lack of effort on Elizabeth Yarwood's part.

Consequently, on the next of the rare occasions that found the whole of the Josefsplatz household sitting down to dine together, Lady Elizabeth broached the subject of the betrothal ball. The topic had arisen before Christmas, but due to the marked lack of enthusiasm on behalf of the two protagonists, only the haziest of plans had been made.

On this occasion, Lady Elizabeth had no intention of letting the matter drop. To Geneva's surprise, her hostess received support from the earl himself. Nothing in Lord Vance's recent behaviour had led her to suppose he wished to cement their supposed engagement in so public a way.

Lord Vance, however, was not as divorced from events as Geneva supposed. Despite his aunt's attempts to shield him, the earl was well aware of the rumours currently circulating Viennese high society regarding the state of his marital plans. The urge to put a peremptory stop to Geneva's regrettable partiality for Fabian Armistead's company was strong, but pride would not allow him to intervene.

That he had totally misjudged Geneva Hartwell, the earl had realized as soon as his temper had cooled, that he loved her took a little longer to dawn on him. By the time it did it seemed to him that it was too late: he had lost her. Geneva went out of her way to avoid his company, and far from being distressed by the loss of the intimacy they had so briefly shared, seemed happy to flirt with every red coat in town.

But for all that, he could not allow her to fall into any trap of Fabian Armistead's making. He had allowed Julien Armistead's nefarious plans to get out of hand; he was not about to make the same mistake with his brother. The earl was in no doubt as to Armistead's motives. Since no one in Vienna was aware of Geneva's fortune, it was obvious that he had singled her out simply to annoy the earl. It would do no harm to show him and the rest of society that the Earl of Brewood's engagement was still very much intact. A betrothal ball was the ideal opportunity to do so.

Therefore when Lady Elizabeth said with a rather challenging look in her brilliant black eyes, that it was high time this engagement was put on an official level, since people were beginning to question its validity and think it excessively odd that some kind of a party had not been thrown, the earl responded with enthusiasm.

'An excellent plan, Aunt Liz! The sooner the better. I feel sure I can leave it in your capable hands. If you will just allow me to look over the guest list before the invitations are sent out.'

Lady Yarwood, who was unprepared for such an easy victory, acquiesced gladly and threw herself into the necessary arrangements with some zeal, eagerly assisted by Lady Isobel. The guest list returned from Lord Vance with only one major revision; the addition in his bold slanting hand of Mr Armistead's name. Lady Elizabeth raised her eyebrows at this but made no comment until she was alone with her husband. Lord Henry merely remarked in his mild way that she might be sure Gus knew what he was about. Lady Yarwood was not entirely convinced, but she knew that for all her husband might prefer to remain in the background, little escaped him, and she had a good deal of respect for his judgement.

Geneva entered into the spirit of things with less enthusiasm than her hostess and understandably so. She could think of nothing more likely to test her self-possession than to be obliged to meet the inevitable battery of curious and sceptical gazes at a ball held in honour of her engagement to Lord Augustin Vance.

For all that it was difficult for a girl of Geneva's sunny disposition to resist the infectious excitement and anticipation that pervaded the household once preparations got under way. The Yarwoods had not entertained on such a grand scale since their arrival in Vienna, and so the handsome ballroom on the second floor had remained under holland covers. Now everything must be polished and cleaned and refurbished. In the week leading up to the ball the whole house was alive with activity, servants and workmen bustling about their tasks under the exacting eye of Lady Yarwood.

The parquet floor must be rubbed until it glowed a rich

golden brown. The three enormous chandeliers must be lowered gently and their countless lustres washed and polished until they sparkled like huge diamonds in the candlelight. Even a coat of paint was deemed necessary to freshen up the pale cream walls and white plasterwork.

The days sped by and all too soon the ball was upon them. The qualms Geneva had resolutely banished could no longer be held at bay. Tonight her every word, her every gesture would come under the critical and merciless gaze of the cream of the European ton. She would be forced to wait at the head of the broad staircase accepting the felicitations and congratulations of an endless stream of guests, and all the time she would know that while her own heart was given wholly to the man at her side, no thoughts of love troubled his heart, no restless yearnings disturbed his dreams. For Lord Vance, Geneva Hartwell was nothing more than an expedient, a convenient means of circumventing society's expectations and getting his own way.

The hours ticked by inexorably, and all too soon Geneva was making her way upstairs to ready herself for the night's proceedings. For one panic-stricken moment she wanted to flee the house, to disappear into the maze of Vienna's back streets. Poverty, starvation, even death, seemed at that moment preferable to being obliged to go through with this dreadful farce. But sanity prevailed. A few hours and it will all be over she told herself sternly.

New gowns for the ladies of the house had of course been a must, and for all her dread of the forthcoming ordeal, Geneva at least had the reassurance that when she left Conway's care, no criticism of her appearance could be made. A white gauze overdress, gossamer light and dotted with seed pearls, floated over a narrow tunic that skimmed Geneva's slight figure seductively, the filmy folds of the gauze parting at the high waist to reveal the rich amber satin beneath. A wreath of tiny satin flowers crowned her soft curls, arranged in the pretty artless fashion that so complemented her youthful beauty.

Geneva arrived at the head of the stairs to find the remainder of the family party already assembled. What a handsome group they made, thought Geneva fondly, suddenly realizing that it was not just the earl she would miss when this deception had finally run its course. Isobel was as pretty and vivacious as ever in powder-blue silk, Lady Elizabeth was striking in deep crimson taffeta, and Lord Henry's understated elegance was perfectly in tune with his quiet scholarly nature. And the earl. He was wearing a perfectly cut, swallow-tailed black coat and close fitting pantaloons. How was it, wondered Geneva, that he could wear the same perfectly correct evening wear as his uncle and still manage to exude a raw masculine power that set Geneva's nerve ends tingling?

She moved automatically to his side as if drawn there by some inevitable force. Lord Vance looked down into her troubled eyes and for a split second the impenetrable barrier between them slipped and his eyes blazed with the fire of his inner passion. But in a moment the earl had regained control and inwardly berated himself for his weakness. However much Lord Vance fought to suppress his feelings for Geneva, he had only to set eyes on her for his love to make an even stronger resurgence, each time threatening to overcome all caution and common sense.

Geneva, unaware of the earl's own inner turmoil, only saw his aloof indifference and felt her throat constrict. She swallowed resolutely and forced herself to speak lightly. 'Well, my Lord, the stage is set. Are you ready to play your part? I must confess to a few last-minute nerves.'

The earl raised a quizzical eyebrow. 'You think our audience will need convincing? But surely not even the most hardened cynic could doubt my desire to secure such a beauty for my wife.'

The earl had intended to match her bantering tone, but he could not prevent a degree of warmth creeping into his voice, and Geneva felt her pulse quickening. But he must not be allowed to see how easily he could affect her;.

'Very pretty, my Lord,' she replied with mocking approval. 'But pray save your best lines for the benefit of the sceptics.'

Lord Vance was spared the necessity of responding by the arrival of their first guests. During the next hour Geneva felt she must have greeted the whole of Vienna. With mounting dismay she curtsied and smiled and accepted extravagant gifts from complete strangers, fervently hoping that either the earl or Lady Yarwood would know which gift to return to which guest once the engagement was terminated. Eventually, to Geneva's profound relief, Lady Yarwood permitted the couple to relinquish their posts, since all but the tardiest of guests had arrived.

Entering the ballroom on Lord Vance's arm Geneva came to an involuntary halt as they crossed the threshold. Lady Yarwood had truly surpassed herself. Ell upon ell of apricot and cream silk hung in lavish swathes from the lofty ceiling, giving the impression of a magnificent Bedouin tent. Hot-house blooms in the same warm hues, their exotic perfumes filling the warm air, stood in pale stone urns along with armfuls of lush greenery. The current mode in Vienna was to decorate one's ballroom in the bright primary colours of Europe's victorious armies, but Lady Yarwood was no slave to fashion and, as she correctly predicted, the subtle shades she had chosen provided the perfect foil for the brilliant array of uniforms and the rainbow shades of the ladies' gowns.

In common with most of the city's townhouses, the Yarwoods' residence in the Josefsplatz was a tall narrow house, but as the ballroom occupied the entire second floor, it was of handsome proportions. An even greater illusion of spaciousness was created by the enormous gilt-framed pier glasses that lined one long wall. Despite the generous size of the ballroom, it seemed likely that the Earl of Brewood's engagement ball would earn that most prized accolade of being deemed a sad crush.

The dozens of delicate gilt rout chairs, their seats newly covered with cream figured silk, had quickly been claimed. Dowagers and matrons sat in little groups, their turbans and aigrettes bobbing vigorously as they gossiped amongst themselves, their emeralds and rubies winking in the candlelight. Shy debutantes in their pale muslins stood in giggling huddles, peeping enviously over their fans at their more daring peers who laughed and flirted with dashing hussars or simpered at ogling dandies. Ministers and diplomats in their sober evening wear gathered in corners to drink claret and discuss politics. Any other young lady in Geneva's position would have been gratified by the number and distinction of the guests who had honoured the occasion. It was a prospect to gladden the eye of any ambitious hostess.

But while it was impossible not to appreciate such a colourful and lively scene, Geneva was prey to other less sanguine emotions. Guilt and dismay as the enormity of her subterfuge was once more brought home to her, but chiefly and overriding all was a painful yearning that all her resolutions could not extinguish. If only it were true, cried out her heart. If only I could look into the cold, dark eyes of the man at my side and see instead the same glow of love which I feel sure must burn in my own eyes for all the world to see. If only this were a real celebration of our mutual love, oh how I would delight in it!

'We had better take our position at the head of the main set. The dancing cannot commence without the presence of the happy couple.'

The earl's harsh irony effectively cut short Geneva's wistful thoughts, and she felt a spark of anger. What a fool she had been to allow a man of Lord Augustin Vance's ilk to touch her heart. Well, she might not be able to dismiss the sorrow it caused her, but no one else would be allowed to guess her folly. Consequently, when Fabian Armistead made his belated appearance, it was to see Miss Hartwell in apparent high spirits, and no sign of any lingering disenchantment between the engaged couple.

Mr Armistead had experienced mixed feelings on the receipt of his invitation to the ball. True it would be the ideal opportunity to further his pursuit of Miss Hartwell and under the jealous eye of the earl, but on reflection he had to admit that his exclusion from the guest list would have done more for his cause. Mr Armistead, unlike his brother, did not underestimate his adversary. He was shrewd enough to recognize the earl's motive and to appreciate his tactics. The Vance pride and temper were notorious, and none who knew him would believe that the earl would countenance the presence of a serious rival in love at his own engagement ball. Yes, Mr Armistead was obliged to own, it was a masterly stroke. Not only would it allay the suspicions of society, it would give Miss Hartwell no reason to take up cudgels in defence of Fabian Armistead. Lord Vance was certainly proving to be a worthy opponent.

Fabian Armistead surveyed the ballroom through his quizzing glass, the epitome of the indolent exquisite. Behind that bored expression however, his fertile imagination was already manufacturing a plan designed to restore his own advantage. His nonchalant gaze fastened on its target, and with leisurely ease Mr Armistead made his way across the room to where Miss Camilla Fortesque sat in icy splendour, her perfect profile displaying none of the dissatisfaction that seethed beneath the surface. It was time to call in reinforcements.

To Geneva's relief, her hazy notions of the behaviour expected of an engaged couple at a ball held in honour of their attachment proved to be sadly provincial. To be going around smelling of April and May with eyes only for one another was considered to be very ill bred. In contrast the Earl of Brewood and his future bride showed themselves to be terribly fashionable by going their separate ways as soon as the obligatory first dance was over.

Mr Armistead, well satisfied with the outcome of what to outsiders might have seemed a highly ambiguous conversation with Miss Fortesque, wasted no time in hastening to Geneva's side. Geneva greeted him with a genuine delight that did not go unnoticed by the interested, but her pleasure was tempered by an irrational disappointment. For all she had laughed aside Lady Yarwood's misgivings and while she herself knew her relationship with Fabian Armistead to be innocent, his presence at the ball could only result in the lowering reflection that Lord Vance was so indifferent to her that he had either failed to notice or did not care that she was obviously enjoying the company of such an attractive and charming gentleman. For some reason this made Geneva doubly determined to be pleased with Mr Armistead, even encouraging him in the light-handed flirtation she usually turned aside.

Mr Armistead was happy to oblige her, although he took wry note of her occasional furtive glances in the earl's direction. It was certainly time for the mighty Lord Vance to be brought down in his betrothed's estimation. Geneva, mindful of her awkward situation, had disclosed few details of her background, but Mr Armistead through some adroit questioning had learned enough to place Geneva in that class of moralistic country-dwelling gentry who could be relied on to deplore the amorous exploits of the earl and his set.

When Armistead led Geneva on to the dance floor it was with one eye on the edge of the room, and when the music stopped he endeavoured to lead his partner from the floor to stand within earshot of Miss Camilla Fortesque and her companion, Miss Clarissa Mansfield. It might be the middle of winter, but beneath the blazing heat of the candles the ballroom had quickly reached tropical temperatures, and Geneva gladly accepted her escort's assiduous offer to procure her a glass of lemonade. Fabian Armistead disappeared into the throng leaving Geneva abstractedly fanning herself, content to observe rather than participate in the gaiety that surrounded her.

Geneva's mood of introspection did not go undisturbed for long. It was quite obvious that Miss Mansfield was not aware of Miss Hartwell's presence when she said in loud intrusive tones, 'As you say, Miss Fortesque, a very lavish affair. But I beg leave to doubt that the marriage will be such an unqualified success.'

'Whatever can you mean, Miss Mansfield?' asked Miss Fortesque, an inflexion of surprise in her well-bred voice.

Miss Mansfield gave a titter of affected laughter. 'Oh really, Miss Fortesque, must I spell it out? It is quite obvious to me that the earl realizes he has made a mistaken. He has had his head turned briefly by a pretty face and depend upon it he is now regretting it.'

Miss Fortesque replied doubtfully, 'Certainly it was a sudden attachment. But even if it is not a love match, well it will not be the first. Lord Vance has reached an age where duty alone demands marriage and an heir.'

'I agree entirely!' said Miss Mansfield, and bent towards her companion conspiratorially. 'But do you really think this Miss Hartwell will be prepared to turn a blind eye to Brewood's little peccadilloes?'

'Perhaps marriage will reform him.'

'Take my word for it, Miss Fortesque, rakes cannot be reformed. Lord Vance would have done better to look within his own class for a complacent wife. Why it is quite obvious that Miss Hartwell is a country-bred innocent who has no notion of what to expect.'

Miss Fortesque seemed to hesitate before replying in a lowered voice, 'Perhaps we underestimate Miss Hartwell. After all there has been nothing in her demeanour to suggest she is unduly distressed by the earl's latest *affaire*.'

Despite a deliberate show of lowering her voice, Miss Fortesque was well aware of Geneva's presence and made sure that every word carried clearly to her rival's ears. Geneva felt her stomach turn, and for one awful moment she thought nausea would overcome her. She dug her nails fiercely into the palms of her hands and tried desperately to turn her attention to the innocuous conversation of two elderly racing enthusiasts at her side. But it was impossible, the insidious words remorselessly dripped poison into her unwilling mind.

Miss Mansfield had given a shocked and delighted gasp at Miss Fortesque's words and begged her to tell all. Miss Fortesque put on a nice display of reluctance but quickly allowed her companion to overcome her scruples.

'Well, Miss Mansfield, I need not say I hope that this is for your ears only. You may be sure that I would not utter another word if I did not know you to be quite the soul of discretion.'

'Oh yes indeed, Miss Fortesque. Your confidences are quite safe with me,' Miss Mansfield assured her, privately resolving to tell no one but her particular friend, Fanny Buxton.

Miss Fortesque continued, apparently satisfied. 'I am a little uncomfortable discussing such matters, for you know we ladies should always overlook the little weaknesses of the opposite sex. But my Lord Vance has been so ... so brazen that it makes it impossible to ignore.'

'Quite, Miss Fortesque. But who is the creature?'

'I believe they call her La Cantonini. An opera dancer at the Burgtheater of all things.'

'La Cantonini! But they say she is quite ravishing!'

'Well, when I saw her driving with Lord Vance I must admit I found her striking, but in quite a vulgar overblown way. But then it is always the same with these Italian beauties.'

'You saw them driving together?'

'Yes indeed, and only a few days after the announcement of his engagement. I believe he is quite without shame.'

'Oh, it is too shocking! How I feel for that poor girl!'

Miss Mansfield continued her spurious sympathy for the unfortunate Miss Hartwell, and Miss Fortesque, satisfied that she had achieved her ends, was content to let her companion chatter on.

Geneva felt as if each word had dealt a fresh blow to her already wounded heart. She was frozen to the spot, unshed tears drowning her violet-blue eyes. A hand on her elbow broke her shocked trance and she turned swiftly to find Mr Armistead at her side. His grave expression was enough to tell her that he too had heard those fateful words.

'Come, Miss Hartwell, I think you would benefit from some fresh air,' he said in a low sympathetic voice.

Geneva nodded gratefully, and allowed herself to be led across the crowded ballroom to one of the long windows that looked out on the square below. Mr Armistead drew aside the curtain to allow Geneva to pass through the open window on to the small railed balcony beyond. Geneva took deep shuddering breaths of the frost-tinged night air, and gradually the numbing shock that had gripped her receded leaving her weak with despair. Mr Armistead said nothing but gently possessed himself of her hands and chafed them comfortingly between his own.

Suddenly the curtain was flung aside and the menacing shadow of Lord Vance fell on the couple. Geneva started and snatched her hands free. But the earl's hard gaze had already taken in the clasped hands and he had come to his own conclusions, Geneva's guilty start only fuelled his anger.

'I suggest, Armistead, that unless you wish to leave the premises over that balcony, you leave voluntarily by a more conventional exit.'

This was said in a low deliberate voice, and Fabian Armistead had no doubt that the earl would carry out his threat given the least provocation. Mr Armistead was no coward but he knew his limitations. It would do nothing for his cause for Miss Hartwell to see him come off the worse in an undignified brawl with Lord Vance. But neither must be beat too hasty a retreat.

'Really Brewood, there is not the least need for such violence. Miss Hartwell merely wished for some air and I offered to escort her.' He bowed over Geneva's hand. 'My dear Miss Hartwell, your very obedient servant.' And with a mocking nod in the earl's direction he was gone, leaving Geneva and the earl alone.

Fourteen

Where the Earl of Brewood led, the remainder of the ton were in general not slow to follow, and so Lord Vance had intended to frustrate Fabian Armistead's mischief-making by refusing to acknowledge him as a genuine rival for Miss Hartwell's affections. This cool resolve was quickly evaporated by white-hot fury when the earl had seen Geneva disappear onto a secluded balcony on the arm of his enemy. Murderous rage overwhelmed him, and cutting short with the barest of civilities the arch attempts at flirtation by a particularly dashing young widow, Lord Vance had wasted no time in interrupting what, in his jealous anger, he did not doubt to be a lovers' assignation.

The sight of Geneva's hands lying unresisting in the ardent clasp of Fabian Armistead had swept away all but the last vestige of his self-control. Only the knowledge that to do so would create the kind of appalling scandal he instinctively shrank from prevented the earl from plucking the rogue off his feet by his coat lapels and depositing him on to the pavement below.

Now as he took in Geneva's sparkling eyes and flushed cheeks, Lord Vance was more than ever convinced that he had disturbed a tender scene. Jealousy and disillusionment twisted his features into a mask of thin-lipped rage. Geneva made as if to speak but the earl ruthlessly cut in.

'I beg you, madam, do not insult my intelligence by offering some feeble excuse. The evidence of my own eyes is all the explanation I require.'

Geneva flinched at his caustic tone, but she would not hang her head in shame. He would be made to listen to the truth.

'Lord Vance, you are mistaken if you believe anything of an

improper nature has occurred. It was perhaps unwise of me to step out here in a single gentleman's company, but nothing untoward has taken place.'

The earl was singularly unmoved by this protestation. Frustration and suppressed emotion had brought his quick temper to breaking point, and he was in no mood to listen to reason.

'You forget, my dear, that you have been unwise enough to be caught alone in my company, so I know how freely you give your favours on such occasions.'

The injustice of his cruel words goaded Geneva beyond endurance. She had been perfectly willing to offer a rational explanation, but it was quite obvious that the earl classed her among the ranks of his opera dancers and was intent on reading the worst into the situation.

'Oh, it is useless to try and reason with you!' she exclaimed angrily. 'You are determined to judge all by your own base standards!'

'My base standards? It is not I who has contrived a lovers' tryst at my own betrothal ball.'

'I see it would be pointless to deny your ridiculous accusations—'

'Quite pointless,' interjected the earl. 'Good God! To think at first I was fooled by your ingenuous ways and displays of outraged virtue! Well I have your measure now Miss Hartwell and it is useless to play the innocent with me any more.'

'Thank you, Lord Vance, you have made your opinion of my character abundantly clear on more than one occasion. Since I can have no possible respect for a man of your morals or character, your insults have no power to hurt me!' Geneva paused for breath but continued before the earl had chance to challenge this blatant untruth. 'However, I would like to know by what right you seek to dictate my behaviour. It would be as well for you to remember that this betrothal is a sham.'

Lord Vance gave a mocking laugh that made Geneva's fists involuntarily clench. 'Oh, I am in no danger of forgetting that. But as I have told you before, while the world believes you to be my future bride I will not tolerate your sordid intrigues.'

'*You* will not tolerate? Of all the insufferable, arrogant hypocritical … oh!' Geneva could have stamped her foot in sheer frustration. Mere words could not express the burning indignation she felt.

The earl sneered unpleasantly, 'Spare me these histrionics, Miss Hartwell. Since you are so careless of your reputation you should be thankful someone is here to save you from the consequences of your own folly.'

This was so preposterous that for a moment Geneva could only stare at the earl in wide-eyed disbelief. She soon recovered the power of speech however. 'Good God, am I now to believe that concern for my welfare is behind this intolerable high-handedness? Nothing but your own overweening pride is responsible for your treatment of me. However much you despise me you cannot stand the idea of another man poaching on your own territory.'

The earl was stung by the injustice of this. He had truly wished to protect Geneva from Armistead's devious plans, but he was not about to admit that now. Instead he resorted to cruel mockery.

'Do you really think Fabian Armistead has anything but the most improper intentions towards you? He is simply using you to be revenged on me for his brother's death.'

Geneva scarcely heeded his words, all she knew was that she had accused him of hating her and he had not denied it. All the anger drained from her and all her efforts could not prevent the tears that filled her violet-blue eyes from spilling unchecked down her flushed cheeks. For all his rage the earl was not proof against such obvious distress. Cursing his own weakness he pulled her into his arms, gently kissing away her salty tears. Geneva was powerless to resist. She knew he did not love her, hated her in fact. She knew he had taken another woman for his mistress, but at that moment love overcame pride and she surrendered to his embrace.

Inevitably the earl's kisses became more demanding, and for all her sorrow Geneva could not suppress the wave of desire his closeness sent through her traitorous body. For the earl, the taste of her sweet lips and the feel of her slender body beneath his roving hands had turned his rage into a passion just as violent in its intensity. The fact that only a length of curtain separated them from a ballroom filled to capacity with the most influential figures in Europe was forgotten in the heat of their desire. Lord Vance's hands travelled downwards, sliding over the swell of her hips and pulling her insistently towards him. Geneva moaned with pleasure and plunged her hands into his dark hair.

Later, Geneva could only conjecture with shame what would have been the final outcome of this steamy encounter, for at that moment the curtain was twitched aside and startled the couple sprang apart, Geneva blushing fiercely and miserably aware of her state of disorder. Their discovery could not have been at more unfortunate hands. The dowager Duchess of Larne was noted for her prudery and now she stared at them through her lorgnette, her piggy eyes round with horror, her chins quivering with indignation. For perhaps ten seconds the three of them were frozen in a farcical tableau of dismay and then in her booming voice the dowager exclaimed one word, 'Disgraceful!' before succumbing to an attack of the vapours.

In the pandemonium that followed Geneva brushed past Lord Vance and back into the ballroom before he had chance to stop her. Geneva walked quickly across the room, her vision blurred by unshed tears. She was painfully aware of the shocked, amused and speculative glances that followed her progress, and her one thought was to escape this glittering cruel world, to be alone with her grief.

Lady Yarwood, who had watched the evening's events unfold with a concerned eye, now hastened to Geneva's side. It was quite obvious that the girl was struggling to contain her emotions; it would be disastrous if she were to break down with all the eyes of the ton upon her. She grasped the girl's hand and gave it a warning squeeze, at the same time exclaiming in a voice intended to be heard by curious ears, 'My dear Geneva, you look quite done up! Is it the migraine? I know how you suffer.'

Geneva nodded speechlessly. She just retained enough presence of mind to realize that her precipitate exit from the ballroom with no credible explanation would only bring an even greater degree of undesirable notice upon herself. Lady Yarwood allowed her to retire before making it her business to inform as many people as possible how poor Miss Hartwell was a positive martyr to sick headaches.

When Geneva awoke late the next day, the throbbing pain in her temples was all too real. She had managed by sheer will power to hold back the tears until she had reached her bedchamber. Then the dam had burst. All the pent-up emotions that had gradually built up since the day of her father's death were now unleashed. Hours later, when the last lingering guest had departed and the house lay still and shrouded in darkness, Geneva lay rigid and swollen-eyed, drained of all emotion and with no more tears left to shed. Only as the grey light of dawn began to lighten the gloom did she at last fall into a fitful sleep.

Now Geneva mechanically slipped from between the covers and drew back the curtains to gaze blankly across the damp grey city. Persistent drizzle fell from a leaden sky. Even the weather seemed to match her mood she thought fancifully. Turning her back on the dismal scene Geneva caught sight of a note lying on her breakfast tray beside the untouched bread and butter and the cold congealed chocolate. Absorbed by her private grief at first she cast only a cursory glance at it but when her eyes fastened on the bold signature of Lord Vance, she sank onto the edge of the bed and read the note avidly.

Geneva visibly paled as she digested its contents. The Earl of Brewood expressed his apologies for the embarrassment he had caused her and since to do otherwise would not be the action of an honourable man, urged her to accept the protection of his name. In short, Lord Vance offered marriage. Geneva stared blindly at those cold dispassionate words and felt that until that moment she had never experienced true pain. The note fluttered to the floor from between lifeless fingers and Geneva abandoned herself to her grief.

It was some time before she could regain her composure. But it was pointless to indulge in self-pity and resolutely drying her tears, Geneva gave herself a mental shake. After all it was her own fault that she was now in this sorry predicament. For Geneva had at last accepted that her love for the Earl of Brewood had begun the moment he had plucked her unceremoniously from that ditch. If she had faced that knowledge at the time then she would never have been so foolish as to accept his bizarre proposal. Instead she had allowed her secret desires to guide her actions, had indulged in the kind of ridiculous fantasies she would have scorned had she found them between the covers of a romantic novel. And what was the result? Her reputation was in tatters, and worse, Lord Vance felt obliged to offer her marriage. Well she would not confirm his worst suspicions of her. She still had enough self-respect to shrink from accepting an unwilling husband however she might love him.

She could not and would not spend another night under the same roof as Lord Vance. The thought of abandoning herself to the mercy of an unknown city no longer had the power to daunt her, anything would be preferable to facing the earl's blistering scorn. The memory of his harsh words of the night before rose fresh in her mind, and for a moment tears threatened to overwhelm Geneva. But that was in the past, now she must concentrate on the future however bleak it might seem.

Once she had reached the decision to leave, Geneva felt slightly better and even able to go downstairs. An enquiry solicited the welcome information from Grieves the butler, that Lady Yarwood along with her husband and nephew had gone out on various errands, but Lady Isobel could be found in the morning-room. Geneva made her way there. She had been too distressed to gauge people's reactions the previous evening, but she feared the worst. Geneva did not feel equal to Lady Yarwood's well-meant enquiries, Lady Isobel on the other hand was in general too wrapped up in her own affairs to notice the problems of others.

Geneva found Lady Isobel pettishly pulling at her embroidery, the threads of which had become sadly tangled. She looked up quickly upon Geneva's entrance and flung her mangled needlework to one side.

'Oh, at last! I am quite bored to death!' she exclaimed, adding as an afterthought, 'I hope your headache is better, Geneva.'

Geneva reassured her on that point and asked with some amusement, 'But why are you alone? At this time of day we cannot usually move for military men!'

Isobel shrugged her shoulders saying petulantly, 'I have told Grieves that I am not at home to visitors. I am in no mood for their empty compliments.'

Geneva raised her eyebrows at this. She had not thought Isobel to be so discerning. 'I am sure they are all quite sincere in their admiration for you, Isobel.'

Lady Isobel gave an unladylike snort and commented with uncharacteristic shrewdness, 'That's as may be, but you may depend upon it, they will be just as sincere when the next pretty face comes along.'

Geneva, glad to set her own problems aside at least for a moment, perceived this was the time to further Oliver Worthington's cause.

'Well you may be right, Isobel. After all they are scarcely more than boys. I think if you wish for serious commitment you should look to a more mature gentleman.'

'Yes but older men are so staid and boring,' complained Isobel.

'Surely not! Only think of Mr Worthington.'

'Oliver?' Isobel gave a peal of laughter. 'But I have known him all my life!'

'Well I don't see what that has to say to anything. And you could not in all fairness describe him as staid and dull,' reasoned Geneva.

'No-o. Not dull, but he is hardly a figure of romance.'

'Well in my opinion figures of romance would not make very comfortable husbands,' Geneva replied matter-of-factly.

Lady Isobel glanced at her slyly. 'Well I may be his sister, but not even I can deny that Gus is the very model of a romantic hero.'

Which perfectly illustrates my point, thought Geneva with grim irony, but was saved the embarrassment of forming a reply by the discreet entrance of Grieves.

'Excuse me, my lady, miss. This note had just arrived for Miss Hartwell.'

Geneva accepted the single folded sheet with a word of thanks. The writing was unfamiliar. She broke the seal and spread the letter out on her lap. It was short and to the point.

My dear Miss Hartwell

After the unfortunate events of last night, I felt I might dare risk offending you by offering my assistance. Forgive me, but I cannot feel your situation is a happy one, and as I am in part responsible for any unpleasantness that may have arisen as a result of our innocent tête-à-tête, I feel duty bound to help in any way I can.

Lady Palmer is to hold a masquerade ball tonight. I will arrange for a hack to be waiting at the corner of Bräunerstrasse at nine o'clock. It may seem a little melodramatic, but it is the one way we can be assured of meeting undetected.

If I have misread the situation then please forgive this impertinence. Believe me when I say I remain,
        Your obedient servant to command,
                Fabian Armistead

Geneva's initial response was to dismiss such an improper suggestion, but then she thought of her dependent state. Without help it was not likely she would get very far. If Fabian Armistead had spoken one word of love, if there had been any hint of ardency in his letter, then Geneva would not have considered it for a moment. But Mr Armistead only offered friendly assistance, and she could certainly do with that.

Geneva folded the note calmly and slipped it into her reticule. Lady Isobel, too polite to quiz her friend on its contents, had returned to her tatting. Geneva watched her for a moment thoughtfully and then exclaimed, 'Isobel! You will ruin it if you pull at it so. Will you not let me untangle it for you?'

Lady Isobel relinquished the puckered canvas willingly and Geneva busily set to work teasing the knotted threads free with nimble fingers. For several minutes they sat in companionable silence until Geneva, her head bent low over the embroidery said with a creditable assumption of nonchalance, 'I believe Lady Palmer is to hold a masquerade ball this evening.'

Lady Isobel gave a sigh. 'Yes indeed. I begged Gus to allow me to go but he would not hear of it.'

'Why ever not?' asked Geneva curiously.

'Well he told me that Lady Palmer and her husband are not at all the thing, and he would hope no lady of his acquaintance would mix in her set.'

If Geneva had harboured any doubts as to the wisdom of attending the masquerade, this information would certainly have sealed her determination to go. It was typical of the earl's hypocrisy. According to his philosophy it was quite acceptable for gentlemen to haunt all manner of unsavoury gaming halls and brazenly set up opera dancers as their mistresses, but his dependent females could not move from the house without his yea or nay and were shackled by every conceivable social rule. Well Miss Geneva Hartwell had no intention of bowing down to his misogynistic tyranny!

Fortunately for Geneva her resolve was not tested by the appearance of the earl himself. On the whole Geneva was relieved when he sent a message to say he would dine at his club. The sooner she was beyond the disturbing influence of Lord Vance the better. But her rebellious heart refused to see things in such a rational light and it would be hard enough to turn her back on her heart's desire without being obliged to see the object of her love in person.

Lord Henry had been called away on Congress business and so it was only the ladies of the house who sat down to dine. Understandably there was a sense of anticlimax now the ball was behind them and they were a fairly subdued party. Lady Yarwood, observing Geneva's wan face, made no objection when she excused herself from their planned visit to the theatre. No more than on the previous evening did Lady Yarwood believe in the existence of a headache, but it would do the girl no good to be seen in public until she had overcome this depression of the spirits. Lady Yarwood sighed inwardly; she had done all she could to promote the match between her nephew and Miss Hartwell, now it was up to them.

Geneva managed to leave the house undetected with relative ease. She was not under constant surveillance as she had been in her guardian's house and so no drastic escape route was needed. She simply slipped out when the servants had retired to their quarters. The hardest part of all had been bidding farewell to Lady Yarwood and Isobel. Geneva had been unable to conceal her emotions and had given both ladies an impulsive hug when, in all their finery, they had appeared in the drawing-room to wish her good night.

'There now, what have we done to deserve this?' exclaimed Lady Yarwood mildly surprised.

Geneva flushed and said in a low stifled voice, 'You have both been so kind, I just wish you to know how grateful I am.'

Lady Yarwood patted Geneva's cheek carelessly, secretly touched by the girl's gesture. 'Really, child, I have simply welcomed you as my nephew's future bride. There is nothing to be grateful for.'

The two ladies departed, and with a heavy heart Geneva went up to her bedroom to change her day dress for a plain white muslin evening gown. She was in no mood to consider her appearance and in a few moments she was ready, a celestial blue domino thrown over the thin gown. It was impossible for Geneva to take any luggage so she had to be content with what necessary items she could cram into her most capacious reticule. Then it was time to leave. Tying the strings of her loo mask and pulling the voluminous hood of her domino over her dark curls, Geneva slipped out into the deserted square, bidding a silent and sorrowful goodbye as she did so to the house in the Josefsplatz that had witnessed so much of the pleasure and pain of her burgeoning love.

Mr Worthington strolled at an easy pace through the narrow streets of Vienna's old town, his shrewd mind pondering on the problem of the Earl of Brewood's engagement. Like Lady Yarwood, Mr Worthington had quickly recognized in Miss Hartwell the perfect partner for his cynical friend. Geneva Hartwell was free of all the worldly conceits that Lord Vance so despised and distrusted, and at the same time she had the strength of character and principal necessary to stand firm against the earl's overbearing ways. Mr Worthington had hoped that the enforced intimacy brought about by their false betrothal would lead to romance. But while he was in no doubt that each had given their heart, it was equally obvious that something had gone badly awry.

Mr Worthington's cogitations were interrupted when he was hailed enthusiastically by an acquaintance. Mr Freddy Bolsover was a gregarious soul and when, as now, he was a trifle up in the world he was inclined to view the world as his friend. Upon learning that Mr Worthington was bound for a certain exclusive gambling establishment, Mr Bolsover immediately offered his company and taking Mr Worthington's arm proceeded to regale him in a slightly befuddled manner with all the latest crim.-con. stories that were circulating the ton.

Mr Worthington listened with half an ear to Mr Bolsover's spicy and often barely coherent titbits of gossip, politely punctuating his rambling dialogue with dutiful exclamations of surprise or disbelief. But his attention was wholly caught when Mr Bolsover touched on the subject that had so recently occupied Mr Worthington's own thoughts.

'Brewood's a friend of yours I know, Worthington, but devil of a fellow, you know, devil of a fellow.'

Mr Worthington prompted him to expand on this cryptic utterance, which Mr Bolsover was very willing to do. He rubbed the side of his nose thoughtfully. 'Seems a queer start to me, like a dog with a bone with the Hartwell chit. Ten to one it's all a hum, for what would Gerry Buxton know? Not as if he moves in the same circles as Brewood.'

'And what does Mr Buxton claim to know?' asked Mr

Worthington with admirable patience.

'Says Brewood's set up that opera dancer, La Cantonini or some such foreign name, as his light o' love. Seen driving her in the park at the fashionable hour, bold as brass, so it seems. Must say the more I think of it the more I think Buxton's got it wrong. Be all over town if it were true. Come to think of it, I would have seen it myself. Always take a jaunt in the park.'

Mr Bolsover rattled on at length in this fashion, and Mr Worthington turned his attention to this new and very interesting item of information. It was, as Mr Bolsover had suspected, all a hum. Lord Vance might not confide in his friend when it came to matters of the heart, but Mr Worthington would certainly have been aware if the earl had taken a new mistress. Then why this unfounded gossip? A sudden vision of Miss Fortesque and Miss Mansfield deep in conversation rose before his mind's eye, and stood in the background, as if carved in stone, the figure of Geneva Hartwell.

The unlikely partnership of the refined Miss Fortesque and the dreadfully vulgar Miss Mansfield had struck him as odd at the time, now it took on a more sinister complexion. Were not Clarissa Mansfield and Gerry Buxton's sister bosom bows? The idea that the superior Miss Fortesque would invent such a scurrilous piece of gossip would have shocked most who knew her, but not Oliver Worthington. He had always suspected that beneath that cool implacable façade there was a totally selfish and ruthless woman. Common sense told him he was allowing his imagination to run away with him, but at the same time he could not shake off the feeling of unease Freddy Bolsover's casual remarks had generated.

The two gentlemen had by now reached their intended destination and, as luck would have it, their arrival coincided with that of two of Mr Bolsover's particular cronies. Mr Worthington was therefore able to extract his arm from Mr Bolsover's fond grasp and relinquish him to their genial company. That done he quickly scanned the dimly lit and opulently decorated card rooms for Lord Vance. Of the earl there was no sign, and Mr Worthington quickly took himself off at a brisk pace intent on visiting all his friend's favourite haunts. The sooner Augustin was made aware of his suspicions the better.

It was well over an hour before Mr Worthington succeeded in running his friend to ground. He had drawn a blank at half a dozen of the city's more exclusive clubs, and was on the point of admitting defeat when he remembered the Louis d'Or. The Louis d'Or was a relatively new establishment that was said to cater for the more hardened gamester. Mr Worthington would not have normally classed the earl in that category but, judging from his mood of the previous evening, it was quite possible he had chosen to forget his sorrows in a bout of heavy gambling.

The Louis d'Or in the Franziskanerplatz was run very competently by a retired French soldier of fortune. The Chevalier de Vambère, as he chose to style himself, was reputed to have switched allegiance between Napoleon's revolutionaries and the supporters of the French monarchy with almost as much frequency, skill and success as that intriguer *par excellence* and France's present Foreign Minister, Talleyrand. The title of *chevalier* was adopted in an effort to disguise his plebeian roots and to attract the aristocracy to his salons. In truth it was an unnecessary expedient since the Louis d'Or's reputation for deep play and excellent claret provided the only recommendation required. The Chevalier de Vambère was more commonly referred to as the Chevalier d'Industrie, but this did not prevent his business from thriving.

A footman dressed in unrelieved black appeared at Mr Worthington's side, and to this sombre individual he relinquished his curly-brimmed beaver and malacca cane. The footman retreated noiselessly, the deep pile crimson carpet and flocked wallpaper seeming to absorb all sound. The morbid livery of the footman exactly suited the mood of the place. The highly charged atmosphere of intense concentration and oppressive silence was almost tangible. Fortunes were being won and lost on the turn of a card or the throw of the dice, and the air crackled with tension.

The earl lounged with his customary negligent grace at the faro table, a glass of claret loosely cupped in one white hand. Mr Worthington remained in the shadows for a few moments, simply observing his friend. To the casual eye Lord Vance would have appeared perfectly sober. He played his cards with a steady hand, his movements betraying no clumsiness. By the litter of notes and vowels at his elbow not only was his judgement unimpaired, he was having the Devil's own luck.

Indeed there was something devilish in his appearance that the dim candlelight and plush crimson decor only emphasized. He certainly had company Satan himself would have envied. The cadaverous Lord Francis Casey, his tall angular frame casting a predatory shadow over the green baize, the Duc de Learmont, a sinister relict of the *ancien régime* in his powdered wig and heavily brocaded coat with its stiff skirts, and Sir Digby Cholmondley, his bulbous features marred by a network of broken veins, the result of years of dissipation.

Mr Worthington recognized the signs of an evening of heavy drinking. The earl's black coat hung open and the arrangement of his cravat had lost some of its immaculate precision. A strand of raven black hair had fallen across his brow which was faintly beaded with perspiration. But it was the earl's expression that caused Mr Worthington his greatest concern. His dark eyes burned with a hectic and reckless light, spots of high colour stained his pale complexion.

Mr Worthington moved quietly across the room and put his hand on his friend's shoulder, speaking in a low voice, 'Gus, a word with you please.'

Lord Vance turned to face him. His voice was slightly slurred but it had lost none of its habitual mockery. 'Oliver, your timing is diabolical. I have a wager with Cholmondley that I will break the bank before midnight.'

Mr Worthington persevered. 'Unfortunate. But I promise you, this is a matter of importance.'

The earl regarded his friend in silence for several moments, a look of questioning alertness replacing the smile of lazy amusement as he took in Mr Worthington's grave expression. Abruptly he stood up, casting his cards carelessly on to the table. 'You win, Cholmondley.'

'Much obliged, Worthington!' wheezed the dyspeptic gentleman who had profited from Lord Vance's default.

Mr Worthington acknowledged this with a brief nod before drawing the earl aside. 'You may think I am reading too much into this, but hear me out and tell me your opinion....'

With that Mr Worthington succinctly related the information so innocently imparted by Freddy Bolsover, and added his own interpretation of events. The earl listened in silence, his features setting into increasingly grim lines as the tale progressed, his long white fingers tightening on the glass in his hand. Lord Vance had indulged freely in the Louis d'Or's famed claret, but it had not dulled his brain and it took him very little time to guess the chief machinator.

The earl spoke softly but there was suppressed violence in the way he set down his glass, a single drop of the ruby liquid leaping from the goblet to stain his cuff.

'Armistead is behind this. Damn him.'

Without pausing to gather up his substantial winnings the earl strode from the club. Mr Worthington hastened after him and catching him in the street tried to detain him.

'For God's sake, Gus! Think before you act! Kill Armistead and you will condemn yourself to permanent exile.'

The earl's expression had indeed been murderous, but at this his features relaxed and there was even a glint of wry humour in his eyes. 'Never fear, Oliver, it is not murder I have on my mind, but love. I have handled this affair remarkably ill, have I not? I am "engaged" to Miss Hartwell, now I intend to beg her to be my wife. A little irregular perhaps, but please God she will forgive me that. Wish me luck?'

Mr Worthington gripped his arm in a gesture of silent compassion before letting him go. Yes, he wished him all the luck in the world.

Fifteen

Geneva found the hack waiting as promised and with one swift backward glance she stepped into the vehicle. Only when the carriage door was shut behind her did a figure detach itself from the shadows and set off in the opposite direction at a jog trot. In a matter of minutes the vehicle had joined the noisy jam of carriages and chairs outside the Palmers' residence. In the blazing light of flambeaux and carriage lamps Geneva could see a steady stream of exotically costumed guests pouring through the open doors into the tall brilliantly illuminated house. The Earl of Brewood might scorn the Palmers' hospitality, but it was clear that a good proportion of Vienna were not so fastidious.

For the first time since Geneva had taken the impulsive decision to accept Fabian Armistead's offer of assistance, she was assailed with doubt. Surely a less public meeting place might have been contrived? Such a lively occasion seemed a little incongruous under the circumstances. Still, she was too grateful for Mr Armistead's kindness to quibble over minor details. The gentleman in question had been watching for the arrival of the hack with an anxious eye, and now he threaded his way through the congestion with alacrity.

'Geneva! I hardly dared hope … I am so very glad you chose to come!' He spoke in a low earnest voice as he handed her down from the carriage, and Geneva glanced quickly up at him, startled and a little unnerved by this odd greeting and by the intensity of his tone. His voice was devoid of all the mocking lightness she had been used to expect. His expression was inscrutable behind his black mask, but through their narrow slanting slits, his eyes seemed to glint with a sinister light. It is nothing more than the effect of his mask and the moonlight, Geneva told herself firmly, but she could not rid herself of a growing unease.

Mr Armistead took Geneva's arm possessively and guided her through the crush until they reached the ballroom. There he led her to a small couch where, he hoped, they might be able to converse in private. With that he went in search of refreshments, leaving Geneva to view the antics of Lady Palmer's guests. Geneva might be new to the fashionable world, but it did not take her long to discover the reason why Lord Vance had steadfastly refused to allow his sister to attend.

While a few guests had like Geneva and Mr Armistead simply covered their conventional evening dress with a domino and donned a mask, the majority had taken the opportunity to indulge in their wildest fantasies. Geneva's eyes widened as she took in the appearance of numerous houris, slavegirls, nymphs and goddesses all dressed in the flimsiest of costumes which left little to the imagination. The circumstance of everyone being masked had imparted a certain reckless freedom to the proceedings. Social etiquette was set by the board, and young blades freely ogled at any lady whose neat figure or well-turned ankle promised a pretty face behind her disguise. The ladies received these blatant attentions with a great deal of vulgar coquetry, and the ballroom was alive with the shrieks and noisy laughter of females as they half-heartedly evaded the bold advances of their partners. Geneva could only blush at such behaviour and wonder at Mr Armistead's choice of rendezvous.

Fortunately, since Geneva was becoming increasingly aware that her solitary state was attracting a great deal of unwanted attention from a particularly raffish set of young bucks, Mr Armistead at that moment returned. He brought with him two glasses of champagne. Geneva would have preferred lemonade, the ice-cold bubbles of the fizzy wine were too frivolous to suit her mood, but she was thankful for his return and so raised no objection. She could not keep a tone of mild reproof from her voice however when she commented, 'I had not expected it to be quite so … so lively.'

Mr Armistead smiled ruefully. 'I would not for the world subject you to such vulgarity unless it were necessary. You have probably gathered that Lady Palmer is not in the habit of entertaining those from the first circles, that in itself should save us from recognition by an acquaintance.'

Geneva's disquiet was appeased to a certain extent by this. In fact Mr Armistead had had quite the opposite intention when he had fixed on the Palmers' masquerade for their meeting. If things went according to plan, Miss Hartwell would be persuaded to elope with him tonight, but it did no harm to hedge one's bets. True, the majority of the guests came from the *demi-mondaine*, but their very position on the fringes of polite society made them all the more interested in the gossip and intrigues of the true aristocracy. Fabian Armistead was confident that the attendance of the Earl of Brewood's intended bride and the identity of her escort would be common knowledge amongst the ton before morning. If that did not cause an irretrievable rift between the happy couple then nothing would.

To Geneva's surprise, Mr Armistead did not immediately turn to the topic that must surely fill both their minds: his offer of help. Instead he seemed intent on confining the conversation to trivia, at the same time plying her with glass upon glass of champagne. A lady relaxed by liberal quantities of alcohol, he reasoned, would be more likely to abandon her country-bred morality and fly with him. Of course he would allow her to assume that marriage was their goal, but in truth he had no intention of being shackled to a girl who, as far as he knew, had no fortune to recommend her. Besides, Lord Vance's humiliation would be all the greater if it was learned that his chosen bride had preferred to sacrifice her reputation rather than marry the earl.

In the end Geneva was forced to introduce the subject herself. She wanted to be as far away from the Josefsplatz as possible before her absence was missed, and precious minutes were ticking away. The earl might not love her, but she knew he would feel himself honour bound to follow her.

'Mr Armistead, your note suggested you might be willing to render me assistance in escaping from a ... an unhappy situation....'

Fabian Armistead gladly took his cue. Clasping her hands warmly, he said sincerely, 'Miss Hartwell, I will willingly do all in my power to help.'

Geneva hesitated, it was not as easy as she had thought to ask such a favour, but the knowledge of the misery it would cause her to remain in Vienna spurred her on. 'Mr Armistead, as I think you suspect, I have come to regret my engagement to Lord Vance. Certain circumstances make it impossible for me to remain in Vienna, and so I must return to England.'

Armistead was forced to bow his head over Geneva's hands to hide his feelings of exultation. This was better than he had imagined! Now was the time to press his suit. 'Oh, Geneva! You do not know how happy you have made me! We will flee tonight.' Unfortunately, since he had taken the opportunity to cover Geneva's hands in impassioned kisses, he did not see the look of blank dismay this lover-like behaviour had brought to her face.

Geneva was too astonished even to snatch her hands from Mr Armistead's grasp. How could she have been such a fool? How could she have so totally misread his intentions? Her mind ran over all the times they had met, surely she had never given him any encouragement, never given him any reason to suspect she felt anything other than friendship for him.

Geneva stood up abruptly, crying in agitation, 'Oh, no. Please, say no more, Mr Armistead! You have misunderstood me. I simply wished for you to provide me with the means to return to England, naturally I would repay you as soon as I was able.'

Mr Armistead, looked up in surprise and saw immediately how badly he had judged the situation. Cursing inwardly he strove to regain lost ground. 'Geneva, my love. I have tried to conceal my feelings for you, but it is hopeless. That you do not return my love is plain to see, but, my darling, you know you could never be happy with Vance. Put your trust in me and in time perhaps you may learn to return my regard.'

Geneva stared at him in horror. 'Oh, Mr Armistead, if I had known, if I had suspected …! I fear my presence here has given you false hope. Please forget I ever asked for help.'

But even as she said it, Fabian Armistead was endeavouring to catch her in his arms. By now surprise had given way to anger and wounded pride. He had exerted all his charm on this little unknown and she had the temerity to shrink from his embrace. The role of lover was abandoned and in one quick movement he twitched Geneva's mask from her face. Breathing hard he fought to hold her. 'You should have thought of the consequences before you agreed to meet me, Miss Hartwell. Why not cut your losses and come with me?

Once news of tonight's little escapade gets out, you may be sure Brewood will be glad to see the back of you!'

Geneva struggled with all her might, and with a cruel laugh Armistead released her. 'Go then, you little fool. I want no unwilling mistress.'

Geneva picked up her skirts and fled nimbly across the dance floor, her one thought to escape the sound of his mocking laughter. Mr Armistead followed her progress across the dance floor with a grim smile, and then set off in feigned pursuit. It was not the perfect revenge he had planned, but enough of Lady Palmer's guests had seen their quarrel and the world would be eager to interpret it as a falling out between lovers. He had done enough to humiliate the mighty Earl of Brewood.

Geneva erupted into the chilly night air, flushed and breathless. She looked wildly round for a hack but the bustle of carriages had dispersed and the square was empty but for one solitary vehicle.

'If you are looking for transport, my dear, I will be happy to oblige you.'

Geneva felt the hairs on the back of her neck stand on end at the sound of that familiar and dreaded voice at her shoulder. She whirled round, a cry of distress dying in her throat as she recognized the hated figure of her guardian. Geneva turned to run but Leonard Boeman was too quick for her. Grasping her arm painfully he yanked her against him, effectively silencing her cry for help by clamping his free hand across her mouth. Geneva struggled helplessly, the effects of her sudden exertion on top of several glasses of champagne had left her dizzy and faint. In a matter of seconds Boeman had thrust her ruthlessly before him into the waiting carriage and then they were moving, travelling at a dangerous speed through the narrow streets of Vienna and out into the hills beyond.

Mr Grieves was enjoying his customary late evening glass of sherry with Mrs Cobb, the housekeeper. Lord and Lady Yarwood might travel the length and breadth of Europe and change residence at a moment's notice, but this particular ritual had but rarely been missed in the fifteen years that these two august members of the household had been in the diplomat's service.

The butler and the housekeeper, very much aware of their superior position, quite naturally deplored any kind of below-stairs gossip as regards their employers, and were quick to quash any such freedom among the servants. But over their single glass of sherry before the cheery fire of Mrs Cobb's snug parlour, a certain degree of delicate speculation about goings on above stairs was enjoyed. The arrival of the Earl of Brewood and the beautiful Miss Hartwell had provided much food for these discreet musings, and the lovers' contretemps were no secret to them.

But tonight their discussion of latest developments was rudely interrupted by a thunderous knocking at the front door. The two servants glanced at each other in silent surprise. It had just turned eleven o'clock, too late for callers and too early to expect the ladies' return from the theatre. Mr Grieves had witnessed the earl's forbidding expression when he had left the house earlier in the day, and both butler and housekeeper were agreed that this was a sure sign that they would see the dawn before they saw Lord Vance.

Their impatient caller repeated his urgent demand for entry rousing Mr Grieves from the comfort of his armchair. Grumbling under his breath at the curtailment of his evening's relaxations, Mr Grieves hastily buttoned his waistcoat and shrugged his portly frame into his coat, before hurrying up the narrow stairs that led from the servants' quarters to the entrance hall. Adjusting his cuffs and taking a moment to recapture his superior composure, the butler signalled to the footmen to open the door, preparing to deliver a suitably cool reception to this impertinent visitor. All thoughts of quelling snubs were forgotten at the precipitate entrance of Lord Vance.

'Devil take it, Grieves! Is the whole house asleep?' exclaimed the earl in exasperation, thrusting his evening cape and ebony cane into the hands of one gaping footman. 'Be so good as to tell Miss Hartwell that I wish to see her.'

'Miss Hartwell retired several hours ago, my Lord,' protested the butler.

But after weeks of doubt and caution, having reached a decision, Lord Vance was not about to let considerations of polite behaviour stand in the way of his future happiness. 'That is of no consequence. Send a maid to wake her, I will wait in the drawing-room.' The earl turned on his heel, the sudden

movement causing his head to reel slightly. Remembering the quantities of claret he had consumed he added, 'And bring me some coffee. Strong!'

This kind of behaviour did not at all suit Mr Grieves's sense of propriety, but he knew better than to gainsay the earl in this mood. Instead he had to be satisfied with injecting a silent reproof into his very correct bow, before issuing several brief commands to his minions.

The earl's coffee made its appearance promptly. Miss Hartwell posed the Yarwoods' servants with a greater problem. In scandalized tones Grieves conveyed the earl's orders to Mrs Cobb. Mrs Cobb, with much tutting and head shaking passed on the message to Conway, who it was decided was the properest person to wake Miss Hartwell. Even Conway's habitual calm was shaken by the sight of Miss Hartwell's empty room and the undisturbed covers of her bed, and although it was entirely beneath her dignity to break into a run, she nonetheless returned to the housekeeper's room with remarkable speed. A lightning search of the house yielded no Miss Hartwell.

Meanwhile the earl's patience was rapidly wearing thin. With an angry exclamation he set his coffee cup down with a force that nearly shattered the delicate china, and strode out into the hall. There he found butler, housekeeper and lady's maid in an agitated huddle. Lord Vance cut through their furiously whispered dialogue, his impatient tones causing all three to visibly start.

'What is going on here? Where is Miss Hartwell?' the earl demanded.

Grieves turned to face him, and at the look of anxiety and dismay on the butler's face, Lord Vance felt his first twinge of apprehension. 'My Lord, Miss Hartwell is not in her room.'

'Well for God's sake where is she? Answer me man!'

The butler wrung his hands together nervously and looked even more wretched. 'I am afraid I could not say, my Lord. Miss Hartwell is not in the house.'

For a moment the earl could only stare at him, cold dread gripping his heart with icy fingers. He was too late. History was repeating itself. Just as his father had driven away his mother, now he with his cruel words and hateful insinuations had driven away the only woman he could ever love. The malicious

plotting of Fabian Armistead and Miss Fortesque had been the catalyst, but the earl knew in his heart of hearts that it was his own unforgivable behaviour which was most to blame.

But he would not make the same mistake as his father. Foolish pride would not stand in his way. He would follow Geneva and find her, and when he found her he would beg her forgiveness on bended knee if necessary.

'You, Conway is it not? Take me to Miss Hartwell's room. I want to know what she has taken with her. Grieves, the news of Miss Hartwell's disappearance must not go beyond this house. Do you understand?'

The sound of the earl's authoritative voice brought all three servants to attention, and the butler straightened his sagging shoulders. 'You may rely upon our discretion, my Lord.' All the servants admired and respected Lady Yarwood's nephew, and they had quickly warmed to the generous heart and unaffected manners of his lovely future bride. If they could help avert scandal then they would do so gladly.

Conway led the earl to Geneva's bedroom. Lord Vance paused involuntarily, the sweet jasmine scent of her favourite perfume hung in the air and the memories it brought almost unmanned him. But this was no time for maudlin despair and as Conway made a swift and systematic examination of Geneva's wardrobe, the earl searched quickly through the drawers of her dressing-table and escritoire, his keen eyes hunting for any clue to her intentions. His search was in vain, there was no note, no hint as to where Geneva might have gone. Then he spied a crumpled sheet of paper half-concealed beneath the draperies of the bed. Eagerly he snatched it up and smoothed away the creases. With a groan of despair he sank on to the edge of the bed, plunging long fingers into his sleek black hair. It was his own note, the one he had sent her that very morning, and as he reread those cold formal sentences he cursed his folly over and over again. How he had laboured over that letter, choosing his words with such care and precision. In his effort to convince Geneva of the necessity of marriage to save her reputation he had failed to mention the real reasons behind his proposal, the fact that he loved her to distraction and doubted he could live without her. No wonder she had fled into Armistead's arms!

He had to find her. He would find her! The earl groaned

again; brave words, but where did he begin? She could be anywhere. Under other circumstances he might have supposed her to be heading for England, but with the threat of her guardian awaiting her there he could not even be sure of that.

Conway interrupted these helpless thoughts. 'My Lord, Miss Hartwell seems to have taken her toothbrush and various other toiletries, but the only clothes that are missing are a white evening gown and a blue satin domino.'

'A domino?' said the earl blankly, but the sound of his aunt and sister returning claimed his attention. In seconds he was ushering them into the drawing-room, ignoring their protests. The moment the door was closed behind them Lord Vance turned to Lady Yarwood. 'Aunt Liz, Geneva has run away. I must find her. If you have any idea where she might have gone, then tell me.'

There was a desperate appeal in her nephew's voice that touched Lady Yarwood's heart, but she did not have the power to reassure him. All she could do was to shake her head silently and sink into the nearest chair, her strong features set into an expression of thoughtful concern. She had to admit that the news did not entirely surprise her; Geneva had too much spirit to meekly submit to Augustin's jealous rages. Lady Yarwood remembered the sentimental farewell Geneva had taken of them earlier in the evening and inwardly berated herself for not immediately suspecting the girl's intentions.

Lady Isobel's more voluble surprise was enough to convince Lord Vance that his sister was not in Geneva's confidence, and with that his last faint hope evaporated. Then he recalled the maid's puzzling information, and with renewed optimism he said eagerly, 'She has taken nothing but a domino. Surely that must give us some clue.'

'A domino?' Lady Yarwood's reaction was as incredulous as had been the earl's own, but it caused Lady Isobel to pause in her fruitless lamentations, an arrested look on her pretty face. The sudden silence of his sister immediately attracted Lord Vance's attention.

'Isobel. Do you know something?' he asked urgently.

Lady Isobel frowned and answered him hesitantly, 'It may be totally unconnected, but this afternoon a note arrived for Geneva. She did not refer to its contents but a little while later she did question me about Lady Palmer's masque.'

'Armistead,' said the earl grimly, at the same time striding across the room and pulling the bell rope vigorously. 'He has an elopement in mind. Well, he will not get far.'

Lady Yarwood and Isobel stared at him in astonishment, but were prevented from questioning the reasoning behind such an extraordinary conclusion by the prompt entrance of Grieves.

'Send a message to the stables. I want the greys harnessed to my curricle and brought round immediately.'

The butler bowed and withdrew, and Lady Isobel at once voiced her disbelief. 'Surely you are wrong, Gus. I know Geneva has shown a partiality for his company, but she does not love Armistead.'

The earl smiled bitterly. 'Maybe not, but Armistead has gone out of his way to be charming and attentive, whereas I....' He could not continue, but clenched his fists and looked even more grim. Lady Yarwood interposed decisively at this point.

'No. I can believe that ... that circumstances may have caused Geneva to leave, but with Armistead? No I cannot believe that.'

The earl gave a ragged sigh. 'I wish I could be so sure, Aunt. But the circumstances, as you so tactfully describe my appalling treatment of Geneva, are worse than you imagine.' With that he gave an unexpurgated history of his supposed engagement to Geneva Hartwell from their first meeting to the malicious rumours spread by Miss Fortesque and the suspected involvement of Fabian Armistead.

Lady Yarwood listened in silence, her expression growing increasingly grave. She had always believed there was more to her nephew's betrothal than he had revealed, but she had never imagined the extent of the deception. It did not change her belief that Geneva was in love with Augustin, but it did put an entirely different complexion on things.

'And so Geneva believes you feel obliged to marry her.'

'But it is what I want more than anything in the world!' protested Lord Vance.

'And if what you suspect is true, if she has fled with Armistead, what then?'

The earl's brows snapped together. 'Then she will swiftly be made a widow, if it is marriage he has in mind, which I seriously doubt.'

'But it may be many days before you trace them,' probed

Lady Yarwood, adding delicately, 'Many days and many nights.'

The earl flushed darkly, obviously in the grip of a powerful emotion. But he simply said in a low fierce voice, 'I love her.'

Lady Yarwood was secretly delighted by this admission, but she shook her head in exasperation. 'But I do not suppose you have told her so, you foolish boy. Do you really think a girl of Geneva's character and principle could accept a husband she believed had been compromised into wedding her?'

A light of hope flickered briefly in the earl's dark eyes as the truth of this dawned on him. 'Then you think it is possible that she does not despise me?'

Lady Yarwood was quite certain that Geneva's feelings for the earl were a good deal warmer than he dared hope, but it would do her nephew no harm to be less than confident of his place in Geneva's heart. Instead she simply said, 'You must discover that for yourself.'

The earl needed no second urging. Snatching up his whip and throwing a many caped driving coat about his shoulders he was gone, manoeuvring his cattle at a smart trot through the traffic of Vienna and to the Palmers' residence.

Geneva was thrown with such force into the carriage that for several moments she could only lie against the squabs dazed and winded. Then the reckless speed of the vehicle as it careered through the narrow uneven streets all but flung her to the floor. Collecting her scattered wits Geneva pulled herself up and took a firm grasp of the strap that swung beside her. It was a moonless night and the figure of her guardian was only just visible lounging on the bench opposite.

'That's right, my dear. Make yourself comfortable. We have a long journey ahead and we do not halt before dawn.'

The indignities she had suffered in the past half-hour had severely tested Geneva's temper, and the gloating triumph in Leonard Boeman's voice brought all her simmering indignation to the surface. The fact that this scoundrel had her entirely at his mercy was momentarily forgotten in her desire to vent her wrath. Geneva's voice was laced with bitter sarcasm as she replied, ''Tis just what I would expect from such a coward! Skulking in the shadows like a rat and then fleeing into the night. Well you had best hope your cattle are swift, for when

Lord Vance hears of this he will waste no time in following your trail. He will run you down and then you will be done gloating!'

In the dark Boeman flushed angrily and there was a distinct edge to his voice when he answered her, telling Geneva that her contempt had touched a nerve. 'You would do well to remember, ward, that you are totally within my power and so curb that sharp tongue of yours.'

'And you would do well to remember, guardian, that the Earl of Brewood is a powerful man, and one who is not likely to let the abduction of his betrothed go unchallenged,' retorted Geneva angrily.

It was Boeman's turn to mock. 'And how will he hear of it? Besides do you really think the proud earl will lift a finger to find you? When he hears of your sordid little affair with Armistead he will be glad to see the back of you.'

'You don't know what you are talking about. There is no affair and Lord Vance is well aware of the fact.' Geneva spoke with commendable bravado, but the truth of her guardian's words had struck home. Lord Vance already considered her a scheming adventuress. He had felt honour bound to offer her marriage, but when the events of this evening became known he would justifiably feel free of that irksome obligation. This depressing thought effectively doused Geneva's anger, and she began to comprehend the hopelessness of her position. But she would not admit as much to Leonard Boeman, she would not give him that satisfaction. Instead she simply asked calmly, 'And what do you intend to do with me? We cannot travel indefinitely without a stop, and you may be sure that when perforce we do halt I will not sit here in meek silence. This is the nineteenth century and I doubt people will turn a blind eye to kidnap.'

Mr Boeman was unimpressed by this. 'Do as you will. But since I am your legal guardian and carry the documents to prove it, I fear your efforts will be in vain. You would do much better to resign yourself to the inevitable. We will return to England and there we will be married without delay.'

'I would rather die,' said Geneva vehemently.

Her guardian shrugged. 'As you wish. It makes no odds to me. Either way your fortune comes to me. Bear that in mind, my dear, and learn to govern your temper. An untimely accident can be arranged as easily as a wedding, and I'll not take a vixen for a wife.'

Geneva could only be thankful that the darkness hid the fear and despair which was surely etched on her pale face. She turned her shoulder on the hated figure of her guardian and stared blindly out of the small carriage window. Already they were leaving the suburbs of Vienna behind, and before them lay the dark shadows of the wooded hills.

Inevitably Geneva's thoughts turned to the earl. If only she had heeded his warnings about Fabian Armistead, but then since the day Lord Augustin Vance had entered her life she had been incapable of making a rational judgement. Now her folly had led her right into her guardian's trap. But it was useless to bemoan her fate. She must rely on her own wits to extricate herself from this coil, for there would be no gallant hero to ride to her rescue this time.

Sixteen

The midnight hour was passed when Lord Vance strode into the Palmers' ballroom. Masks had long been discarded, as indeed had all semblance of modest behaviour. The earl surveyed the debauched scene with ill-concealed disgust. It more resembled London's infamous Cyprians' Ball than the party of a society dame. The fact that he too had not been averse to such entertainment in the past was forgotten; Armistead would pay dearly if he had exposed Miss Hartwell to this display of gross impropriety.

Lord Vance pushed his way through the revelling crowds without ceremony, his superior height allowing him to survey the ballroom for any sign of the blue domino. Time and again he would glimpse a flash of blue silk, and each time he fought his way through the heaving mass of bodies to the lady's side, it was to find himself looking into the face of a stranger.

His lordship's peculiar antics did not go unnoticed, particularly by his vigilant hostess Lady Palmer, an unlikely Cleopatra with her plump figure and improbable guinea-gold curls, who could hardly contain her glee at the gratifying presence at her ball of one of the most notoriously top-lofty members of the ton. The fact that his only reason for honouring the occasion was quite obviously to remove his wayward betrothed did not detract from her elation one jot. The very public disagreement between Miss Hartwell and Fabian Armistead had, as Mr Armistead hoped, been interpreted as a lovers' quarrel. Their sudden exit had sent a delicious ripple of speculation around the room. Add to that the appearance of the deceived earl himself, and Lady Palmer was quite justified in thinking her ball would be the most talked of event of the season.

Her round face flushed with triumph, Lady Palmer bustled

self-importantly to the earl's side, and laying one plump bejewelled hand familiarly on his arm, exclaimed in affected accents, 'Why Lord Vance! What a delightful surprise, I did not dare hope you would grace my little entertainment.'

His lordship was in no mood for exchanging polite inanities with his hostess, whom he knew to be little more than a Convent Garden abbess who had tricked her foolish titled husband to the altar. He simply looked down his long aristocratic nose at her and favoured her with a curt nod. But Lady Palmer had no intention of being deterred by his disdain and continued to prattle on until the earl ruthlessly cut in.

'Madam, I have simply come to escort Miss Hartwell home, so if you are able to tell me where she is, I would be obliged to you.'

Lady Palmer, taking in the grim cast of the earl's features, responded to this with a nervous giggle. Much as she was relishing the scandalous incidents of the evening, she would have preferred not to have been the one to tell Lord Vance that his betrothed had left in some distress with the ardent Mr Armistead in hot pursuit.

'Oh dear, I believe Miss Hartwell has already left,' was all she could manage to say.

'And Fabian Armistead?'

Lady Palmer's eyes widened at the directness of the question, but Lord Vance was past caring what the gossips might think. His only concern was to find Geneva; he was indifferent to his own humiliation.

'I believe Mr Armistead left at around the same time,' replied Lady Palmer falteringly.

'Your servant, madam.' The earl turned on his heel and strode from the room, oblivious to the interested gazes and whispered comments that followed him.

Leaping into his waiting curricle, Lord Vance ordered his groom to 'Stand away from their heads', and the vehicle leapt forward; the objective, Fabian Armistead's lodgings.

Mr Armistead had indeed pursued Geneva like the ardent lover the world supposed him to be, but he had missed her struggle with Leonard Boeman and had only been in time to see Geneva climb into a travelling chaise with a handsome blond gentleman. Armistead had quirked a sardonic eyebrow, but had thought nothing more than that some gallant young fool had offered to escort Miss Hartwell home. If asked he would have answered that doubtless Miss Hartwell was at present back in the bosom of Brewood's family, worrying at how best to hide her illicit outing from her jealous fiancé. What he did not expect was to be disturbed at an ungodly hour by the arrival of the wrathful earl.

While Lord Vance did not for a moment imagine Armistead would have the audacity to conduct the seduction of a gently bred female in his own home, he hoped by calling there to learn from Armistead's servants their employer's destination. In consequence, he was somewhat taken aback when having demanded in fearsome tones of the butler the whereabouts of his master, he was conducted to the master's study, where Mr Armistead was seen to be enjoying a solitary glass of brandy.

The earl was not at a loss for long. In three long strides he had crossed the room and was gripping Mr Armistead by the lapels of his handsome brocade dressing-gown.

'Where is she, Armistead?' It was scarcely more than a whisper but it was loaded with menace.

Armistead was taken by surprise, but his quick brain was rapidly reviewing the situation. Miss Hartwell had quite obviously not returned home which pointed to the single alternative: the blond gallant. It seemed the earl was after all destined to be the cuckold. Despite the uncomfortably vice-like grip the earl held him in, Armistead achieved a mocking smile.

'Such violence! My dear Brewood, you forget that I know what a murderous fellow you are. Do you think I would be such a fool as to bring the delightful Miss Hartwell here?'

The earl laughed harshly. 'Your deviousness knows no bounds. I would put nothing past you.'

Armistead would have shrugged had his position allowed it. He contented himself with an ironic lift of his eyebrows. 'You are welcome to search the premises, Brewood, but I fear you would be simply wasting your time while the real villain of the piece made good his escape.'

The Earl thrust him back into his chair, but continued to loom over him threateningly. 'What nonsense is this? Can you deny you were at the Palmers' ball with Miss Hartwell? That you left with her?'

'The former I cannot deny, the latter I do emphatically.' Mr Armistead adjusted his mangled cravat with deliberation before continuing. He was enjoying this. True it would be more circumspect to feign ignorance, but he could not resist the opportunity to tell the arrogant earl that his beloved had flown with another man.

'It seems, Brewood, that we have both lost out. If it had been a straight contest between the two of us then I believe my charm of manner would have prevailed, but unfortunately Miss Hartwell has a taste for blond Adonises, and so we are both worsted.'

Armistead had hoped to confuse the earl with this whimsical speech. It would suit him very well for Lord Vance to be forced to beg for information. He was destined for disappointment.

'Blond Adonises ...? Boeman! Of course!' Armistead's perfidy was instantly forgotten as the earl digested this new revelation.

Irked by the earl's superior knowledge, Armistead sneered nastily, 'So you know the young pretender. 'Tis a merry dance the parson's daughter has led you.'

Lord Vance spun round to face him, his face pale with anger. 'I have more pressing matters to attend to, but you may be sure, Armistead, that when I return you will be made to pay for this night's work.' With that he was gone, leaving Mr Armistead with mixed emotions about the success of his manipulations.

The travelling chaise rattled on through the night, its reckless speed never slackening. Once they had left the suburbs of the city behind them, and were following the winding curve of the Danube that led through Austria and into neighbouring Germany, Mr Boeman made himself comfortable and settled down to sleep. There had been no sign of pursuit and he was already congratulating himself on the success of his mission.

Leonard Boeman had arrived in Vienna a week previously, but he had bided his time and lain very low. A servant had been employed to watch Miss Hartwell, and Mr Boeman could hardly believe his luck when the spy had returned with the intelligence that his ward had stolen out of the Yarwood resident apparently unseen and unescorted, dressed for a masked ball. Servants' gossip had brought Boeman the news of the earl's rocky relationship, and he had almost convinced himself that far from chasing her across Europe *ventre à terre*,

Lord Vance would be secretly relieved to have Miss Hartwell off his hands.

Sleep was the furthest thing from Geneva's thoughts. She was determined to foil her guardian's evil schemes, and her mind worked busily, forming and discarding various plans of escape. Taking advantage of her captor's slumber, Geneva stealthily searched the interior of the chaise for any weapon she might use to defend herself. Up to now Mr Boeman had evinced no designs on her virtue, but Geneva guessed that it would only be a matter of time, for how else did he hope to force her to the altar? Not surprisingly the holsters fitted to the inside of both doors proved to be empty, and she could not hope to gain possession of Boeman's own pistol without waking him in the process. Geneva bit her lip in vexation and thought again. Since her guardian had divulged his intention to travel without break until dawn, it seemed likely that her virtue was safe at least until the following night. It was imperative therefore that she make her bid for freedom during the day.

That decided, no immediate solution sprang to mind. A brief look at the rough road hurtling beneath the carriage wheels had been enough to convince Geneva that throwing herself from the moving vehicle must be a last resort. Death might be preferable than life as Mrs Leonard Boeman, but Geneva had every intention of avoiding that ordeal with life intact, if only to prevent her despicable guardian from getting his hands on her fortune.

Her situation seemed quite hopeless, but while it was tempting to give up and repine the loss of all hope of future happiness, Geneva was made of sterner stuff. The depressing thought that without Lord Vance's love, life was hardly worth living anyway, was not allowed to intrude for long. Geneva's father had always taught her to make the best of her lot, and while she was too spirited to face life's disappointments with Reverend Hartwell's quiet resignation, neither was she one to mourn what could not be mended. Geneva forced herself to concentrate on escape, it did not pay to think beyond that.

The sun was just peeping above the horizon when a vague plan began to take shape in Geneva's mind. The champagne she had drunk the previous evening had combined with the jolting of the chaise to render Geneva acutely discomfited. The carriage must halt soon for a change of horses, and then whatever her guardian might have planned to the contrary, he would be obliged to let Miss Hartwell answer the call of nature. Surely he must relax his vigil at that point! Geneva counted on it, for it offered her only realistic chance of escape.

The sun rose slowly in the sky, dispelling the thin crust of frost, and at last Mr Boeman yawned and stretched and rubbed his stubbled chin. Geneva, who had been watching her guardian anxiously for any sign of movement, now quickly transferred her gaze to the pretty Austrian countryside. She was determined that she would not give this scoundrel the satisfaction of seeing her fear. Indeed the haughty profile and cool indifference that greeted Mr Boeman's awakening annoyed him, and once he was sufficiently alert he could not resist trying to goad her.

'Where is your bravado now then?' he jeered, and when she vouchsafed no reply added with false magnaminity, 'Still I don't mind a bit of spirit in a female as long as she don't push me too far. You're not an ill-looking wench though a mite skinny for my taste. I don't doubt we'll deal very well together as long as you remember who is master.'

Geneva bit back a scathing retort and lowered her eyes to veil the flash of contemptuous anger in their depths. It would do no harm for this conceited coxcomb to believe he had forced her into submission. Adopting defeated tones, Geneva murmured, 'My fate is clearly in your hands, guardian. There is little sense in bemoaning the fact.'

Mr Boeman was irritated by her meekness but to Geneva's relief, abandoned his attempts to taunt her. The horses had slowed to a trot, their necks dark and lathered with sweat, great plumes of steam issuing from their dilated nostrils. They were nearly spent and Boeman turned his attention to a halt and to his breakfast. A milestone informed them that Linz lay ten miles ahead, but Mr Boeman did not wish to draw attention to himself in a large town and so he instructed the coachman to stop at the very next posting house.

Half an hour later they pulled off the road into the yard of a small isolated inn. Too isolated for Geneva's liking, she had hoped for a small village at least, where even if help could not be found she would have a fair chance of concealing herself. Still, this might be her only chance and so she resolved to take it. From the instructions her guardian gave to his coachman it was clear that he had no intentions of leaving the carriage. The coachman was to hire fresh horses and order breakfast. Her heart pounding in her breast, Geneva fought to prevent a note of panic creeping into her voice when she pleaded, 'Mr Boeman, may we not step into the inn for a moment? I would like to wash and repair my appearance.'

Boeman laughed unpleasantly and shook his head. 'No need to make yourself pretty on my account, my dear. Save that for our wedding morn.'

Nothing was more likely to spur Geneva on than this reminder of what lay ahead. Lowering her eyes and blushing rosily she said meaningfully, 'But Mr Boeman, I beg of you, I really must leave the carriage. Urgently.'

This time Boeman took her meaning. For all his planning this was one factor he had not considered and he was momentarily nonplussed. Then he replied, 'Very well, but remember I am your legal guardian so do not think that anyone will come to your aid if you create a scene.'

With that warning he handed Geneva down and keeping a strong hold of her arm, led her into the inn. A serving wench promptly appeared to guide the lady to the washroom, but Mr Boeman did not relax his grip.

'I am afraid my ward is feeling a little faint and needs the support of my arm. If you would just point the way.'

They were directed through the public parlour and down a long narrow passage to a small room at the back of the building. For an awful moment Geneva thought her guardian intended to accompany her all the way, but he contented himself by warning her that he would be right outside and thankfully Geneva closed the door on him.

Completing her ablutions as hastily as possible, Geneva looked about the poky little room for an alternative exit. Her eyes immediately fastened on the small hatch-like window. It was set high in the outside wall, but with the aid of a convenient stool she would be able to reach it easily. Geneva wasted no time. Tucking up her skirts and tying her reticule securely about her waist, she mounted the stool and set to work on the window catch. It was rusty and stiff, and to Geneva it seemed an age before it eventually gave way. The window was scarcely a foot and a half wide, and Geneva thanked heaven for her slight build. Gripping the narrow sill, she took a deep breath and heaved herself upwards. She succeeded in getting her head and shoulders through the narrow gap, and with a great deal of wriggling she was eventually half in and half out of the window. The smallness of the window made it impossible for her to manoeuvre at all, and Geneva realized she would be forced to drop head first into the bushes below. Closing her eyes and bracing herself for the fall she resolutely thrust herself out of the window, landing in an undignified heap. Fortunately the bushes served to break her fall, and only slightly winded, she was quickly on her feet and planning her next move.

The landscape offered little cover. They had left the wooded hills behind, and all that could be seen for miles around was gently undulating grassland, punctuated by the occasional red tiled roof of a farm house. Geneva looked around her swiftly, there was no time for dithering. At any moment Leonard Boeman might lose his patience and force open the flimsy wooden door.

Wishing she was wearing something less distinctive and more practical than a white muslin gown and blue silk domino, Geneva set off at a stumbling half run. Her target was the thick hedgerow that lined the road which would hopefully serve to conceal her. Heart in mouth she struggled through the long grass, dreading the sounds of fury and activity that must inevitably erupt sooner or later from the inn behind her. The distance between her and the safety of the hedgerow she judged to be no more than a few hundred yards, but in satin evening slippers and narrow skirts it seemed longer. At last gasping for breath and almost faint with relief she pushed her way into the heart of the dense foliage and crouched there waiting for the pounding of her heart to abate.

She had little time to catch her breath for no sooner had she concealed herself than there came the sound of a horse and carriage approaching from the direction of the inn. Geneva froze in panic before common sense told her that even if Mr Boeman had discovered her flight, he would hardly have pursued her at such a sedate pace. Parting the branches carefully she peered out to see a farmer's cart drawn by a lazy-looking cob rounding the bend. It carried a young couple, who judging by their humble transport and their attire were peasants.

Geneva's initial impulse was to hail them and beg a lift to the next village, but then she hesitated. Her guardian would catch this ponderous vehicle in no time. A better idea came to mind and in an instant she was scrambling out into the road and flagging down the car. The occupants gazed at this bedraggled apparition with some awe and suspicion, but by dint of some very tortured German and a great deal of vigorous miming, Geneva managed to convey the message that all she wanted was to swap her conspicuous blue domino for the young woman's rough brown cloak. The woman was very willing to oblige her; the unprecedented luxury of finest silk easily outweighing the practicalities of brown worsted. Well pleased with her bargain, it took little urging on Geneva's part to convince her to don the garment immediately, and in a moment the happy but doubtless bewildered couple were once more on their way, the silk domino standing out very satisfactorily against the green landscape.

Rather proud of her ingenuity Geneva returned to the obscurity of her bush pulling the cloak about her. Now all that was needed was for the cart to get a good start on Mr Boeman without disappearing entirely from sight. Almost at once sounds of furious activity began to emanate from the inn yard. By cutting across country Geneva had rejoined the road, which followed a more circuitous route, a good mile further on. But even from that distance it was possible to distinguish muffled shouts and the clattering of hooves as a horse was hastily backed between the shafts of a vehicle. It would not be long before Leonard Boeman was on her trail. Geneva could only pray that he would be fooled by the tantalizing glimpse of bright blue still visible as the cart wended its way into the distance.

Her prayers were answered. Boeman, receiving no response to his impatient hammerings, had put his shoulder to the washroom door. Cursing loudly he had done a speedy circuit of the inn's environs and then had caught sight of the cart and its occupants. With a grim smile he had called for the landlord and wasted no time in appropriating that gentleman's gig and horse. Both were solid and reliable, but neither were built for the speed Mr Boeman demanded. All his cursing and urging could not make the animal break out of its shambling trot.

Geneva only waited for him to pass her hiding place before

emerging from the hedgerow and beginning to walk back along the road at a brisk pace. For all the sluggishness of her guardian's transport, it would not be long before he caught up with the cart and discovered his mistake. Then he would not rest until he had tracked her down. Leonard Boeman was obviously a desperate and dangerous man who would go to any lengths to achieve his ends. He had given her a choice; marriage or death. But, judging by his murderous expression, Geneva was fairly certain that marriage was no longer an option.

There was little point dwelling on her guardian's likely retribution, she must simply evade capture. Unfortunately there was nothing simple about it. With no transport and no money Geneva was at a decided disadvantage. All she could do was to push on and hope she might reach a village where at least she might have a chance of concealing herself. And what then? asked the pessimistic voice in her head. It is a month to your birthday, do you really think you can remain in hiding for a month? Even if you could, how would you live?

There was no answer to these daunting questions, and Geneva's spirits which had been temporarily boosted by the success of her escape plan, now began to flag. She began to realize just how exhausted and cold she was, and to notice how painful her feet were, the thin soles of her slippers being no protection from the stony surface of the road.

Geneva tried to distract her mind from these physical discomforts, and inevitably she had the most success when she allowed herself to think of what she had left behind in Vienna. Plodding on with half an ear listening for the dreaded sounds of pursuit, Geneva gradually slipped into a dreamlike trance, into a fairytale world where everything worked out according to the heart's deepest yearnings.

Geneva was warm and cosy, curled up before a roaring fire. The figure of the earl appeared before her and he was gazing at her with a tenderness that made her pulse quicken with joy. He enfolded her silently in his protective embrace and she was safe and warm. In the security of his arms she knew no fear; wicked seducers and avaricious guardians did not exist. The earl's love was Geneva's armour against all the evils of the world.

The unmistakable rumble of an approaching vehicle roused

Geneva from this pleasant reverie, and she turned to see her guardian bearing down on her. Leonard Boeman was in a savage temper. It was not until he had wrenched the innocent farm girl from her seat that he realized how completely he had been duped. Not surprisingly, the lusty young labourer took exception to this treatment of his fair wife, and Boeman had found himself sitting in the dust with a bloodied nose.

Knowing he had neither the courage nor the ability to defend himself against such a formidable opponent, Boeman had focused all his impotent rage and hatred on Geneva; she would be made to pay for this! Scrambling to his feet, Boeman turned the unwieldy gig and lashed the unfortunate horse into a terrified frenzy. Now as she stood there frozen in terror, he urged the horse faster and faster, his face a mask of murderous rage.

For a split second, Geneva could only watch helplessly as the maddened horse thundered towards her, her limbs numbed by horror. Then she flung herself desperately to one side out of its path. The gig careered past and Boeman cursed violently and sawed at the reins. While he fought to hold the demented animal, Geneva ran blindly, lungs bursting, in one last desperate attempt to get away. But in minutes, Boeman was out of the gig and after her and gaining with every stride. With a grunt of triumph he caught her around the waist and flung her to the ground pinning her there with the weight of his own body.

Geneva struggled helplessly. With a manic laugh Boeman's hands closed around her slender throat and squeezed mercilessly. Geneva clawed frantically at his hands but his grip only increased. She choked and gasped, her strength slowly ebbing away. His face swam before her in a red mist and she was dimly aware of the sound of hooves and shouting before blackness overwhelmed her and she slipped into unconsciousness.

Seventeen

If it were possible, the news that Geneva was at the mercy of Leonard Boeman, heightened Lord Vance's determination to find her even more. She had rejected Fabian Armistead and that gave the earl a momentary lightness of heart, but it was swiftly supplanted by fear for her safety. In Armistead's hands her virtue would have been at risk, in Boeman's hands her very life was under threat. The thought of Geneva alone and desperately afraid was so painful to the earl that, although it would have broken his own heart, he could almost wish she had eloped with Armistead, a willing mistress, rather than be subjected to Boeman's cruelty.

Lord Vance could only hope that Boeman still planned to gain Geneva's fortune through marriage and not through more sinister and violent means. With a month of his guardianship still to run, the earl guessed Boeman would concentrate on gaining the relative safety of English soil before arranging a wedding. This gave Lord Vance a chance to catch up with them. If he intended murder then the earl might already be too late.

All these thoughts ran like lightning through the earl's brain in the time it took him to exit Fabian Armistead's lodgings and mount his curricle. By sheer luck Lord Vance had discovered Geneva's abduction just two hours after its execution. Boeman could not have expected that and the earl hoped that he had elected simply to head for England with all possible speed, in an attempt to outrun any pursuers, rather than bothering to cover his tracks.

The earl had deduced correctly. Boeman had left Vienna in haste, and in doing so had drawn attention to his flight. A travelling chaise cannot speed through a city at dead of night and escape notice. Judicious enquiries of various linkboys and night watchmen furnished Lord Vance with a fair description of the carriage and a good idea of its direction. His expression stern and full of purpose, the earl set his team in motion, weaving his way through the narrow city streets at a strict trot until Vienna and its suburbs lay behind him. Only then did he drop his hands and give his horses their heads, allowing them to plunge forward surefootedly into the darkness, their long eager strides eating up the ground.

The earl's horses were in prime condition, fresh and willing. The temptation was to gallop full tilt in hot pursuit, but Lord Vance did not succumb. For all his start, Lord Vance reasoned, Boeman was probably equipped with inferior cattle, and while the earl's team had only a light sporting curricle behind them, Boeman was in a heavy cumbersome carriage. The earl was also the better horseman, and so where Boeman demanded reckless speed and ran his poor beasts into the ground, Lord Vance nursed his greys and conserved their energy for the long chase ahead.

Consequently the earl was gaining ground rapidly and steadily, but when dawn finally broke across the Austrian countryside he knew he must change his horses. Their grey flanks were heaving and dark with sweat, they had already covered more than two stages and for all he was reluctant to change them for job horses, the earl really had little choice. He allowed the weary beasts to drop to a walk and with his attention no longer needed to guide them through the darkness, his thoughts naturally turned to Geneva.

The possibility that he might lose her had banished all the earl's doubts and prejudices. The barrier he had built up over the years since his mother's desertion, to protect himself from emotional pain, had crumbled, leaving him blindingly aware of what Geneva Hartwell meant to him, had always meant to him.

The earl now believed he had started to love her at that very moment when their eyes had met across the Harbury Tea-Rooms. Naturally he had been attracted by her beauty; its freshness and vibrancy had illuminated the dreary gentility of the place, but it was more than that. It was the expression in those remarkable eyes. Wide with amused wonder as she took in the startling appearance of that vulgar doxy, and then candid and questioning as she had turned to find his gaze upon her. Geneva's whole personality glowed in those luminous orbs, they shone with the innocence and integrity of her inner being. Their changing lights reflected her every mood. Sparkling with humour and mischief, burning darkly with anger and passion. And when he had lashed her mercilessly with his cruel jealous tongue, the earl had seen his own pain mirrored in their violet depths.

What a blind fool he had been! How could he ever have looked into that lovely face and believed her capable of any of the vile calculating ploys he had accused her of? If only he were not too late to put things right. She might not love him, but perhaps she would forgive him. If only he were not too late. That agonizing thought drummed remorselessly through the earl's brain and made it impossible for him not to urge his horses onward. The sooner he reached a posting house, the sooner he would have fresh horses in the traces, the sooner, please God, he would have Boeman in his sights. His mind was so focused on his object that when he rounded the next bend to find the road ahead completely blocked, it took him a moment or two to fully comprehend the extraordinary scene before him.

What at first sight appeared to be a bewildering medley of vehicles and horses was revealed at a second glance to be in the main a single and very impressive entourage. The centrepiece was a large, almost spherical carriage hung between four enormous gilded wheels, and was the kind of vehicle in general reserved for the use of fairytale princesses. The main body of the coach was painted a delicate eggshell blue, as yet little marred by the dust and mud inevitably accumulated on a long journey. It was lavishly ornamented with elaborately carved and gilded woodwork and was drawn by four showy chestnuts, which Lord Vance's critical eye judged to have been selected more for their superficial glamour than for their quality.

Two postillions and no less than four outriders accompanied this magnificent equipage. They were recognizable as such by their very distinctive pale blue and gold livery, and by their slightly pained expressions which suggested they little relished taking to the road in company with such a monstrosity. A second carriage of more plebeian and practical design was heavily laden with a great quantity of luggage, but its occupants had, to a man, decanted onto the roadside and at present were huddled anxiously around an object or person unseen on the grass verge.

The third and final vehicle, a humble gig pulled by an equally humble brown cob, was entirely unattended, and the cob, perhaps embarrassed to find itself in such exalted company, more likely tempted by a patch of particularly lush green grass, had taken advantage of its abandoned state to detach itself from the main group.

The earl took all this in with a bemused eye as he slowed his team to a walk. His first thought was that one of the vehicles had met with an accident, but there was no obvious sign of damage, and as Lord Vance drew nearer his eye was drawn to a highly dramatic scene being enacted in the middle of the road.

A portly gentlemen of slightly more than middle age, exquisitely attired in canary-yellow breeches and a navy-blue coat of exaggerated cut, had adopted an heroic stance a little at odds with his dandified appearance. His noble head was thrown back, its carefully coiffed and pomaded curls gleaming in the sunlight. One plump soft hand rested on his hip in defiant fashion and in the other he wielded a wicked-looking rapier, its deadly point hovering inches above the chest of a second man who cowered helplessly in the dirt at his feet.

The second man was Leonard Boeman. The earl no sooner recognized him than he sprang from his curricle, flinging his reins to his astonished groom.

'What has happened here?' he demanded, his anxious eyes searching in vain for any sign of Geneva.

The portly gentleman did not abandon his dramatic pose but merely turned his head stiffly to face the earl, barred as he was from freer movement by the preposterous height of his shirt collars and the cascading folds of his cravat. He was of foreign appearance, heavy-jowelled and baby-faced and his olive skin was stained with florid colour. He had a tiny cupid's bow mouth, at the moment pursed in strong disapproval. From his black pumps and intricately clocked stockings to his broadly striped puce and silver waistcoat hung with half a dozen fobs and seals, he was a veritable Pink of the Ton, the archetypal dandy. But something had evidently occurred to offend his delicate sensibilities and he held his lethal weapon with a great deal of purpose.

The exquisite considered taking offence at the earl's abrupt questioning, but his desire to unburden himself of the indignation he felt was greater, and he replied in heavily accented English.

'Sir, you see before you' – here he indicated Boeman with an eloquent and graceful sweep of his free arm – 'a scoundrel so base, so depraved,' – the gentleman's voice throbbed with emotion – 'so wicked, that he would take that delicate flower of youth and beauty and crush all life from it—'

'Then the young lady is ...?' The earl could not bring himself to say it, to think it.

'Dead? Alas I fear the worse, but I tell you, I Vincenzo, Comte di Fiorelli, I will avenge this monstrous crime, this villain will pay with his life!'

The count fixed his glittering eyes on the cringing Mr Boeman, the tip of his sword quivering threateningly. In desperation, Boeman pleaded to the earl, 'Brewood, for heaven's sake, he is mad! Don't let him kill me, I never laid hands on the wench, I swear it.'

'Why you lying dog, *scellerato, assassino, birbante*—' The count's fury was greater than his command of English and he lapsed into his mother tongue.

The earl ignored Boeman's plea favouring it with no more than a contemptuous curl of his lip. Anger had driven the earl relentlessly onward through the night, but fear for Geneva thrust all thoughts of revenge from his head. He would deal with Boeman later. Now he interrupted the Italian's harangue, demanding ugently, 'Count! The young lady, where is she?'

The count gestured towards the huddle beside the road and replied grandly, 'Never fear! My people are attending to her. *La Bellezza* could not be in better hands. Ah! To think of that fair creature in the clutches of this *malvagio!*'

But the earl was gone, thrusting his way through the count's gaggle of servants. On the ground Geneva's body lay still and lifeless, the livid bruises around her neck in awful contrast to her deathly pale face. With a groan of despair Lord Vance sank to his knees and gathered her inert body in his arms. The count's servants' ministrations seemed to have been limited to wringing their hands and bemoaning the poor girl's fate in voluble Italian. Now the earl took charge.

'Move back all of you, give her some air!' He turned to a thin elderly gentleman whose modish attire suggested he was the count's valet. 'You, fetch me some smelling salts and a blanket, and some brandy if you have it.' Recognizing the voice of authority the little man scampered back to the servants' carriage and in a few moments the earl had tenderly wrapped Geneva in a fur-lined travelling rug. The movement seemed to rouse her a little and her eyelashes fluttered briefly against her waxen cheeks.

'Geneva! Geneva wake up!'

The voice was urgent and insistent but Geneva wanted to ignore it. She was deliciously warm and comfortable, she wanted to sleep. With a moan she snuggled further into the warm softness that surrounded her. But the voice persisted.

'Geneva, you must wake up. Please open your eyes.'

Reluctantly Geneva obeyed. Bright sunlight made her wince and she turned her face away.

'Geneva look at me, please.'

Geneva opened her eyes cautiously and squinted upwards. An involuntary smile touched her lips. Why she must be dreaming for here was Gus looking down at her, and with such a tender, loving expression. But he looked worried as well. Frown lines creased his brow. Geneva felt an overpowering urge to smooth them away and, as it was a dream, she did just that. Or would have done had Gus not grasped her hand in his and pressed it passionately to his lips.

'Oh, my darling, my little love. Thank God!'

Geneva listened in delight to these loving phrases. Really, this was the most wonderful dream she had ever had. But she just could not keep her eyes open a second longer, and with regret she sank once more into oblivion. For one brief dreadful moment, the earl feared the worst, and then his anxious fingers found her pulse, strong and steady, and closing his eyes he sent up a silent prayer of thanks.

The whole of this touching scene was witnessed with a great deal of surreptitious sniffles and sighs by the count's servants, and his valet, a man of great susceptibilities, wept unashamedly. Lord Vance himself had no time for such sentimentality, his priority was to see Geneva in a place of warmth and safety. Much as he was loath to leave her even for a second, the earl surrendered his beloved to the care of two of the more capable-looking maids and returned to the count's side.

That volatile gentleman was still engaged in berating Leonard Boeman in an eloquent polyglot of English and Italian. He had worked himself into a grand rage, and it would be hard to say who was most likely to survive the encounter, for while Mr Boeman's death on the end of the count's vengeful sword seemed imminent, the count himself was in danger of succumbing to an attack of apoplexy.

A fortunate interruption came in the form of a plaintive feminine voice, emanating from the depths of the whimsical carriage.

'Vincenzo, is it safe for me to descend? I would be very happy to render the unfortunate girl my poor assistance, but if there is blood....' The voice trailed off expressively.

The count seemed very struck by this. Much as he would have liked to skewer the villain at his feet, he had exceedingly nice notions when it came to the fairer sex. It would not do to expose the ladies to bloodshed, and on consideration, such violence would inevitably wreak havoc with the unsullied perfection of his stockings.

The earl seeing his dilemma stepped in promptly. 'Count, happily the young lady, Miss Hartwell is, thanks to your courageous actions, still living. But I believe it necessary to her continued welfare that she be immediately conveyed to some inn or dwelling and a doctor summoned. My curricle is hardly adequate for such a task. If you and your lady wife,' the earl hazarded, hoping this was indeed the status of the lady in the carriage and that he had not stumbled across some illicit affair, 'would be kind enough to take her up in your carriage, you may rely on me to deal with this scoundrel.'

The count seized upon this eagerly. 'Ah, you phlegmatic Englishmen! But you are right of course. However I might wish to put an end here and now to this miserable cur's existence, the young lady's health should be our primary concern. I will immediately consult with the contessa.'

With that the count sheathed his sword and hurried across to the carriage. Boeman was visibly relieved by his departure. Struggling to his feet and dusting down his clothes, he addressed the earl confidentially. 'My thanks to you, Brewood. The fat fool would murder me in cold blood. Now we may discuss this matter like reasonable men.'

Lord Vance replied with dangerous calm, 'And what makes

you think I will be more reasonable than the count, Boeman?'

Seeing the warning gleam in the earl's dark eyes, Boeman gave a nervous laugh and tugged uneasily at his cravat. 'Well, there is no harm done after all. The girl lives.'

The earl made no answer but continued to stare at Boeman in that same unnerving fashion. Boeman cleared his throat, before adopting a wheedling tone, 'Come now, Brewood, we are both men of the world. We are not going to come to cuffs over some silly chit you and I both know you would sooner be rid of.'

'You will have to explain the reasoning behind that, Boeman, I don't quite catch your meaning.' It was said with the same deadly calm, but Mr Boeman began to feel unaccountably hot. Despite the sharpness of the winter air, he was strangely reminded of the warm oppressive atmosphere that presages a sudden, violent storm.

With less confidence he blundered on, 'Brewood, my dear chap, let us speak plainly. The girl spun you some tale and you chose to believe her, not that I blame you for she's a taking piece. But I know you aristocrats, and you don't shackle yourselves to second-hand goods—'

Mr Boeman got no further, the storm broke above his head and he found himself for the second time that day lying in the dust nursing a bloody nose. But the earl had a far greater grievance than the farm labourer, and before Mr Boeman had chance to recover his wits he was being pulled violently to his feet by his shirt front. Only the count's intervention prevented another bone-shattering left fist.

'Sir, sir, I beg of you,' he remonstrated in agitation, 'pray think of the contessa's sensibilities!'

Reluctantly the earl let Boeman fall to the ground before contemptuously turning his back on his sorry victim, and transferring his attention to the count and his lady. He was in time to see one dainty white hand laid lightly on the count's proffered arm, and then from the dim interior of the coach emerged the elegant figure of the Contessa di Fiorelli. The earl's startled gaze took in the slender frame in its modish pomona-green walking dress, the golden curls topped with a dashing bonnet, a gracefully curved ostrich plume quivering against one smooth cheek.

'Good God!' he ejaculated in blank amazement. 'Mama!'

* * *

When Geneva next opened her eyes, the throbbing pain around her throat was sufficient to tell her this was no dream. Her senses gradually informed her that she was no longer spreadeagled on a hard road surface, but lying comfortably on a soft mattress. What had brought about this change of circumstances was a complete mystery to Geneva. Her last memories were of her guardian's twisted and evil face as he inexorably choked the life out of her. Oh, and then there had been that exquisite dream, when Gus had looked at her so tenderly and said such lovely things. In her half-waking state Geneva chose to dwell on that more agreeable memory.

'Oh Gus, if only you were really here,' she sighed, not realizing that she had spoken aloud that heartfelt desire. The next instant her wish was granted. Lord Vance was gazing anxiously down at her. Suddenly Geneva was wide awake and struggling to sit up.

'Hush now. Lie still, you have had a shocking experience,' said the earl gently restraining her.

'But what happened? Why are you here? Where am I?'

'Everything is fine, Geneva, you are quite safe. Your despicable guardian tried to throttle you but fortunately help was at hand. I am here because I followed you, of course! As to where you are, well I cannot answer that exactly, suffice to say we are in the best bedchamber of an inn whose name temporarily escapes me, somewhere between Vienna and Linz.'

'My guardian, where is he?' Geneva could not keep a note of panic from her voice, the memory of his attack was too vivid for her fear to be quickly assuaged.

'Believe me, you have nothing to fear from Mr Boeman. He has been persuaded that if he wishes to live he should remove his miserable carcass to the Americas; he is already on the way to the coast, under escort naturally.'

There followed an awkward silence. So much was unsaid, unexplained between them. Geneva longed to thank the earl for pursuing her kidnapper, but was very much afraid that it had been an unwilling action motivated only by duty. In the end blushing hotly and lowering her eyes to the counterpane, all she could bring herself to say was, 'Then – then you rescued me?'

The earl grimaced ruefully. 'I wish I could take credit for that, but all our gratitude must be reserved for another. Though God knows, there is no one I would less like to be in debt to!'

Geneva looked up at him questioningly, unable to understand the bitterness in his voice. The earl forced a reassuring smile and said by way of explanation, 'Your rescuer was the Comte di Fiorelli.'

'Oh?' Perhaps she was being abominably dull-witted, but the name meant nothing to Geneva.

'The Comte di Fiorelli is the man' – the earl seemed to struggle with his emotions – 'is the man who eloped with my mother.'

'Oh!' Impulsively Geneva laid her hand sympathetically on the earl's. 'Oh, how dreadful for you!'

Lord Vance looked down at the hand so artlessly given to him, and quite suddenly the painful reunion which had just taken place seemed to lose its sting, indeed as he relived it in his mind, he realized it had been almost farcical.

The earl's silence worried Geneva, and she asked anxiously, 'What will you do?' She was not well versed in the subtle nuances of male honour. With the father no longer living, did it fall to the son to exact revenge on the lover?

'Will I call him out, do you mean?' The earl could not suppress a grin at the thought of himself and the dandified count facing each other across twenty yards of turf. 'Well, as he is now my stepfather, I think it would be wisest to let well alone. Besides he is a very dangerous fellow, I am not at all eager to meet him!'

Geneva looked at him suspiciously, there was a definite glint of wicked amusement in those dark eyes. Before she had an opportunity to question him further however, the count himself, accompanied by his countess, surged portentously into the room. Geneva had no difficulty in recognizing the Contessa di Fiorelli as Lord Vance's mother. The golden curls, the wide china-blue eyes, the vivacious manner were all Isobel. The count was another matter.

Geneva's eyes widened in frank disbelief. Ever since Lady Yarwood had disclosed the tale of Lady Vance's fall from grace, Geneva had pictured the count as a rather mysterious and dangerous character, all flashing dark eyes and hot Latin temperament.

The count clapped his plump hands together in delight at the sight of Geneva. 'Ah, my dear lady! I am so happy to find you well.'

Geneva thanked him faintly and watched bemused as he possessed himself of her hand and raised it to his lips with rare finesse. Geneva could not prevent her eyes straying over his bowed head to the earl, who was watching her amazement with barely concealed mirth. Geneva quickly averted her eyes and bit hard on her trembling lower lip.

She found her introduction to the earl's mother less amusing. The contessa seemed to have no consciousness of the acute awkwardness of her position, but rather exclaimed on it as if it were no more than a diverting coincidence that she should meet up with her estranged son after all these years. Geneva felt a spurt of anger at this feckless lady whose selfish behaviour had caused her family so much pain. But while Geneva could not warm to her, it was impossible to remain angry with the contessa for long. She had such a carefree charm and such a blithe disregard to the consequences of her actions.

Without the slightest hint of shame or embarrassment she explained that she was now a lady of considerable consequence in the society of Northern Italy. For, contrary to popular consensus, the Comte di Fiorelli was in fact entitled to his aristocratic name. His family's impecuniosity had obliged him to turn his gambling skills to good effect, but his days as proprietor of a gaming house were long gone. The count and his lady now lived with the utmost respectability on the profits of his industry.

The contessa would have rattled on indefinitely, but the earl, seeing that Geneva was beginning to flag, thought it time to intercede, and the couple were ushered from the room. Lord Vance shut the door behind them and, returning to the bedside, possessed himself of Geneva's hand, saying gently, 'Now, my love, if you are not too tired, I think it is time that you and I did some talking.'

Geneva was still trying to take in the revelations of the past few minutes and she answered distractedly, 'Yes of course. But is that really the man your mother ran away with? Was he always so – oh! What did you call me?'

The earl watched the colour come and go in Geneva's cheeks with tender amusement and chose to answer only the last, and he correctly judged, the most important of her questions. 'I called you, my love. And unless you have any objections, indeed even if you do, I will continue to call you that as well as my dearest darling, my reason for life, and, if you will forgive me and have me, my sweet wife.'

'Oh, but you do not wish to marry me!' exclaimed Geneva despite all the evidence to the contrary.

'My dear and only love, I wish it more than anything else in the world. But if you cannot forgive me then I do not blame you.' The earl watched her expression anxiously.

'There is nothing to forgive, my Lord. Indeed please do not feel you must offer me marriage.'

Lord Vance shook her gently and said in exasperation, 'Good God, Geneva, for once will you listen to what I am saying and try not to misunderstand me! I love you! I want to marry you!'

Geneva shook her head in bewildered wonder. For so long she had convinced herself that her love was not, could not be reciprocated; now she found it impossible to accept. With an exclamation of frustration the earl pulled her into his arms and kissed her with a thoroughness that left her breathless and dizzy with joy. When he finally released her, Geneva could only snuggle against his shoulder, dazed and happy. He really did love her.

'Now are you convinced?'

Geneva looked up at him mistily. 'Oh Gus, I do love you!' Then her eyes sparkled with mischief. 'But I think you may have to convince me a little more!'

The earl grinned in relief. 'Baggage!' he murmured appreciatively, before proceeding to leave her in no possible doubt as to the strength of his feelings.